the RIGHTEOUS

This book is a work of fiction. Names, characters, businesses, organizations, places, events, and incidents either are the product of the author's imagination or are used fictitiously. Any resemblance to actual persons, living or dead, events, or locales is entirely coincidental.

Printed in the United States of America.

Published by Thomas & Mercer
P.O. Box 400818
Las Vegas, NV 89140

ISBN-13: 9781612182186
ISBN-10: 1612182186

the
RIGHTEOUS

MICHAEL WALLACE

ACKNOWLEDGMENTS

I want to thank my fellow writers from the Gibraltar Point writing retreat, who gave me encouragement to press forward with *The Righteous* when I was otherwise discouraged. Thank you to Laurie Channer, Rebecca Maines, John McDaid, Elizabeth Mitchell, David Nickle, Janis O'Connor, Steve Samenski, Robert Stauffer, Peter Watts, and of course Pat York, who passed away tragically, but always provided support.

I also want to thank Jeffrey Anderson and Grant Morgan, who provided excellent feedback on an early draft of the book that helped clarify my vision as a writer. Thanks also to my agent, Katherine Boyle of Veritas Literary, who knows when to express enthusiasm and when to apply the jaded, professional eye.

To build a writing career takes years of effort, much of it spent laboring in the dark. During those long, lonely years, one person was always at my side. Thank you, Melinda.

CHAPTER ONE

Amanda Kimball drugged her three-year-old daughter before putting her to bed. She dissolved half an Ambien tablet into a cup of warm milk and sat her daughter at the table to drink it.

Sophie Marie wrinkled her face after the first sip. "I'm not thirsty, and anyway it tastes funny."

"Just drink it," Amanda urged.

Other children passed in and out of the kitchen, completing the nighttime ritual of getting drinks, saying goodnight for the third time, complaining about their siblings, and using a hundred other tricks to delay bedtime. Twenty unwilling children made bedtime a trial in the Kimball house. It took half a dozen women working together to get all the diapers changed, teeth brushed, and squabbles settled. Normally Amanda would have lent a hand, helping her sister wives with their children.

But not tonight. Tonight Amanda could think only of her own daughter.

Within a few minutes Sophie Marie grew blinky and began to yawn. Her eyes had already closed by the time Amanda carried her upstairs to bed.

A terrible feeling had settled in Amanda's stomach by the time she tucked the girl in bed. "Go to sleep, my child," she whispered. "Tomorrow will be very different for us."

Amanda joined the sister wives in shutting down for the night. Elder Kimball had returned from Salt Lake with two of his older sons that evening, but they had already retired to the men's wing of the house. That left the wives in charge of nightly prayers and scripture study.

But Amanda could not focus on the Book of Mormon tonight. She couldn't help but look from face to bowed face within the circle. Which of these women could she trust? Any of them? Fernie? Fernie was not only her sister wife, but her cousin. Amanda had other friends among the wives of Elder Kimball, but over the past weeks she had begun to question all of them. Charity was the first wife; how could she not know what was happening in Blister Creek? Clara Sue was the youngest and prettiest. Delores, Elder Kimball's favorite. Maybe all of them knew. Maybe even Fernie.

Amanda had taken the cell phone call that afternoon. "Amanda Christianson Kimball," the man said with the voice of an executioner. "Having violated thine covenants, thou hast been sealed unto death. Prepare thyself to stand at the Judgment Bar."

The man had hung up. There had been no argument. No mercy offered. She had been sealed unto death. Only the manner of that death remained in doubt.

How had they known what she planned to do? Had they watched her? Had they followed her?

"Amanda?"

She started in her chair, realized that the other women were staring. She stared back, open-mouthed. Were her thoughts so transparent? A bead of sweat crawled down the small of her back.

"It's your turn to read," said Charity, frowning at the open book in Amanda's lap.

"Oh." Amanda dropped her eyes to the page but had no idea which verse they were on. She scanned the page furiously, trying to recall the last words spoken.

"It's the next page," Fernie whispered. "Verse seventeen."

Charity's frown deepened, her lips thin. She said nothing, but she'd doubtless have *plenty* to say to Elder Kimball when he next visited her room.

* * *

Upstairs, Amanda sat at her desk and pulled a sheet of paper from the drawer. She had to believe that Fernie was still true to her.

She thought for a moment, then began to write.

Fernie,

If you read this, then I'm already dead. My blood has atoned for my sins.

Dear God, why am I so alone? I don't know where to turn. I will tell the prophet, but maybe he already knows. That is what they say. You are my cousin, my sister wife, and my friend. And you are a good woman. Maybe I'm making a mistake. Maybe someday we'll laugh about this together. But if you discover this letter in your dresser and something has happened to me, you will know why I died and by whose hand.

First, go to my room and get the manila envelope under my mattress. It will help you understand the rest of this letter.

She paused. *What do I say next? How do I explain this?* She put pen back to paper three times, but always lifted it again, her mind a blank. Finally, she gave up. She folded the half-completed note and tucked it into her Book of Mormon. Perhaps it was better this way. Better not to draw Fernie into this mire. Maybe this stupor of thought was Heavenly Father's way of stopping Amanda from making a grave mistake.

Yes, that was it. That was surely it.

Amanda went to bed fully dressed. She lay in bed with her eyes open as the house settled in for the night. Little voices hushed, and then women went to bed one by one. Creaks diminished, then ceased. Soon, all that remained was the occasional cough. Amanda listened to Sophie Marie's soft, slow breaths as she tried to calm her own racing heart.

When she could wait no more, Amanda slipped out of bed. She reached between the mattress and pulled out a manila envelope. She opened it to make sure she had the right one, and not the second envelope that she'd meant Fernie to find. Yes, this was it. Inside was her evidence, together with a wad of bills stolen from her husband.

Her plan was to leave town and head west until she reached the highway. From there, she'd hitchhike to Cedar City and then catch a bus to Salt Lake City, or south toward Las Vegas.

But she had one stop to make before she left town. She had to see the prophet. She had to believe he didn't know—he couldn't. Amanda gathered Sophie Marie. The girl did not stir, but lay in her mother's arms, leaden and limp. Only her deep and regular breathing betrayed life. She would make no noise as they fled.

The floorboards in the hallway groaned underfoot. Amanda tried at first to take slower steps, but this only prolonged the anxiety, so at last she clenched her jaw and hurried down the stairs, which creaked a warning to anyone who might be listening.

She let out her breath when she reached the living room and saw that it was empty. She made her way straight for the front door. In a moment, she was outside, down the driveway, and into the street.

The pavement radiated heat underfoot, even as the desert air cooled rapidly. A breeze came from the Ghost Cliffs to the north, bringing with it the smell of sand and sage. Houses, each a multi-winged compound designed to hold several wives and their children, stood like dark and silent sentinels along the street. There were no cars on the road and only the rare streetlight to puncture the darkness. Outside the cone of lights, the stars glittered overhead.

She'd spent a year at the church's Harmony, Alberta, settlement as a child, but had lived the rest of her life here in Blister Creek. She knew every inch of the surrounding hills, had hiked the burned sandstone of the Ghost Cliffs and the red rock of Witch's Warts. She loved the blue skies that stretched from horizon to horizon. The smell of the desert was home. The cottonwood trees along the creek, the pockets of green sprinkled across the red landscape, even the scorpions and rattlesnakes that came in from the desert at night spoke to her of home.

She might never see it again. Out of the community, she would be excommunicated, her name stricken from the names of the saints. Her only hope lay in the envelope tucked under her arm. That the prophet would come to her rescue.

Sophie Marie grew heavier in Amanda's arms as she slipped from shadow to shadow on her way west. The prophet's home lay on the western edge of Blister Creek. Beyond that, ten miles of desert to walk with a sleeping child in her arms before she reached the highway.

When Amanda reached the prophet's home, she looked down at Sophie Marie and knew she couldn't take the girl inside. If she was wrong, if the prophet knew what these men were doing and had sanctioned it, as impossible as that was to believe, then he might take the girl from her. Better to leave her daughter here, sleeping, to be snatched up when she fled. She laid the girl on the grass. Sophie Marie sighed, but did not wake.

A light burned in the front room, and she walked up to the house and looked in through the window. The prophet sat by himself at a small worktable with slivers of colored glass spread in front of him like pieces of a jigsaw puzzle. Brother Joseph, now eighty years old, had retired from his work on the ranch, but kept busy making stained glass windows. Almost every home in Blister Creek had a window made by the prophet. The Kimball house held a stained glass window of the Nauvoo temple from before it had been burned by a mob in the days of Joseph Smith. Sunbursts, desert sunrises, and scenes from the Book of Mormon hung in other houses.

At the age of eighty, Brother Joseph had the look of an Old Testament patriarch: white hair, piercing eyes, and a full beard. But Brother Joseph looked like any other man as she saw him now, and not a prophet of God. He worked intently as he took advantage of the quiet after his wives and children had retired to bed.

She had felt the man's hands on her head and his gentle voice as he had given her a prophet's blessing. And she knew in her heart that he couldn't be caught up in these conspiracies. He would rebuke the men who would kill her. The papers she carried in the manila envelope would convince him. She turned to glance at her daughter before going inside.

Sophie Marie was gone.

There was nothing where she had lain, only an indentation in the grass. It was as if a wild animal had carried her away without a sound. Heart pounding, she ran to the spot and looked into the darkness, wild with fear.

"Missing something, Amanda?"

She whirled and saw three men standing in the darkness just beyond the light coming from the window of the house. Shadows masked their faces. One of them held her daughter, still asleep, in his arms.

"Give her back." Her voice was brittle in her ears.

"Certainly," the first said. "She is yours, after all. A gift from the Lord."

"A gift you seem to scorn," the second man said.

The man holding her daughter said nothing.

"What do you want? Please, I'll do anything. Just give me back my daughter."

The first man said, "The envelope in your hands. Give it to me."

She held out her hand, shaking. He stepped forward to take it, then dropped it at her feet. "Don't worry. Your daughter will be safe."

She took a step backward, but this took her farther from the house. The man took a step in unison, keeping her close.

Scream, she implored herself. *Scream, for the love of your daughter. Scream!*

But terror had taken her and she couldn't move. And then his hands moved with the speed of a striking snake. They closed around her neck. She flailed with her hands, but the second man closed in. He wrenched her arms behind her back. She tried to hurl herself to the ground, to wrestle herself free, but the two men held her upright.

The hands tightened until she couldn't breathe, though she opened her mouth and gulped for air like a fish thrown up on the riverbank. Lights began to pop in her head. The hands released. She drew a single, ragged breath before her attacker tightened his grip again. They didn't want her to die. Not yet.

The second man released her arms. She flailed at the man choking her, but the strength had left her limbs and her efforts amounted to nothing. The man who had released her arms took a pair of pliers from his pocket. He reached the pliers into her gaping mouth and seized her tongue. Her daughter slept peacefully in the third man's arms.

No, she begged silently through the pain and terror. *Not like this.*

"Amanda Christianson Kimball," the man with the pliers said. "In the name of the Savior, Jesus Christ, we do exercise righteous judgment upon thee. Let the blood of the wicked be spilled to justify the souls of the righteous."

The pliers bit into her tongue. And then an excruciating tearing in her mouth. She screamed. The tongue held. Blood streamed from her mouth. The man with the pliers grunted while the other two held her limbs and head. He jerked back and forth, forced to readjust his grip until he finally ripped her tongue out by the roots.

Through the pain, Amanda darted a glance toward the home of her would-be rescuer. *Look out the window,* she pleaded to the prophet. With all her will, she silently begged. *For the love of God, look.*

Inside, the prophet of the Church of the Anointing set down his soldering iron and lifted the stained glass to the light. The man and his work shimmered as seen through her watering eyes. The window was a white dove with an olive branch in its mouth.

Brother Joseph did not look toward the window nor see into the darkness outside.

CHAPTER TWO

Eliza Christianson woke with a strange warmth spreading through her body. Her hand was on her crotch, and she had the horrified suspicion that she had been touching herself down there. Sweat stood out on her forehead, and she was breathing hard. A vague memory of a dream. She'd been kissing someone, and his hands had been on her body.

She froze, afraid to move. Only gradually did she come to her senses. It was dark. Her sisters still breathed quietly in their beds. She moved her hand to a more chaste location. At least it had been on the outside of her pajamas and not next to the skin.

Eliza made her way to the stairs, intending to go downstairs and get a cold drink from the fridge. Something to clear her head. No girl she knew admitted to dreams like that. In fact, most girls her age suffered from a naïveté about sexual matters. When they did talk about boys, the most their imaginations could muster was a chaste embrace or a close-mouthed kiss.

Eliza's thoughts were more dangerous. Impure. Lustful.

There was a light on downstairs. Eliza thought at first that it might be her mother, who suffered from insomnia. But something made her hesitate at the top of the stairs.

She heard men's voices. It was an animated conversation, and Eliza could never resist eavesdropping on the male world, so she crept to the next landing and peered through the bars of the stairs.

Her brother Jacob sat at the dining table with his textbooks scattered around him. It was the only time he had to study without the younger children begging him to tell stories or asking for help with their algebra or piano lessons. Father had picked up one of Jacob's pencils and tapped it nervously against the table. His other hand stroked his beard.

"I need your support in this," Father said. "Even the prophet was asking me if we'd chosen a husband yet."

"But surely Liz can do better than Elder Johnson," Jacob said.

Eliza hardly dared to breathe. They were talking about her. She had turned seventeen two weeks earlier, and the murmurs for her marriage had risen to a dull roar. But she'd had no idea the matter had progressed this far.

"He's a good man," Father said. "Righteous, too."

"But so old. And she'd be what? His twelfth wife?"

"Thirteenth," Father corrected.

Thirteenth wife, three hundredth, what did it matter? All she could think was old, old, old. Elder Johnson had to be in his seventies. The thought of lying naked next to that wrinkled, sagging old man, his breath smelling of Ensure and Scope, his hair thin and greasy, made her flesh crawl.

"It's unhealthy for a girl to wait too long to marry," her father said. But there was still something in his voice. Hesitation? He wanted Jacob to convince him. "You know an unmarried girl turns to masturbation. Lesbianism. All manner of pernicious sins. Leave a woman unmarried and she'll either turn lustful or bind her natural urges so tight she'll be prone to hysteria."

Jacob snorted. "Pseudoscientific claptrap." He was a medical student at the University of Calgary and would know something about the subject, which Eliza found reassuring. "She's not going to become a lesbian. She won't grow a mustache or male genitalia. She won't suffer hysteria. It's all nonsense and you know it."

Only Jacob could get away with talking to Father like that. Abraham Christianson was head of the Quorum of the Twelve and second only to the prophet himself. Most people approached him with the proper deference. Eliza certainly did.

"Okay, then," Father said. "So it's nonsense. And I'm not dead set on Elder Johnson."

Eliza breathed a sigh of relief from the stairs. It was just talk. She was about to return to bed when Father continued.

"But you'll have to admit there's a danger in waiting. Wait too long and she might start thinking about following her brothers to college. She's a smart girl. She waits a year or two and she might decide to wait ten or twenty."

"So what you're saying is that you want to snuff her ambitions. Knock Liz down before she gets any ideas." Jacob gave Father a serious look. "Let's be very clear what you mean."

Father sighed. "Jacob, don't be difficult. However you look at it, Eliza can't stay unmarried forever. Neither, I might add, can you. Only your position is much more tenuous, isn't it? There are never enough wives to go around. Liz has value, to put it crassly. She'll never have more value than she does right now. And that can help you find your first wife."

"Ah, so we want to move the goods before they spoil. Okay, fine. But leave me out of it for the moment. What's wrong with giving Liz a choice?"

"A choice? It's not her decision, Jacob."

"Okay, maybe choice is the wrong word. But we can take her opinion into consideration. There's no harm in that."

"Maybe." He didn't sound convinced. "That is, until she fixes on the idea that it's all up to her."

"Liz knows better than that," Jacob said. "Listen, how about this? She comes with me tomorrow to Utah. She can meet the other two men and see how they stack up to Elder Johnson."

"I don't know. I can imagine the foolish questions. Not to mention the murder."

Murder? Eliza was still dealing with the excitement of leaving Canada and going to Utah to meet two potential future husbands when the word *murder* hit her like a brush with an electric fence.

Jacob shook his head. "You can't claim both that Liz is mature enough to get married and that she's a naïve, giggly girl who's going to make a fool of herself."

"Why not? Why can't she be both mature and immature? Ready to get married. Not ready to navigate the minefield waiting in Blister Creek."

"You might have that exactly backwards, Dad. But seriously, don't underestimate Liz."

"That still doesn't answer the question of the murder investigation," Father added.

"Investigation?" Jacob winced. "I'm not a detective—I'm not even a doctor yet. I'm going to take a look at the medical facts, try to figure out what they tell us."

"Call it whatever you want, but I need to know what's going on in Blister Creek, and Eliza is bound to get in the way."

"She won't get in the way. And she needs a chance to know all three men before we decide."

Father was silent for a long moment. His hand returned to his beard. At last he nodded. "Okay, Jacob, but be careful. This murder is an ugly business. And I don't trust the Kimballs. Oh, and could you try not to infect Eliza with your cynicism? It won't help matters." He rose to his feet, and Jacob reached for his textbooks.

Eliza scrambled upstairs before her father could see her. Lying in her bed, she had no more lustful thoughts. Instead, she thought about leaving Harmony, driving from Alberta and south to Utah. To perhaps meet her future husband.

And a murder, she remembered. She would accompany her brother while he tried to solve the crime. She couldn't help but be frightened by the prospect. And excited.

* * *

"God hates women," Jacob told Eliza. "It's a pity, because women have always been His most devoted followers."

Eliza, sitting next to him in the Toyota Corolla sixteen hours into a twenty-hour drive between Harmony, Alberta, and Blister Creek, Utah, was dry-eyed and cramped. She'd expected them to spend the night in White Valley, Montana, where the church kept a small community of a dozen or so families, but Jacob had driven straight through. Eliza had drifted in and out of sleep all night as they'd passed through Salt Lake City and Provo. They were on I-15, somewhere south of Nephi, where trees gave way to sage-brush and puddles of illusory water glimmered on the blacktop as the summer sun lifted in a ball of fire over the desert.

"Are you going somewhere with this?" she asked, gathering her wits. "Or are you trying to goad me?" Always hard to tell with Jacob.

"Every father wants a son. Most mothers, too. A daughter is a disappointment. A boy grows up, he's stimulated and challenged. A girl, ignored until puberty, then guarded like a bitch in heat."

Eliza knew Jacob wanted the argument, if only because debating with himself would be boring. Fine, she'd play along. "And what about the boys? What's our brother up to these days? Still coked out in Las Vegas, living with a transsexual stripper?"

"Wouldn't be a surprise. They drove Enoch from town like a mad dog." Jacob was fond of oscillating between crass, almost crude language, and an archaic style. He made one such switch right now. "Alone, he succumbed to the wiles of the adversary. Debauchery is the mistress of temptation." A shrug. "So, perhaps it's not easy being one of God's chosen people. Man or woman." He stared straight ahead. "But sadly for your sex, it's not a man lying in a pool of his own blood, but Amanda Kimball."

Eliza had questioned him about the murder as soon as they'd left Harmony. He'd told her about Amanda Kimball, and the whole matter had become suddenly real. Amanda was her cousin.

During that year that Eliza had spent in Blister Creek, Amanda had been like a cool, tomboyish older sister. She'd known the best places to look for arrowheads, and she'd once taken Eliza to an Anasazi ruin she had discovered in one of the canyons. They'd climbed to the ruin via six-hundred-year-old handholds carved into the sandstone wall. They had found a crumbling, two-room house with baskets and a broken pot lying in one corner. The house was perfectly preserved by the desert air; there were still dried corncobs in one of the baskets.

And now her cousin was dead. Murdered.

"So God really hates women?"

"Of course not, Liz. God loves and cherishes women. You know that."

They stopped for lunch at a greasy spoon in Cedar City. Polygamists were fairly common through central and southern Utah, but they still drew looks. The Mormons—those who followed the fallen prophets in Salt Lake City, that is—dressed like gentiles, while a daughter of God like Eliza wore no makeup, kept her hair waist-length, and wore a dress that fell to her ankles with a high collar and sleeves to her wrists. In Montana, someone had asked if they were Mennonites. Nobody made that mistake in Utah.

"They're ashamed of us," Jacob said when they reached the car.

"How do you mean?"

"The Salt Lake Mormons can't forget that they were once like us. They were the polygamists who fled into the desert. It's why they're so eager to appear normal to the world. All the Osmonds, Marriotts, Steve Youngs, and Mitt Romneys were just like we are. It's why they've rushed so fully into the embrace of Babylon and why they look at us like that. They're ashamed, and they blame us for their embarrassment."

"You see embarrassment, I see pity," Eliza replied. "Poor, simple-minded girl, brainwashed into a fundamentalist cult. Bet she can barely write her own name."

Jacob chuckled at this.

But she'd meant it only half jokingly. She'd never noticed the stares until a few years ago; now she was conscious of every glance and whisper. The snickers of teenage boys were especially irritating.

They passed the last gentile outpost thirty miles east of Cedar City. The land was stark and beautiful. There were red cliffs streaked black with desert varnish. The road turned gravelly and then became a dirt road. The air-conditioning blasted full force; it cut the heat but did not fully filter the road dust.

It had been three years since Eliza had seen Blister Creek, so it was fresh to her eyes. The setting was spectacular. The town sat at the base of the Ghost Cliffs, which soared vertically two thousand feet above Blister Creek Valley. The cliffs glowed in the late afternoon sun. Irrigated green fields made a quilt across the valley floor.

The houses were much like back home: large farmhouses with extra wings and outbuildings to hold wives and a multitude of children. The houses, the school, the town office, the mini-mart, and the town store were all made of red brick.

The exception was the temple. A white fortress in the desert, perched on a hill in the center of town. The golden figure of the Angel Moroni crowned the single spire. It was here that the saints performed their sacred rituals: baptism for the dead, washings and anointings, the endowment, eternal marriage, and the second anointing.

The sight of the temple always sent a chill down her spine. It was here that Christ would reign in the Millennium.

Her great-grandfather, Henry B. Young, had ordered its construction. The Church of the Anointing were those who had fled to the desert after the Church of Jesus Christ of Latter-day Saints had renounced polygamy and fallen into apostasy. In the early years, Brother Henry had believed that the mainstream Mormons would eventually come around. They hadn't. Only a remnant had remained true and faithful to the eternal principle of plural marriage.

Two women with waist-length hair, four children in tow, looked at their car as they passed, no doubt noting its Alberta plates. A young man and his son, unloading two-by-fours from a pickup, stopped their work and frowned. Faces appeared in windows.

"Into the belly of the beast," Jacob murmured. It was a phrase usually reserved for a foray into the towns and cities of the gentiles. They continued down Main Street. He turned to Eliza. "Don't forget that we're here to look into a murder."

"We?" She felt a mixture of excitement and dread.

"Absolutely, we. That business about checking out potential husbands is Dad's reason, not mine." He shrugged. "Okay, so we can't forget that entirely. But the murder is your top priority. I need eyes and ears among the women. They might tell you things they wouldn't tell a man."

"I thought we already knew the identity of the murderers." According to Jacob, the prophet and Elder Kimball thought that Mexican day laborers had raped and murdered Amanda. Brother Joseph wanted Jacob to figure out which one before deciding how to administer justice.

"Do we?"

* * *

Elder Kimball resembled a bald, sweating Pillsbury Doughboy, well on his way to baking to a golden, flaky consistency in the brilliant sun. Jacob let himself run with the imagery for a moment. He needed to see Kimball not as an elder of Israel, but as a suspect. He paused, surprised at how he was already thinking of suspects and evidence. Maybe Father was right and he needed to think of this as an investigation.

Jacob and Eliza had parked the Corolla next to the temple and stepped from the chilled interior of the car into the suffocatingly hot, dry air of the desert. He had brought his bag from the trunk.

Witch's Warts stretched in a jagged, bumpy scar from just beyond the temple halfway to the Ghost Cliffs. It was a collection of sandstone fins and hoodoos, interrupted by dry washes, natural arches, and sand dunes. A hell of a place to lose a cow, as they said.

Or a body. A boy had found Amanda just inside. Wild animals had uncovered her body from a shallow, sandy grave.

Kimball waited at the murder site with his two sons. One was about twenty, the other, Taylor Kimball Jr., a few years older, closer to Jacob's age. He was taller than his father, broader at the shoulders, and thinner, but with the same sallow complexion. Taylor Junior was one of Eliza's suitors, although Jacob hadn't yet told her as much.

Elder Kimball eyed him with irritation as they approached. "You said ten o'clock. It's a quarter to eleven already."

"I said *about* ten," Jacob corrected. "We've been driving all night. I had no way to know exactly when we'd arrive." He looked around. "So it's just you and your sons?"

"I don't see anyone else, do you?" There was a rough edge to his voice. "Brother Joseph said to keep it quiet until you came. So I did."

He was grateful for that, but Elder Kimball and his two sons were still three people too many for his taste. Jacob could see the body some thirty feet further into the maze of stone; it had been covered by a plastic tarp. Footprints mucked up the sand around it.

He turned back to Elder Kimball. "I was sorry to hear about your wife. I hope I can figure out how she died."

Elder Kimball said, "I don't see the point of this, frankly. It's been almost two days since we discovered the body. We know the culprit. We should act at once. Vengeance is mine, sayeth the Lord."

"Believe me, I want to figure this out quickly," Jacob said. He forced himself to remain patient. Sweat trickled down his neck and along his ribs. "Nothing would make me happier than swift justice. But we've got to be very sure before we act. Besides, we don't know *which* Mexican might be responsible."

"Does it matter? The other two are accomplices at the least. And justice is simple. Burn their trailer in the middle of the night. It would be a righteous judgment."

"Not a good idea."

"How so? They're illegal aliens. Nobody will know or care that they are gone."

Jacob was taken aback. "Right, because no illegal alien ever had a mother in Guadalajara, or a wife who received Western Union payments and twice-weekly calls from *El Norte*. Not to mention friends in Los Angeles, cousins in Phoenix, and so on. They may seem like vagabonds to you, but each of those men has about thirty friends or relatives who'll come looking for him if he disappears." He shook his head. "That kind of attention is the one thing that my father and Brother Joseph insist must not happen." He looked back to the tarp. "Can you stay here, please, while I take a look?"

Elder Kimball said, "You're wasting your time. It's obvious what happened here. The only thing to be gained by your mucking around is to desecrate the body of my wife."

"And I'm very sorry. But I've got to have a look for myself. It's the only way to answer my questions. I'll treat the remains with complete respect."

"I told you. I'm not going to let you bother her."

Jacob met the man's glare without looking away. "Elder Kimball, I'm not backing down."

The muscles on Elder Kimball's jaw tightened. His two sons glowered from over his shoulder. "Are you defying me, boy?"

Jacob fought down his anger. "Yes, as a matter of fact, I am."

"And you are *who*, exactly? Someone important, perhaps?" It was a rhetorical question. Elder Kimball knew every detail of Jacob's family to the third generation. He knew exactly who Jacob was or was not. It wasn't Jacob's lineage that was at question, but his standing in the community. "No, I didn't think so. You are a young man, unmarried. I am a member of the Quorum of the Twelve Apostles, since your tone of voice indicates that you need reminding."

"And my father is the *senior* member of the Quorum, since *you* need reminding. The *prophet* called my father and asked if I could come. And if I fail," Jacob added, "and word reaches the outside world, everything we work for would be in jeopardy. Which is why Brother Joseph insists that you allow me to continue."

"Does he?"

Again, Elder Kimball knew the answer, but Jacob would have to force the issue or the investigation would be a sloppy affair, followed by a rush to judgment. Which was, no doubt, Kimball's intention. Jacob took out his cell phone. "Should we call him?"

When Elder Kimball said nothing, Jacob moderated his tone. "Look, I know you're not happy I'm here. Of course you just want to take your wife and give her a proper burial. But this is terrible, unprecedented." He shook his head. "Brother Joseph needs to be sure. As a medical student, I've seen a lot of cadavers, and the prophet thought I might help.

"And Elder Kimball, if the gentile authorities show up, you know who they'll question first. The first suspect is always the woman's husband." He held up a hand to fend off the sputtering retort. "I know. It's preposterous. They wouldn't understand your special calling as a servant of the Lord."

Elder Kimball's response balanced on the edge of a knife for a long moment before Eliza stepped in. She took Elder Kimball by the arm. "I'm so sorry, Elder Kimball. We were all shocked to hear the news. I hope my brother finds the man responsible. That's all he wants."

His face softened. "Ah, Eliza Christianson. I didn't recognize you at first. It's been a few years. You've grown into a lovely young woman. These are my sons, Taylor Junior and Ammon."

Elder Kimball's sons fixed her with a hungry gaze like a praying mantis about to snatch a grasshopper from a leaf. She smiled chastely.

Eliza had proven her worth already. Jacob took advantage of the break in tension to approach the tarp. It was cooler within the sandstone fins, especially here, where they narrowed and stretched overhead to partially block the sun.

Behind him, her voice echoing through the sandstone, Eliza said, "Thank you, Elder Kimball. I'm still just a girl, though."

"Nonsense. Why, three of my wives were younger than you when we got married."

Jacob stood in front of the tarp. It bulged. The dead body. Faced with the unpleasant task, he hesitated.

"Your poor wife," Eliza continued. "And the mother of your daughter Sophie Marie. You must be devastated."

"I've been very anxious to get your brother here and resolve matters." An abrupt reversal. Nevertheless, he actually sounded sorry for the first time. "Terrible business what these Lamanites have done. The old curse still holds, I'm afraid."

Navajo and Paiute were always Lamanites—so called because they were descended from the tribe of the same name in the Book of Mormon who had been cursed with dark skin for rebelling against God—but some people called Mexicans Lamanites as well, as they were partly of the same heritage.

"When is the funeral?" Eliza asked.

"As soon as possible. Maybe tomorrow, maybe Monday."

"It must be so hard for you and your family."

Meanwhile, Jacob removed the stones weighing down the corners of the tarp one by one. He took out a pair of surgical gloves from his bag and put them on, then pulled a surgical mask over his face.

It's just meat, he reminded himself. *Like a slaughtered animal.* It was what he had to tell himself before dissecting a cadaver at school. He loved to study human anatomy, to see how muscle, tendon, and bone all came together to form the machine that was the human body. Even better was pathology, to see a clogged artery or an enlarged kidney. How quickly such an elegant machine broke down from one diseased member. But he'd had to train himself to cut into the waxy flesh of a cadaver.

He couldn't allow himself to think of Amanda's body as human. *Just meat.* Think of it as a human, a poor woman murdered in a moment of terror and pain, and he would never be able to go through with this.

He looked back to Eliza, standing next to Elder Kimball some thirty feet back, and made a sudden decision.

"I need my sister for a moment," he called back. "She knows how to use this silly Japanese camera." He held out a hand to stop Elder Kimball and his sons. "No, please, stay there. You'll block the light and confuse the situation. I need to think clearly. Please, I insist. Liz."

She approached with a squeamish expression. It was cruel to make her look. The emotional burden, if nothing else, rested more heavily on her shoulders than his. Eliza had spent a good deal of time with her cousin's family as a child and had been unusually close to Amanda.

"Come on, Liz," he encouraged in a voice meant only for her ears. He handed her a surgical mask. "We only have a few minutes."

And then he could see, as she stepped forward, that it wasn't just the momentum of the situation that carried her forward, it was curiosity.

"Brace yourself," he told her when she stood by his side. He swallowed hard, then peeled back the tarp to reveal the murdered body of Amanda Kimball. Eliza let out a gasp.

CHAPTER THREE

Amanda's eyes stared forward, dry and glassy. The skin on her face was pale, like wax paper. She wore a yawning gash beneath her chin that stretched from ear to ear like a second mouth. Blood caked with sand stuck to her flesh.

And the smell. Like pork that's gone rancid. Eliza swallowed hard and turned away, then swallowed hard again. Her stomach roiled, and she stripped off the surgical mask to get more air.

Jacob handed her the camera, but it was a moment before her head cleared and she could take it with trembling hands. "What's wrong with the camera?" she asked.

"Absolutely nothing. Just take some pictures. I wanted to talk to you. Now let me tell you what's obvious. And don't throw up."

She nodded. The lightheadedness was passing. "What do you know?" She was surprised he had already gathered information while she had been fighting to stay on her feet.

"Just the basic stuff. First, she wasn't killed here. Not enough blood."

He sounded very calm…too calm, she thought. She could tell that he wasn't altogether well, but only because she knew him so well.

Eliza felt ready to look at Amanda again. She turned slowly, ready to look away if it proved too much. Blood soaked Amanda's dress. "Looks like a lot of blood to me."

"With her throat cut like that? I know it looks like a lot, but there's maybe a half pint on her clothes, that's all. If she'd bled out here, she'd be swimming in blood. The sand would be clumped all around her, and not dry. A woman her size has roughly eight or nine pints of blood. It made a terrible mess, wherever it happened. I've slaughtered enough pigs at the farm that I knew it right away." He turned to look at her. "It helps, you know, if you try to think of her like a slaughtered pig."

"What are you talking about?" she asked, revolted by the image and thinking that she must have misheard him. She was growing lightheaded again. "A pig?"

"Just for the moment. An image of an animal slaughtered. You've seen that before; you can stomach it. Later, this body can be Amanda again. For now, it's meat."

"I see." She turned to look at the body again, trying to take his advice.

He nodded, then continued. "Two, I don't think she was raped. We'll scrape for semen—don't look at me like that, Liz,

I'm training to be a doctor—but look, her temple garments are in place." Amanda's dress rode up her thigh, and Eliza could see that he was right as Jacob bent to brush away more of the sand around her legs.

Temple garments were the underwear, complete with covenant marks, that Mormons wore after taking out their endowment in the temple. The Salt Lake Mormons wore garments that went to the knee and just off the shoulder, but true garments went to the ankle and wrist. Eliza had not yet taken out her endowment—women did so at marriage, men when they received the Melchizedek Priesthood—but she'd done plenty of laundry in her life and knew almost everything about them except what the marks signified. People did not discuss such details outside of the temple.

"The camera," he reminded her. "Hold it up. They're watching. So could a Mexican have figured out how to take off her garments, then put them on properly once he was done raping her?" Jacob asked. "And why bother? No, she wasn't raped."

She didn't know what to make of this information. If not rape, then what had been the motive? But before she could voice this question, Jacob glanced over his shoulder at Elder Kimball and said in a low voice, "What of him? Strange emotions, yes? You'd think he'd lost a horse, not one of his wives."

Eliza followed his gaze. Elder Kimball was stewing. "You know what I think?" she asked in an even lower voice. "He's not here out of any sorrow. Maybe a sense of duty?"

Jacob pulled down his mask and took a step back. "Duty? Maybe. Or maybe he's here to muddy the waters, tell us his own version, throw us off the scent."

"What do you mean?"

"He knows that some people will blame him when they learn that Amanda was murdered. Even if people find out it was the Mexicans, they'll say he should have kept an eye on her." Jacob bent over the body. "What an idiot, thinking he could burn them to death while they slept. Not to mention barbaric. A servant of the Lord should do better. You know what I can't figure out?" he asked abruptly. "Why the throat? Yes," he repeated. "Why the throat? Such a deliberate cut."

She started to say something, but he shushed her and straightened. He let out a low breath, then reached for his bag. Jacob had just finished his second year of medical school. Eliza suspected that the University of Calgary would have expelled him had they known the scope of Jacob's medical experience. He had set bones, administered vaccines and eye exams, performed autopsies, even performed hernia operations and extracted wisdom teeth. None of that made him a coroner or forensic anthropologist, but he was the closest to one who would ever look at Amanda's body.

He removed a screwdriver, which he inserted between her teeth and used to pry open her jaw. Eliza swallowed, hard, but forced herself to watch. Jacob stuck his gloved fingers into her mouth, poked around for a moment, and then removed a thick, blackish something which he held between his thumb and forefinger. It was Amanda's tongue.

Eliza turned away with a moan. She desperately needed to be sick.

"Do *not* throw up," he told her again. "That will bring Elder Kimball right over."

Her stomach heaved twice, but she fought it down. A bitter taste came into her mouth. Jacob put a hand against her back, which helped steady her legs. A moment later her eyes cleared and the static subsided from her ears.

"Good, now take some pictures," he told her. "I want the tongue and the open mouth."

She obeyed, trying not to look straight on as she lifted the camera to her eyes. "I don't understand. What…why?"

When she finished, Jacob pushed the tongue back into Amanda's mouth. He put away the screwdriver and forced her rigid jaws closed. "It's simple enough to understand. Someone cut out her tongue. Or, more accurately, they tore it out by the roots."

Eliza was determined not to show any more signs of weakness. "Yes, but how did you know to check her mouth?"

A moment of hesitation. "I can't tell you."

"What do you mean, you can't tell me? Something told you to check her mouth. That's got to be important."

"Yes, of course it's important," Jacob said. "But I can't tell you. It's something we don't talk about. Not here, not with someone who hasn't yet…" His voice trailed off as he waited for her to draw her own conclusions.

"With someone who hasn't gone through the temple yet. That's it, isn't it?"

"Exactly."

Meaning that there was something in the temple rituals, something about the cut throat that had told him to look in Amanda's mouth.

Jacob pulled the tarp over Amanda's body. "No rape. Murdered in a certain way known only to certain people. It wasn't the Mexicans, that's for sure. No, it was a church member." He raised his eyebrows, looking at Elder Kimball and his sons, who had lost patience and begun trudging through the sand toward them. "We know where to start looking, don't we?"

Eliza followed his gaze. Elder Kimball? Was it possible that one of the Lord's Anointed was involved in the murder of his own wife? The mother of his child?

* * *

Charity Kimball, senior wife of Elder Kimball, eyed Eliza with thinly-veiled hostility. Jacob had dropped Eliza and the luggage at the Kimball house. Charity had sent two boys upstairs with their bags, then called Eliza into the kitchen, where the other wives were preparing dinner for forty people. Women shucked corn, rolled dough, chopped potatoes, and cut watermelon and tomatoes.

As she had graduated into the ranks of the young women, Eliza had grown accustomed to the animosity of the older women. Some were open about it, like Charity, while others were sickly sweet to her face, then spread rumors behind her back. The burdens of plural marriage were borne on the shoulders of the earlier wives. A typical man might marry one girl at twenty-five, maybe another at forty, and a third at forty-eight, each new bride a teenager.

And how could an older woman compete against the freshness of a sixteen-year-old girl, to say nothing of all the wives between the youngest and wherever she sat in the hierarchy? Her solace was that she could command the younger wives as she saw fit.

"Two months since my husband deflowered his latest wife and already he's ensnared fresh meat," said Charity. She removed the cloth from a large bowl of rising bread dough. Her hands punched down the dough as if it were Eliza's head. "Are you one of the Ernie Young girls?"

"No, Sister Kimball, I'm Eliza Christianson."

Her face softened. "Ah, Abraham's daughter. It's been a few years, hasn't it? I've heard you're more than a handful, girl. But look at you. Grown up and looking for a husband, are you?"

"Not looking, no. I'd rather take my time."

There were a few chuckles, including one from Fernie Kimball, who was Eliza's half sister, but through her mother, unusually. Their mother had divorced after Fernie's father had suffered a nervous breakdown and run off to California with some gentile woman. Mother had remarried Abraham Christianson. Eliza didn't know Fernie very well; Fernie had been out of the house for several years.

Eliza had already asked casually about Amanda. But the women said they didn't know what had become of her cousin, only that she had disappeared the day before yesterday. She had not come down to breakfast, and Elder Kimball had told them that she'd gone to visit an elderly aunt for a couple of days. No knowledge of the murder, then.

Children played, fought, bullied, and whined around the feet of the women, but they were ignored until they misbehaved to the point of earning a swat. The older girls worked with their mothers in the kitchen, and those just a few years younger than Eliza watched her more keenly than any.

"Taking your time? Are they all so naïve in the Christianson household, Fernie?" one of the wives asked.

"I certainly wasn't," Fernie said.

Charity said, "You'll be married by Christmas, Eliza." Her tone was gentle. "Jacob needs a wife, and it's always that first one that's

the hardest for a man. Wait too long and he'll find himself among
the Lost Boys. Nobody wants that. Not for Jacob. That means you
must do your part."

"Yes, I see."

"God only knows how you've remained a maiden as long as
you have. Now here, we've got work to do," she said as she stepped
to the sink to wash the dough from her hands. "Make yourself useful and fold the crescent rolls. The first shift eats at six."

The men and older boys always ate first, followed by the
women and children in subsequent waves. It was Saturday night,
which meant the men had a priesthood meeting. Jacob would be
back for dinner and then gone again.

During Eliza's last visit, she'd thought the Kimball women a
grim lot, all thin lips and sour expressions. Wives tended to reflect
their husbands, and Elder Kimball was a stern, domineering man.
The reality was more complex.

With no men in the house, the women laughed and gossiped,
told ribald jokes, and teased one of the wives about the red hair of
her youngest child. "Where did that come from, anyway?" Charity
asked with a sly smile. "The Kimballs don't have any redheads and
you're blonde." Two other women discussed the best curriculum
for homeschooling their children in trigonometry. Someone else
talked about a Shakespeare reading group that she'd organized.

The Church of the Anointing believed that "the glory of God is
intelligence," as the first prophet of the Latter Days, Joseph Smith,
had taught. Eliza had met members of the Fundamentalist Church
of Jesus Christ—one of those counterfeit churches always in the
news for incest and marrying off twelve-year-old girls—and had
also known a couple of girls from the True and Living Church,

another polygamist sect based in Manti, Utah. She'd thought them mentally feeble. For whatever reason, native intelligence or the intellectual emphasis of their prophet, the company of her own people was superior.

The men came to eat. There were three men and four priest-hood-holding teenage boys, plus her brother Jacob, but they ate a mountain of food in about twenty minutes before they went to shower and dress for their meeting. Children poured into the dining room when they left. They cleaned up after the men and reset the table. As Eliza worked, she found Elder Kimball's wives warming to her as she had already warmed to them.

"Which one is Sophie Marie?" she asked her half sister Fernie as the children ate.

"The dark one with the curly hair," Fernie said. "They say she looks like Amanda's older brother who died in a fall as a child. She certainly has a different look to her. Something in the eyes."

Sophie Marie was a quiet eater in the midst of chaos.

"She's a bright one," Fernie said. "Reminds me of my Daniel, already reading at four." Fernie hiked her baby into a high chair and gave her older son a bowl of mashed potatoes and a few pieces of roll to feed the baby.

"Is your brother coming back around?" Charity asked a few minutes later as the women settled into their own meal. Older children helped the younger ones and cleared dishes.

Eliza didn't understand the question. "You mean, is he staying here tonight?"

"I don't mean Jacob, I'm talking about Enoch. My daughter saw him at the church house last Tuesday. Maybe he was talking to the bishop? I don't know."

This was news to Eliza. She hadn't believed the rumors about cocaine and strippers, but she had believed the part about working in a casino. Probably drank and gambled, too. It had been two years since she'd seen him.

Eliza had been in tears when she'd heard they were holding a church court to try Enoch in absentia. She'd found Father as he was leaving the house, grim-faced and wearing his nicest suit. In tears, she'd grabbed his arm.

"Don't let them do it," she pleaded. "He'll come back, I know he will."

"The master of the house gave talents of silver to his servants," Father said. His grip was firm but gentle as he pried her hand free. "When he returned, he found that one servant had buried his talent in the ground. The master took the talent from the slothful servant and gave it to the faithful servant."

"Enoch's not a parable from the Bible, Father. He's my brother. Maybe I could talk to him. He'd listen to me."

"Eliza, you're a smart girl, so listen. Enoch made his choice. The rest—trial, excommunication, shunning—is just a formality. Enoch buried his talent in the ground."

They'd called Jacob as a witness, and he'd later shared the details with Eliza. The first charge was violation of the Word of Wisdom, the health code that proscribed alcohol, tobacco, and hot drinks like coffee and tea. Enoch had been caught drinking beer.

The second was immorality; by his own admission, Enoch had participated in "immoral acts" with a gentile girlfriend.

Most serious was the charge of disobedience to a priesthood leader, in this case, his own father. His relationship with Father had been deteriorating for several years. First, he'd lost his scholarship, and then he'd disappeared for several weeks; it later came out that he had gone to London, of all places, with a couple of gentile friends, including his girlfriend. Father had called him to repentance. They had argued.

Enoch had ended the fight by making an obscene gesture at Father and his Grandpa Griggs as he'd climbed onto the back of a friend's motorcycle and roared out of town. The next day, the court.

Eliza had never expected to see Enoch again. Name stricken from the records of the church. Marked for damnation. Last she'd heard, he'd taken up with some Lost Boys in Las Vegas, including Gideon Kimball and Israel Young.

And now he'd been seen in Blister Creek? Surely not.

Charity Kimball must have read the skepticism on Eliza's face. "The Lord is merciful, and the prophet is just. Perhaps your brother has repented. Like the Prodigal Son."

But Father had been right. Lost Boys did not simply rejoin Zion. It wasn't a matter of faith, contrition, and repentance. Who would let Enoch take a wife when there were so many men who had kept their covenants?

So what had brought Enoch to Blister Creek? Maybe Jacob would know.

CHAPTER FOUR

It took a strong man to stand before the prophet and tell him that he was wrong. Jacob didn't know if he was that man.

Fake it till you make it.

Jacob repeated those words to himself all through the Saturday night priesthood meeting. The meeting itself was more of the same: faith, obedience, and how to be a good husband and father. He'd never heard this particular lesson, but he nevertheless knew its mind-numbing details by heart. Instead of listening, he repeated his refrain until he had half convinced himself.

When Jacob was twelve and his father was interviewing him for worthiness to receive the Aaronic Priesthood and be ordained a deacon, he had confessed his doubts. His testimony was weak, maybe even nonexistent. If he applied the same standards to the gospel that he did to any other religion, then the Church of the Anointing would be found wanting.

"Well, of course," his father had said. "You don't use logic to measure the truthfulness of the gospel; you rely on faith."

"But I don't have any faith," he had said. "That's my whole problem."

"My advice is to fake it till you make it."

Father had explained. Pray, fast, study the scriptures. Behave, that is, as though he already had a testimony. State publicly his faith in the Lord and his willingness to obey the prophet. Over time, the testimony would come.

It was an odd theory, and one that had never worked, not completely. But he did notice one curious thing in following his father's advice. As soon as he "faked it," so to speak, people treated him differently. They admired his knowledge of scripture and the strength of his testimony. Eloquence with words was assumed to be a mirror of one's convictions.

It was a lesson that had followed him to college and then to medical school. Act as if you know what you're talking about and people will assume that you do. Pretend you have no fear and you will appear confident to others.

And that was what was needed now, Jacob reminded himself as the meeting closed with prayer and a hundred men and older boys dispersed from the chapel. He must stand up to Elder Kimball in front of the Prophet of the Lord, and he, a young man of twenty-six, must convince them—or the prophet, at least—of his moral authority.

Brother Joseph remained after the chapel emptied, together with Elder Kimball. Jacob made his way through the pews and climbed the stairs to the podium. Brother Joseph didn't rise, but gripped his cane and idly rubbed at the polished brass beehive handle. The cane was said to have belonged to his great-grandfather, Brigham Young. At the age of eighty, Brother Joseph had lost some of his physical strength, but remained mentally sharp. He stroked his white beard as Jacob approached.

"Jacob, you are looking well," the prophet said. His voice trembled with age. "I've always thought you looked like your father, but just now, as you came walking up through the pews, the resemblance was uncanny."

Jacob took that as a compliment. "Thank you."

Elder Kimball spoke up. "You've seen the body." He sounded—what? Exhausted? Resigned? "I take it you're agreed then, that the Mexicans are to blame? Yes, of course," he said, answering his own question. Kimball turned to the prophet without taking a breath between sentences. "My boys have taken my wife's body to the house. I'm going to tell the rest of them what happened when I get home. It'll be good not to keep it secret any longer. Charity will dress Amanda in her temple robes, and we can do the burial first thing in the morning, before sacrament meeting. We'll keep the murder hush-hush, so as not to attract state or federal attention. As for the Mexicans..."

Jacob cut in. "Excuse me for interrupting, Elder Kimball, but we're getting way ahead of ourselves." He was not happy that they'd moved Amanda's body. What he needed was a professional investigation to catch the things that he might have missed, but at the very least he'd wanted the body to stay untouched while he considered new angles.

He'd planned to boot up the laptop when he got to the Kimballs' tonight and Google a few of the loose ends. Monday, he would send the sample he'd taken from Amanda's vagina to a friend of his at the University of Calgary, although he didn't expect that would turn up anything. Maybe he'd take another look at the crime scene to check out the footprints, but there'd been enough traffic at the site to obliterate clues.

Elder Kimball asked, "Ahead of ourselves? Are you suggesting we hold off on the funeral?"

"No, go ahead with the funeral." There was no way he was stopping it; as the body had been moved already, the site contaminated, it was best not to waste his capital objecting. "But you're wrong about the Mexicans. They're innocent."

Elder Kimball sputtered, but Brother Joseph lifted a hand to stop him. "Explain, please," the prophet said.

It was here that Jacob steadied his breathing. He must appear very calm; any doubt would ruin his argument. Memories of Amanda's slaughtered body were still fresh in his mind. He owed the woman justice.

He chose his words carefully. "The manner of the murder points in a different direction. Her throat was cut from ear to ear, and her tongue..." He paused to let their minds catch up. "Her tongue had been torn out by its roots."

The two men recoiled with visual horror. Elder Kimball, if anything, looked the more stricken of the two, and when he recovered it was only with doubt on his face where once there had been certainty.

Jacob knew the words from the temple endowment had come to their minds as surely as they had come to his own. *We, and each of us, covenant and promise that we will not reveal any of the secrets of this, the First Token of the Aaronic Priesthood, with its accompanying name, sign, and penalty. Should we do so, we agree that our throats be cut from ear to ear and our tongues torn out by their roots.*

The bloody penalties had troubled Jacob the first time he'd gone through the temple, shortly after receiving the Melchizedek Priesthood from his father. They were a relic of an earlier time, when enemies and apostates harassed the church from every side. By compelling the members to take their endowments under covenant, they could ensure loyalty and protect the sanctity of the temple. But until yesterday he had always taken them symbolically, not literally.

"Are you certain?" Brother Joseph asked sharply. "Both the throat and the tongue?"

"I have pictures on my digital camera. It's in the car if you'd like me to get it."

"That's not necessary, Jacob," the prophet said. "We trust you."

"So you see," Jacob continued, "it can't be the Mexicans. It's got to be one of the saints."

Elder Kimball had nothing to counter this, but Brother Joseph shook his head. "The evidence isn't conclusive. It might be an apostate. It might be one of the Lost Boys who learned the temple covenants through deceit. It might even be a Salt Lake Mormon. They've debased the endowment, but until 1990 the wording was similar in that regard."

"It might even be one of the Lamanites, still," Elder Kimball added. He still clung to his discredited, and no doubt racially motivated, theory. "Many Mexicans are Salt Lake Mormons."

"All possible," Jacob conceded. "Just barely. But all those others you mentioned—what's their motive? And it doesn't matter. There aren't any Salt Lake Mormons, Lost Boys, or apostates in

Blister Creek. That leaves the Mexicans, but enough people have seen them working in tank tops or drinking beer to make it obvious they're not Mormons." He shook his head. "No, it has to be a church member."

"You might be right," Brother Joseph said. "Nevertheless, you must rule out these possibilities before we look within our own community. Continue your investigation, and I'll pray to the Lord for guidance when I visit the temple tonight." He fixed Elder Kimball with a sharp look. "In the meanwhile, leave the Mexicans alone. But we can't have them around during the funeral. They'll be curious. And they might talk."

"I've got some flagstone waiting in St. George," Elder Kimball said. "I don't usually work them on Sunday, but I could send them out in the morning with the truck. That would take most of the morning."

Brother Joseph said, "Good enough."

He levered himself to a standing position with his cane. Even diminished as he was by age, the prophet was still a commanding physical presence, and Jacob had to look up to meet his gaze. He placed a hand on Jacob's shoulder. "See me after church tomorrow and I'll give you a blessing to help you in your search."

Jacob would have rather had more evidence or, better, a legitimate suspect or even a few leads, but he would take the prophet's blessing. "Thank you."

The prophet's eyes hardened. "I have faith that God will deliver this evildoer into your hands. And then we will exact the Lord's vengeance."

* * *

The angel came to Elder Kimball that night while he was in bed trying to fall asleep. There came a bright light, so strong that it hurt even though his eyes were closed. They flew open in terror. For a moment it was so bright that he could see nothing, and then the angel came into view.

It had been a rough couple of days since they had discovered Amanda's murdered body. Taylor Young Kimball was not a sentimental man. He had lost three children under the age of five, and his wives had suffered half a dozen miscarriages over the decades. The first loss had been the one that had almost destroyed him. He'd had two children already, both by his first wife Marielle. Gideon and Taylor Junior. Both were colicky, unhappy children to match their mother's sour disposition.

His love had been Charity, his second wife, and the first of his own choosing. These days Charity had long been his senior wife (Marielle had died of breast cancer in 1988), but the early years had been a trial. Charity had been like Rachel from the Bible story, with Marielle as Leah. Bullied, hated by the first wife.

Charity had borne him a beautiful son named Joel. The boy, only a toddler, had fallen into an irrigation ditch when it was swollen from a storm. They'd found his body wedged in a snag of sticks.

Kimball had thought his heart would burst from his chest. For two weeks he had retreated from Zion and had pointed a gun at his own head on more than one occasion, knowing full well that God would not forgive him for taking his own life.

At last, his uncle, Brother Heber, the prophet of those days and father of Brother Joseph, had come into Kimball's bedroom where he lay on his bed, staring at the ceiling.

"Some of your cattle are free in the Ghost Cliffs," Brother Heber had said. He'd been born and raised in the days when the saints would have scoffed at modern conveniences like indoor plumbing and air-conditioned pickup trucks. Together with his father, two uncles, a handful of family friends, and a number of wives, the Kimballs and Christiansons had forged the community of Blister Creek and done so in the face of betrayal and excommunication by the Salt Lake church, federal opposition, and the brutal realities of the desert itself.

"Your brother was going to round them up for you," continued the prophet, "but I told him it was time you got off your sorry ass and got to work. It's a hundred and ten out there, and those cows are too dumb to find their way to water."

Kimball had said nothing. Let the cows shrivel and die for all he cared. It would not bring back his son Joel. It would not undo the hatred he felt for Marielle and her two sons or erase the bitter words he had spoken to Charity. He closed his eyes as he remembered their fights, their incriminating words, each one blaming the other.

"Life is pain and hardship, boy. This isn't the first time God has tested his elect, and it won't be the last. Now, I'm not going to leave this room without giving you either a blessing or a horsewhipping. It's up to you. After that, you can decide if you're willing to obey the Lord or if you'll fall away and suffer eternal damnation."

He'd chosen the blessing. He still remembered some of the words. "And bless you, Brother Kimball, that you will discern good from evil, according to your faithfulness. Let the Lord stiffen your resolve against the suffering of the world, that you remember the eternal perspective."

Kimball had left that room a new man. He never again forgot the eternal perspective. He had lost a child, but only for this life. He would have that child again in the next life, and the other children that he had lost. Amanda would belong to him in the next life as well. He would right all of the wrongs in the next life, when his work here was done. He would be the father and the husband that he could have been had he not spent his life building Zion.

Nevertheless, he felt pangs of guilt and sorrow when he thought of Amanda's murder. Had he not feared that something like this was coming? The path they'd chosen had not been without risks, and his actions had put his wife in danger.

It took an angelic visit to set him straight. When his eyes adjusted and he saw the angel in all its dazzle and glory, he felt terror. Had it come to punish him for Amanda's death?

"Elder Kimball," the angel said. Its voice was cold. "The Lord is greatly displeased."

Kimball had been ordained to receive the ministering of angels when he joined the Quorum of the Twelve, but he'd never expected to actually see one. The first time, there in the temple with his son, had been a surprise, and not altogether a pleasant one.

It occurred to him, not for the first time, that he might be hallucinating. Prophets and apostles had seen angels, even Heavenly Father and Jesus face to face, but he also knew the world was full of crazies who claimed to have seen everything from aliens to the Virgin Mary.

Still, he didn't think he was crazy. He had a more fundamental fear. Kimball did not feel holy or righteous whenever it appeared. Perhaps it was Satan or one of his minions. Would he know the difference?

There was a scientific answer to that question. Joseph Smith had received instructions on this matter: which he'd recorded in the Doctrine and Covenants thusly: *If it be the devil as an angel of light, when you ask him to shake hands he will offer you his hand, and you will not feel anything; you may therefore detect him.*

Nice, in theory. What the scripture didn't account for was the sheer terror a man felt in the presence of an angel armed with a sword. Who had the courage to demand that an angel shake his hand as some supernatural lie detector test?

He was trembling as he sat up in bed. "I didn't do it. I didn't kill her. I did everything you asked."

The angel floated several inches above the floor of Kimball's room. His hair was white, and he wore white robes. His face was too bright to look at.

"Thou slothful servant," the angel said. "You may not have murdered your wife with your own hands, but your cowardice led to her death. Worse, you have broken the veil of silence and your enemies are looking for a way to destroy you."

"You mean Jacob? He is a boy and will be easily intimidated." Unfortunately, he knew otherwise from the experience in Witch's Warts. He, elder of Israel, had been the one intimidated.

"Do not be a fool, Taylor Kimball. He is protected by his father and by the prophet, who, sadly, are misguided in their devotion to the old ways. You must keep an eye on his sister as well."

"Eliza? What are you talking about? She's just a girl. All she needs is a husband and she'll fall into line."

The angel drew his sword. The sword was the opposite of the angel itself, so black that it wrestled with the light of the angel and sent weird shadows crawling across the floor like snakes. And cold enough to chill the air. "Fool. Do you question me?"

"No, of course not." Kimball cowered. "I see that you are right. Yes, of course. I had overlooked the girl." If Jacob and Eliza were a danger, why didn't the angel threaten *them* with a sword?

The angel said, "This is the most important moment for two thousand years. The Lord demands your obedience. You have been called to serve Him. But if you will not, He will strike you down and find someone worthy of His blessings."

"I will serve Him. What should I do?"

"You will either drive Jacob from town or see him dead. I have other plans for the girl."

"Yes, I understand."

The angel flared brighter than the sun, and Taylor Kimball fell back, stunned. When he opened his eyes again, it was black and his head was fuzzy. He had the impression of waking from a dream. Had he really just promised that he would kill Abraham Christianson's son if necessary? Or had he just dreamt the whole thing?

CHAPTER FIVE

There was no better way to fill a labor shortage than a truckload of Mexican illegals. They did not agitate for health insurance. They would not complain to the police if shorted on their pay. As they generally spoke little English, they were unlikely to meddle in church business. They would do their work and then disappear.

Blister Creek was a town in perpetual need of muscle power. Out of eight hundred people, fewer than sixty were adult males. When Blister Creek needed lifting, pulling, chopping, carrying, or digging, it turned to strong Mexican backs and shoulders to bear its burdens. And yet, as outsiders, it was natural that the Mexicans should also bear the brunt of suspicion for any crime.

"Spiritual guidance," Jacob said to Eliza as they walked down the sidewalk after sacrament meeting, heading toward the Mexicans' trailer on the north end of town. "It'd be useful if it helped with more than finding lost car keys."

She shrugged. "You were expecting something new at church today?" It was hot, and she was frustrated that they'd spent practically their whole Sunday in church meetings when they had so much to do.

The day had begun with Amanda's funeral. Her cousin had been dressed in her temple robes, and her face was veiled, but Eliza knew what to look for and could see the stitches under the chin even through the veil. After the funeral, a procession of meetings: morning devotional, relief society, Sunday school, and finally sacrament meeting.

Jacob said, "No, not really. More of the so-called milk of the gospel and none of the meat, but when isn't it? So Brother Roberts claimed that God told him to check his oil before he was about to drive to Phoenix. Lucky for him. He might have destroyed his engine, otherwise. A true tragedy. And then the Lord told him where to look for his keys. Nice."

"Well, why not?" she asked. "He prayed, and the Lord gave him an answer. Isn't that the essence of spiritual guidance?"

Jacob persisted. "It's a smallish God that worries about lost car keys. Either He's oblivious or He's more concerned with minutiae than the big picture. Let's see, help Brother Roberts find his car keys or prevent the Indonesian tsunami. Tsunami, car keys. Hmm. What will it be?"

"God doesn't tamper with free agency. He can't stop every bad thing from happening."

She knew it was a weak answer even before Jacob slapped it down. He asked, "How does it tamper with free agency to whisper in a quarter of a million people's ears that now might be a good time to walk away from the beach?"

"Maybe He did whisper and people didn't listen. It's called the still, small voice for a reason."

"Okay then. How about, 'Run like hell! NOW!' People could still obey or not."

"What are you saying, Jacob? That God doesn't exist?"

"Hardly. I'm saying that maybe God is more inscrutable than we imagine. Maybe He does help people find their car keys while letting hundreds of thousands of people drown from a tsunami, but we're fools to think we know why."

"So it's all random," she said. "Is that what you're saying? No, I can't buy that."

"You're missing my point, Liz. I'm not talking about the tsunami or car keys. I'm talking about us. About Amanda. There won't be any divine aide in finding Amanda's murderer. I could see you thinking that during Brother Roberts's talk. You were thinking, 'Maybe we could pray to find out who did it. Maybe Jacob could use his priesthood.'"

That was, in fact, exactly what she had been thinking. "So we can't pray for an answer? Okay, then maybe God can help in some other way."

"How do you mean?"

"Maybe that's why God sent you to medical school," Eliza said after thinking about it for a minute. "You told me you were drawn to pathology. Maybe that's why. To teach you how to look at bodies. To think about what goes wrong with things."

Eliza enjoyed his hesitation. She'd given him something that he hadn't yet considered.

At last, he laughed. "Excellent, Eliza. Okay, first things first. Let's rule out the Mexicans. Should be easy enough."

It wasn't as hot as it had been yesterday, but it was warm enough. By the time they reached the Mexicans' trailer, sweat trickled down her back and dribbled along the edge of her bra. She let Jacob walk ahead so she could fiddle with the darn thing. Once she went through the temple, she would add an extra layer of clothing in the temple garments. She didn't know how the women of Blister Creek could stand it.

The Mexicans had returned with Elder Kimball's flagstone that afternoon, and they lounged in the shade of a cottonwood tree where they'd parked the trailer. It was a fifth wheel, raised on cinderblock. They had a panel truck, in which they'd hauled their supplies of carpet, linoleum, and bathroom fixtures. A beat-up Ford F-150 was parked next to the panel truck.

The four men looked up from a card game. One man hastily shoved a beer into a cooler at Jacob's approach. Elder Kimball was a fanatic about that sort of thing, but Jacob wouldn't care if they drank or smoked. Why should a gentile obey the Word of Wisdom?

Jacob addressed the men in Spanish. *"Buenas tardes. Hay alguien acá que hable inglés?"*

"I speak English," one of the men said. He raised his eyebrows. "You speak very good Spanish." He glanced at Eliza, then dismissed her with his eyes and turned back to Jacob. "Where did you learn?"

"Spent a few years in Mexico when I was a teenager. But my Spanish is rusty."

The Mormon colonies in Mexico had been established with the same thinking as the settlements in Alberta, to hide polygamists from the federal government. The colonies had mostly gone mainstream, but they still had a few unaffiliated polygamists. Jacob had spent several years in the colonies as a child during a series of raids similar to those that had once sent Eliza to Blister Creek.

"But what about you?" Jacob asked. "You barely have an accent."

"I've been in the U.S. off and on since '89. Worked in Atlanta for a few years, then Phoenix." He smiled. "Thought a few months in a polygamist cult would make a good change of pace."

She didn't know if he was trying to bait Jacob, but her brother just chuckled. "Just don't cross the cult leader or they'll burn down your trailer in the middle of the night." He said it in the same joking tone of voice that the Mexican had used, except that Eliza knew that Elder Kimball had been planning just that.

"My name is Manuel. These other three don't speak English."

"I'm Jacob, and this is my sister Eliza." He turned to the others and introduced himself in Spanish. Eliza understood enough to hear their names as Jaime, Martín, and Eduardo.

Jacob turned back to Manuel and said in English, "I'm not from Blister Creek. Are these people easy to work for?"

Manuel shrugged. "Sure." He said something to the other men, and they continued their card game without him. "I mean, they've been paying us on time, which is the most important thing." His tone was friendly enough, but reserved, just shy of suspicious.

Jacob continued with the small talk for a couple of minutes, then casually asked if they'd ever met any of the women in the town. Did they know a woman named Charity Kimball? How about her sister wives? What about Amanda Kimball?

"Is that what this is about?" Manuel's tone had grown defensive. "You think one of my men has been messing around with your women?" He shook his head. "We're so busy most days we barely have time to sleep, and these guys are never out of my sight, except when a couple of them drive to St. George for supplies or to hit the bar."

Jacob said, "Nah, I don't think that. I'm looking for a man. Someone said he was back in town."

"Who is he?"

"He's one of what we call the Lost Boys. They're young men expelled for wrong-thinking or bad behavior." He shrugged. "Or maybe they're just dumb. Our standards are strict."

"Yes, I've noticed. So who is he?"

"He's my brother, actually. Name is Enoch. He's been in some trouble, and I thought he might have come around looking for me."

"What's he look like?"

"He'll be easy enough to recognize. Red hair, and if you shook his hand, you'd notice a crooked thumb."

As Jacob spoke, Eliza watched the other three men. They occasionally glanced her way or to the conversation between Jacob and Manuel, but mostly paid attention to their game.

Except for the one named Eduardo. He was a young man, maybe early twenties, with dark hair and brown eyes. He wore a tank top, and his arms and shoulders were bare and muscled and very tanned. He caught her eye and then looked back at her a moment later.

Go ahead and stare, she thought, refusing to look away or feel embarrassed. Gentiles were all the same. They gawked at her conservative clothes and lack of makeup as if she had just stepped off a nineteenth-century frontier homestead.

"Well, good," Jacob said as Eliza tuned back in to the conversation. She had missed something. "Thanks for the information." He shook hands and gave his farewells to the others in Spanish.

"I missed that last part," she said as they walked away. "He's seen Enoch?"

"Yes, with two other young men. They were probably Lost Boys, too. Could have been Tuesday. Maybe Monday. He wasn't sure. Saw them coming out of the temple."

"What? The temple?"

"Yeah, I know." Enoch had been excommunicated, so he couldn't go into the temple. They reached the sidewalk, and Jacob said, "Apart from that, there was something odd about that exchange. Seemed like Manuel was pumping *me* for information."

Eliza didn't say anything, still off-balance from the news about Enoch. She was sweating again now that they'd left the shade of the cottonwood tree.

Jacob said, "Which begs the question, what? Has Manuel heard something? Is he just curious, or does he know more than he's letting on? I was certain that the Mexicans weren't involved. Maybe I was wrong. Did you see anything?"

"Just that the young one—Eduardo—kept staring at me. Reminds me of that place we stopped in Cedar City. You'd think we were a carnival exhibit or Amish or something."

"Maybe he thought you were cute," Jacob said. "He was probably just checking you out."

"Oh, shut up. I can tell the difference between gawking and checking out."

"If you say so. But it seems like he's seen enough polygamists now that he's past the gawking stage. If that's all it was."

"Anyway," she said in an exaggerated tone. "What's next?"

They passed the church building, together with a few women coming from a late meeting. There were a handful of elderly women, and two mothers pushing strollers. Eliza and Jacob exchanged friendly greetings with these women.

Jacob waited until they were alone again before answering. "What's next? I guess you'd call it following up on leads. I've got a couple of phone calls, that stuff to send to the lab, and perhaps you could ask Amanda's sister wives some questions."

"Fernie might know something. I'm kind of afraid to talk to the others."

"It won't hurt to ask Fernie, although I thought I'd give her a call myself," he said. Eliza remembered that Jacob, while not related to Fernie by birth, had spent more time with Eliza's half sister than she had. He continued, "But don't worry about the others. Be yourself and they'll warm up. Start with Charity Kimball."

Easy enough for him to say, but she knew she had to make herself useful. The other women knew about the murder by now. It was her job to talk to them. "Okay. I'll see what I can find."

He nodded. "Good. Maybe someone noticed Amanda acting strange or saw her talking to someone. I'd also like a second look at Witch's Warts. See if I can find the spot where they killed Amanda. Now," he said in a change of tone. "What's up with our brother, and how does he fit in?"

"Enoch?" she asked in surprise. "He's not mixed up in this."

"Are you sure? I'm not saying he's the murderer, but what's he doing kicking around Blister Creek? He doesn't belong here. And he wasn't alone, either. Remember?"

She studied the expression on Jacob's face. "Do you know something already?"

They were approaching the Kimball house, and they slowed their pace. Jacob turned. "I don't know everything that Enoch's been up to. But this isn't the first time he's been seen running with other Lost Boys. Gideon Kimball, for one. And now he shows up in Blister Creek. It's the last place he belongs. And the timing. According to Charity Kimball, one day before Amanda's murder."

"That could be coincidence."

"Sure. But it's the best lead we've got at the moment."

"So how do we find Enoch?" she asked.

"Manuel saw him drive off in some piece of junk with Nevada plates. We'll look around town, but I think we'll have more luck if we track him down where he lives. Don't have his address, but I know where he works."

They had reached the Kimball house. Children played in the front yard, in spite of the heat, and women set up tables on the veranda for Sunday dinner.

"So where are we going?" Eliza asked before they came within earshot of the others.

"Babylon. The Great Whore of the Desert. Legs spread wide, she gives teat to drunks and pornographers. Gambling, drugs, and all other manner of vice call it home."

Eliza was shocked, both by his crudity and by what he was implying. "You don't mean..."

He nodded. "Las Vegas."

* * *

It cooled quickly as they gathered with the Kimballs for their Sunday evening meal. They ate watermelon and pork ribs, together with potatoes, corn on the cob, raspberry pie, and gallons of lemonade.

In spite of the week-ending feast, the mood was somber. Most of Elder Kimball's wives had only learned of Amanda's death that morning. The mood at the funeral had been grim. Someone planted the rumor that Amanda had died of exposure in the desert, but this didn't take. Sharp eyes had spotted trauma on the body, and the service had turned into a gossip fest. Eliza had heard a few theories about the murder, all of which she took into account, but none offered new information.

And many of the women in Blister Creek did nothing to hide their anger. They were angry that the men had kept a stranglehold on information. Women and girls had walked around for three full days without knowing there was a murderer in town.

Eliza was eating watermelon and thinking about Las Vegas when one of Elder Kimball's weaselly sons, Taylor Junior, slid in next to her. She looked for her brother. Jacob was talking with Fernie Kimball, Eliza's half sister. Fernie laughed at something that he said. Neither looked Eliza's way.

"You look lovely today, Eliza," Taylor Junior said. His voice was hoarse, as if he were just getting over a cold. He sat close enough on the bench that his leg touched hers.

She shifted to remove her leg from contact and said, "Thank you," then turned back to her food.

"I noticed you in Sunday school. That woman has nice hips, I thought. Perfect ratio of hips to waist and legs of the right length and size. Not too skinny, but not overweight, either. One look and I knew you'd be both a good lover and fertile."

Eliza never ceased to be astonished by the sheer, awkward rudeness of the young men of the church. A laugh came out of her mouth before she could stop it.

Taylor Junior looked annoyed. "What's so funny?"

"I'm sorry," she said. "But perfect ratio of hips to waist? Come on, you need to work on your pickup lines."

"What are you talking about? That wasn't a pickup line."

"Small talk, then. Whatever you call it, it was incredibly rude."

She'd tried to put a gentle tone to her words, but Taylor Kimball sputtered angrily as he rose to his feet. He seemed a lot bigger, more threatening than he had a few moments earlier. "Are you looking for an invitation written on a silk napkin, delicately perfumed? This isn't about pickup lines. And you don't have any say in the matter. You're just a girl. And you won't stay single forever, you know."

"No, but *you* might if you don't stop acting like such a jerk." She was angry now. "There's not a woman in the world who will go for that kind of come-on."

Other women had overheard the conversation, and they smirked as Taylor Junior grew even more huffy and red, if that was possible. Eliza was beginning to wish she'd kept her mouth shut.

"I'll tell you something, Eliza Christianson," Taylor Junior said. He had lifted his voice so that everyone in the surrounding area could hear. "No, *two* somethings. In the first place—"

But before he could posture any further, Jacob arrived at the table. He put a hand on Taylor Junior's shoulder. "Here, have a seat. It'd be a shame to waste this good meal with an argument."

Taylor Junior brushed away Jacob's hand. "Your sister needs to learn her place." The women at the table tried to hush him.

Their amusement had turned to embarrassment. But Taylor Junior ignored them. "Did you hear what she said to me?" he said to Jacob and anyone who would listen. "Your sister—" and he spat this word for a second time, "just told me—"

"Whatever it was, I'm sure it was nothing." Jacob returned his hand to Taylor Junior's shoulder. "Sit down, Brother Kimball."

"Don't touch me. And don't give me that brother garbage. You're not my brother, and you're not my priesthood leader." Taylor Junior stared Jacob in the eye.

Jacob's voice lowered then. "Careful, *Junior*. Very careful."

"Yeah, whatever. You don't have a wife either, so who are you to threaten me?"

"I'm not threatening you," Jacob said. The flash faded from his face. Only the grim set to his mouth remained to show he was angry. "But let's be clear. You're not going to marry my sister. Now or ever. I don't want to see you sitting with her when I come back. Or talking to her."

He turned and walked away. There remained silence, before the women turned back to individual conversations, each of which began jarringly, like a lawnmower sputtering to life. Eliza looked down at her food, waiting for Taylor Junior to leave.

He looked around, then stared at the back of Jacob. A shuffle. He made to leave, but before he did, he put his hand on Eliza's knee and gave a viselike squeeze. She winced.

"You little bitch," he whispered. "I won't forget this. And when you *do* become my wife, your wedding night will be one to remember. Your cunt'll be so sore you won't be able to sit for a week." He got up and stomped toward the house. She was left trembling.

Jacob was cheerful when he returned, having missed Taylor Junior's parting shot. "I hope Father isn't disappointed. Because that little display disqualifies Taylor Junior from the marriage sweepstakes. Wouldn't you agree?"

Eliza looked up in alarm. "He isn't...he wasn't..."

"Yes," Jacob said, his face suddenly serious. "He was."

She glanced at Taylor Junior, now slamming the door of the house behind him, and then back to her brother. Elder Johnson, Taylor Kimball Jr. Who was the third choice?

CHAPTER SIX

By the time they left Blister Creek on Monday, Eliza could not stop thinking about Enoch. Surely he couldn't be involved in Amanda's murder.

She had once felt the same way about Enoch that she now felt about Jacob. As a young girl, she had idolized them both. They were like Book of Mormon heroes. Captain Moroni with his Standard of Liberty. Ammon, who had cut off the arms of the Lamanite bandits and converted an entire nation of unbelievers. They knew everything. They could do anything.

And what girl ever had two brothers like Jacob and Enoch? They never teased her or told her to go play with her dolls. They had read her stories and later taught her to read by herself. They had taught her to ride and groom a horse. They had taken her fishing at the beaver pond and when the brook trout weren't biting had spun preposterous stories about a colony of gnomes that lived in Father's beard, surviving on crumbs of toast and bits of jam they found clinging to his whiskers. Jacob used big, delicious words like *juxtaposition* and *defenestrate* with no sense of irony. Enoch whispered brainteasers in her ear during sacrament meeting just when she thought she would slip into a coma through sheer boredom.

But she was older now. For all that she loved Jacob, she saw that he was only human. He made mistakes. He could be condescending. He wrestled with his doubts. Despite what had happened to him, Enoch still somehow remained forever perfect in her mind.

So it was with reluctance that she raised her fears about Enoch with Jacob as they hit I-15 and headed south toward St. George. An hour and a half beyond that waited Las Vegas.

"Please tell me that Enoch is not involved."

"I hope not, Liz." Jacob sounded troubled. "Maybe he knows something, maybe not. But even if he does, it doesn't mean he's directly involved."

"He doesn't belong in Blister Creek. You said it yourself. And in the temple? How could it be random? Maybe it's tied to the murder. But why? Why Enoch?"

Jacob said, "It's like the story of Lehi's dream in the Book of Mormon. He let go of the iron rod and is wandering strange paths through the mists and darkness. A Lost Boy."

Jacob fiddled with the radio and settled on an AM station with an evangelical preacher, spinning nonsense about miracle springwater that could cure whatever ailed you, depending, of course, on your faithfulness. She wondered if the springwater were an out-and-out fraud, or if the whole outfit was a tool of the devil. The show was grating, and she was relieved when Jacob finally switched it off again.

"And why are they called Lost Boys?" Jacob said about twenty minutes later, as if there had been no pause in the conversation. "Lost sounds accidental. You lost your compass. Maybe someone gave you bad directions."

"Are you saying that the Lost Boys intentionally lost their faith?"

"No, nobody does that. I'm saying it's convenient that so many boys fall away. Boys, never girls."

Eliza didn't like the train of his argument. "Many are called, but few are chosen. It's difficult to walk the straight and narrow path."

"Get beyond the platitudes, Liz. When a young man leaves Zion, it's a one-way trip. We don't celebrate the return of our prodigal sons with a feast. We build fences. I have an uncle, for example, who was caught masturbating to an underwear catalog."

"Which uncle?" she asked. "I never heard about that."

"Not your uncle, my mother's brother. He was young, and all young men are tempted by masturbation. The point is, he was caught. He'd always been the golden boy. Future church leader, they said.

"But heaven forbid you admire a few hotties in a J.C. Penney catalog. My grandfather bought him a one-way bus ticket to Calgary. Not too different from Enoch's story, except that he killed himself a few months later."

Eliza didn't know what to say. It was a tragic story.

"In contrast, what happens when a girl flees in the middle of the night?" Jacob asked.

"They track her down. She's not let out of sight until she's married and pregnant."

"Right. She's certainly not allowed to make her own way in the world. That's because young women are valuable and young men are a threat."

"But it's still a choice," Eliza said. "Nothing forces boys to rebel."

"Nothing but human nature. That, and a conscious effort by older men to alienate the mentally slow and the morally weak." He shook his head. "They're not lost, they're expelled. That's the simple truth of the matter."

"So if not Lost Boys, then what?"

"Bachelor lions."

"Bachelor lions?" she asked.

"A lion pride consists of a handful of male lions, often brothers, and a large number of females."

"Yes, of course. And the females do the hunting, kind of like we do all the work in the church, yes?" She smiled. "And?"

"The Lost Boys are like the males expelled from the pride. The bachelors. They lurk on the outside, making periodic threats. Eventually, they drive off the old males. They then murder the cubs of the pride so as to insert their own genes as quickly as possible into the population."

"Okay, so the Lost Boys are bachelor lions," Eliza said. "But doesn't the fact that they're mentally slow and morally weak, as you put it, make it unlikely that they'll try to take over the pride?"

"Not everyone who is morally weak is mentally slow and vice versa. And it's all relative. Our outcasts are more intelligent and capable than those of other polygamist groups."

It fit with what she'd thought about the girls from other communities and their lack of intellectual spark. "But why? Why are they more intelligent?"

"It's simple evolution, Liz, to borrow from the atheists of the world."

Eliza scoffed. "Now I know you've lost your mind. We are created in God's image, not descended from monkeys."

"Are you sure about that?" he asked with one of his half smiles that may have indicated sarcasm or may have just indicated that Jacob was, in fact, an evolutionist. "But that's not what I'm talking about. Look, if a man is tall, his children are more likely to be tall, more so if his wives are also tall. What if he's intelligent? What if he remains in the community precisely because he is intelligent, while his dumber brothers are expelled?"

Eliza thought about that for a moment. She'd talked to a young woman once from the Fundamentalist Church of Jesus Christ of Latter-day Saints, and she'd said that it was the elder brothers who became church leaders in her church, while the younger sons were expelled. In the Church of the Anointing, it didn't work that way. More like a pride of lions, as a matter of fact. Tooth and claw.

"By that logic," she said, "we're all growing more spiritual as well, aren't we? More likely to throw all our energy into the church? After all, we kick out the spiritually dull, too."

"Yes, you could make that assertion."

"Then what about you?" she asked. "Nobody would question your brains, but spiritually you're not exactly conversing with angels."

"Every village has its idiot, Liz."

"So why? Is it just accident? Or is there some purpose behind this evolutionary stuff?"

"Why do we practice plural marriage, Liz?"

"To bring about the fullness of the gospel," she said. "It was a practice of the ancient church of Abraham and Isaac, and it's a requirement of the Celestial Kingdom."

"That's the spiritual reason," Jacob said. "But what's the temporal reason?"

"To raise up a righteous seed. Proverbs says, 'Raise up a child in the way he should go, and when he is old he shall not depart from it.'"

"Almost. There's also a quasi-Darwinian viewpoint in the concept of a 'righteous seed.' If it were just a question of teaching correct principles, why not encourage adoption into the families of the church leaders? No, it's believed that to grow a righteous people, it is necessary to have two ingredients: first, the proper soil—that is, a proper spiritual upbringing—and second, a good seed. Hence, a man reproduces according to his moral and intellectual strength."

"And a woman?" she asked.

"She reproduces according to her ability to get pregnant." Jacob raised an eyebrow. "It's a stud service, not a full-on breeding program. Gentiles experimented with something like this," he continued. "They call it eugenics. Good genes."

"Like the Nazis."

"Right. It's not the science that's suspect—farmers have used selective breeding for thousands of years—but stuff like what the Nazis did, or in the United States when they sterilized retarded people. It's morally repugnant."

A guilty thrill coursed through her, the feeling that she was discussing forbidden knowledge, even stepping near the edge of blasphemy. Eliza felt she should turn the conversation to something safer, but couldn't help her curiosity.

"It's not very effective, in any event," she said. "I mean, in the church. If you just select from the male half of the population, aren't you doubling the length of time to improve the stock?"

"That is an admitted flaw to the system."

And with that, they settled into silence as they left Utah and passed through the northwest tip of Arizona as I-15 made its way into Nevada. Jacob found CNN on the radio. The news was a typical snapshot of the world's misery. There was more fighting in Iraq and Afghanistan. A coup in Africa and a typhoon in China. A man in Ohio with body parts of a dozen people stored in freezers in his basement. They had caught the guy through the recipes he had mailed the local paper, which were rip-offs of Thirty-Minute Meals, but with human flesh substituted for whatever meat Rachel Ray had selected.

And the drumbeat continued its grisly tempo, some of it closer to home. Three dead in a drive-by shooting in Las Vegas. A train had derailed in Denver, killing eleven. Someone had kidnapped an infant from a hospital in New Mexico. It was the child of a prominent Los Alamos scientist, eerily familiar to a pair of earlier abductions in California. The two babies had been kidnapped by a satanic cult and killed as part of a black mass.

Eliza was congratulating herself on standing apart from the misery that afflicted the world, when she remembered Amanda. Her ghost-white flesh, the jagged grin that gaped from ear to ear.

"Can you shut it off?" she asked when she could take it no longer. "It's too depressing."

He shrugged and turned off the radio, then returned to his thoughts. They stopped for dinner, then continued. Twilight approached. At last, Las Vegas. Her first visit.

The city was a gaudy bauble, glaring with such light that it banished the night. It was cool outside the city as the dry air bled the heat into the night sky, but when they pulled into the city they had to turn the air-conditioning back on to cope with the heat stored in the asphalt and cement.

They drove down the Strip.

She gaped at the flashing lights, at the crowds, and at the spectacle: erupting volcanoes, replicas of Paris and New York, casinos and hotels that competed against each other to attack the senses with a garish display of wealth and worldliness. They stopped at a light, and a young man pressed a glossy flyer to Jacob's window flaunting a naked woman pinching her nipples. The ground was littered with such filth.

They parked and made their way into the crowds. There were people of all imaginable races and classes on the streets and coming and going from the casinos. Homeless, tourists in shorts and tank tops, slick young men, scantily clad women, men in business suits. Even, she was shocked to see, families with children. Lots of them.

The prophet had taught that there had never been a city more wicked than Las Vegas since the days of Sodom and Gomorrah. She shuddered and wanted to return to the car.

"What are we doing here?" she asked, gripping Jacob's arm and refusing to meet the eye of a tout who tried to pass them something. "Doesn't Enoch live in a crack house somewhere? Not here, surely."

"Come on, Liz. Do you believe that? Look, if you're scared, just shut your eyes and think about how righteous you are. The Lord will protect."

"Jacob, don't."

He must have heard the hurt in her voice, and the fear, because he turned to face her. "Sorry. You didn't deserve that. Listen, we're safe here. Maybe safer than we were in Blister Creek. But you've got to get a grip on yourself." He pulled a scrap of paper from his pocket. "This way."

"Where are we going?"

"Place called Caesar's Palace. It's one of these monstrosities along here."

"But how do you know where to find him?"

"Father kept an eye on him for a while. I told him to send money, but you can't do that, of course. Father doesn't know, but I came down once, tried to talk Enoch into getting out of Las Vegas. But he'd already, I don't know, fallen in with the wrong people. It didn't go well."

They found Caesar's Palace. Eliza approached with growing dread. They entered a room of a size to swallow thousands of people. Stretching from one side of the enormous room to the other were slot machines, video poker games, roulette and black-jack tables, digital displays churning with ever-growing jackpots, together with the sound of machines spitting out coins or blaring wins with light and electronic sound. Gaudy, faux Greek statuary pocked the room, joined by scantily clad cocktail waitresses and smooth young men wearing parodies of togas or gladiator costumes. And everywhere, people.

They milled from machine to machine, some excited, others glassy-eyed zombies who didn't appear to know if it was night or day. Two men swept past her in robes, and she thought them employees of the casino until she got a closer look and saw they were Arabs.

Jacob looked down at the paper again and regained his bearings. They picked their way through the casino.

"Where is he, exactly?" Eliza asked.

"Uhm, a security station near the slot machines." He frowned, glancing through the vast maze of clinking, chiming slots. "That doesn't exactly narrow it down, does it?"

Eliza forced herself to hold her head high instead of cringe or bury her face in her brother's shoulder. Nevertheless, she gripped Jacob's arm as they pushed from one bank of slot machines to the next, sometimes being bumped or jostled.

"This way," Jacob said. "I've got it now." They approached a man in a suit standing behind a bank of television screens. Each screen showed a different part of the casino. It took a moment to recognize her brother.

Enoch and Jacob were not twins, but being only ten months apart, they looked so alike they might as well have been. The primary difference was the color of their hair. Jacob's was strawberry blonde, and Enoch's a dark shade of red. Enoch glanced back and forth from the monitors to the people stepping up to an oversized slot machine in the shape of Zeus, where each person turned in a coupon to take one pull at the handle. A crash of thunder sounded every time a lightning bolt settled into position, but nobody came close to getting all six bolts and the $100,000 prize. Enoch turned as they approached, and a frown settled over his face.

"Hello, Enoch," Jacob said.

"What are you doing here?" He looked at Eliza and his face softened slightly, then hardened again when he turned back to Jacob. "And Liz? You brought Liz?"

"Do you have a few minutes?"

"I'm working. You know, a job. Someday you should try it."
He looked them over. "We see all kinds here, but I swear I recognized you the instant you came through the doors. It wasn't just
the clothes, either. There's that self-righteous way that you carry
yourself. You don't want to be polluted by accidental contact."

His words stung, even though they weren't directed at
her.

"Nice to see you, too," Jacob said, smiling. "Isn't there someone else who can cover for a few minutes?"

"There's a hundred. The economy is crap—I'll bet we can find
all sorts of people who want my job. So I'll walk away from my
post, we can chat, and I'll get fired. How does that sound?" He
directed his attention to Eliza. "Liz, what are you doing? Is this how
you want to live your life?"

She took Jacob's arm, upset by how angry Enoch had become.
"I'm with Jacob."

"Figures."

"Leave her alone," Jacob said.

"Right, I've got no beef with Liz. It's you, Jacob. It's because
of you that I'm here."

"No it's not."

"Sure it is. If you hadn't been so damn good at everything,
not to mention smug about it, I could have been just a normal kid.
Instead, I was compared to you every step of the way."

Jacob said, "And all the times you got into it with Father? That
was my fault too? Oh, yeah, and the beer and cigarettes? Are you
going to claim that I bought them for you and forced them into
your mouth?"

"I made a few mistakes," Enoch said. "Big deal. I believed in the gospel—I still believe in it."

Eliza was struck with the incongruity between Enoch's words and his behavior. Enoch, who claimed he still believed, had taken a job in the heart of Babylon. The belly of the beast. Why?

Enoch said, "But that's the funny thing. I believe and I've been kicked out. Nobody knows what you believe, Jacob. I don't think even *you* know."

"That's not true," Jacob said, but the way his words came out Eliza could tell that Enoch had cut him with that last remark. "I know what I believe. Just 'cause I don't run into the street and shout my beliefs to the world doesn't mean that I don't have them."

"You're a doubter."

"I'm waiting for God to direct me."

"Hah! That's your way of saying that you do whatever you want because God hasn't yet revealed Himself to you. As if you need a personal invitation. God's plan is freely available in the scriptures and from the mouths of the prophets." Enoch had raised his voice, and now he looked around as if concerned with who might be watching. "Now, what are you doing here? I've got a job to do, and my boss is going to walk through here in about five minutes, and I don't want to be talking to a couple of people from the old country when he does."

Jacob said, "What were you doing in Blister Creek last week?"

"What are you talking about? I haven't been to Blister Creek in three years, and I don't intend to ever set foot there again. Now, can you go away? Please. I can't talk right now."

"That's fine. What time do you get off work?"

"What's that to you? You planning to wait?" Enoch asked.

"Yes. As long as necessary. I've been sent by the prophet," Jacob added. "If you still believe, as you claim, then you will obey his will and speak with me."

Enoch rocked back on his heels. Surprisingly to Eliza, this seemed to catch him more off guard than Jacob's mention of Blister Creek.

"The prophet sent you?" A long pause. "But I...why would he have sent you?"

Jacob stayed silent, and Eliza realized belatedly that this was his tactic, to let Enoch keep talking and revealing information. But before her mind could catch up to Jacob's, she said, "You know something, don't you?"

"About what?" Enoch looked newly guarded.

She had grown frustrated. "About Amanda's murder, Enoch. What do you think?"

His face turned pale. "Amanda Kimball? Murdered? No."

"Murdered," she repeated. "Two days ago. With her throat cut from ear to ear and her *tongue ripped out by its roots.*" She didn't know yet what that meant, but Enoch would, if he'd really been at the temple.

Enoch took two steps back, as if he were trying to flee, and knocked into a cocktail waitress, who dumped her tray with a cry. Drinks spilled to the floor, but Enoch paid no attention to the mess or to the waitress sprawling at his feet. He buried his face in his hands.

CHAPTER SEVEN

Enoch lived in a brick apartment building two miles northwest of the Strip. He was too shaken to drive, so they left his car at the casino and went in Jacob and Eliza's Corolla. Enoch had retreated to the casino restroom and emerged a few minutes later, looking pale. He'd begged out of the rest of his shift on account of illness. Once the three of them were in the car, Eliza realized that he hadn't had to concoct that story: her brother smelled strongly of vomit.

When they reached the apartment, Enoch retreated to the bathroom and locked the door. They could hear running water from the sink and more sounds of their brother being sick. He looked terrible when he came out. He went straight to his bedroom to change his clothes.

Meanwhile, Eliza had taken a look around the apartment. It was not what she was expecting. It was just a small, clean apartment with no crack pipes, no ashtrays overflowing with butts, no empty beer cans lying around, and no evidence of a roommate, transsexual stripper or no. The only evidence of a worldly lifestyle was a television and a stereo. So much for the rumors. Eliza and Jacob waited on the couch.

When at last he joined them, Enoch was pale but in control. "Sorry about what I said earlier. I'm so tired of lectures. I thought you'd come back for more of the same and brought Eliza to dish up an extra helping of guilt."

Eliza said, "You're my brother. I love you. I thought I'd never see you again. And I didn't come all the way from Canada to tell you to shape up."

"Well, maybe that would have been better. Not this other stuff."

"You wouldn't have listened anyway," Jacob said. "You weren't interested in advice, remember?"

"You still could have helped in some way," Enoch snapped. He seemed to catch himself, and when he spoke again sounded tired. "I didn't need a lecture, but yeah, I could have used help, Jacob. I was destitute, forced to drop out of school. And I didn't know jack about how to survive out here. You have no idea how low I sank."

"We can't help you," Eliza said. Her anger had faded, and now she felt guilty. "You were excommunicated. We have to shun you."

"Have to? That just kills me. Who came up with that shunning crap anyway?" Enoch shook his head. "But that doesn't matter. No thanks to you, I survived. I found help."

"Meaning you took up with the Lost Boys," Jacob said. "Is that it?"

"Ah, so I should have waited for my family to come around. They would have helped. Eventually. Right?"

"We can go around and around," Jacob said. "But that's not why we're here. Someone murdered Amanda Kimball last Wednesday. You know something about that, Enoch. What?"

He said nothing, so Jacob tried again. "Why target Amanda? What possible reason would they have to kill her, and as a traitor, too, with her throat cut and her tongue ripped out?"

"They told me they weren't going to kill her," Enoch said. "Just frighten her. Remind her of her covenants and let her know the prophet wasn't pleased."

"What do you mean, the prophet?" Jacob asked. "Is Brother Joseph involved in this somehow?" He said it casually, but Eliza found herself shaking her head. There was no way that the prophet would be involved in something so horrible.

"Yes, of course. Well," and here he paused, "okay, I've never spoken to Brother Joseph directly."

Eliza couldn't hold her tongue. "Is the prophet in the habit of killing those who disobey him?"

Jacob lifted his hand. "It's okay, Liz." He asked Enoch, "How about the Lost Boys? Is Gideon Kimball involved? Israel Young?"

Enoch ignored the question, as he had ignored Eliza's. "It's not easy being an outcast. Hated by everyone. Even your own family." He shook his head. "Who would choose such a life? Yet there are still ways to serve the Lord. Is there not a mansion in the Lord's kingdom for all who obey His will?"

Jacob said, "Enoch, what are you playing at? You have information. We need it."

"Why? This doesn't concern you."

Jacob fixed Enoch with a hard stare. "Listen. Whatever you think you were doing was not serving the church and most certainly isn't the will of the prophet or of the Lord."

"How do you know that?"

"By their fruits, you shall know them," Jacob said. "An evil tree bringeth forth evil fruit. What's the fruit of these friends of yours? A young mother murdered by a corruption of the temple endowment."

"The Lord's ways are not our own, Jacob. What of God smiting Pharaoh with plagues, or in the Book of Mormon, of Nephi beheading Laban to obtain the Brass Plates? By God's own command."

Jacob said, "Whatever moral turpitude has polluted your thoughts, Enoch, let me reiterate, the prophet doesn't know anything about it. How do I know? I already told you. Brother Joseph and Father sent us to investigate Amanda's murder. If both the prophet and the senior member of the Quorum of the Twelve aren't running this, then who is?"

"Perhaps you've fallen under the influence of the Adversary," Eliza suggested. In general, it bugged her when people blamed their bad behavior on Satan, but in this case it seemed appropriate.

Jacob said, "You don't feel good about what happened, Enoch. Look at your reaction when you heard the news. Whatever you thought would happen, it wasn't murder. And I know that it's not you. Do you remember that time when we were kids, when you found Israel Young taping firecrackers to toads? You gave him a beating he wouldn't forget. And what about the time with the injured kitten? You always had a gentle soul, Enoch. Please, tell us what you know," Jacob urged. "It'll lift a weight off your conscience."

Enoch said nothing, and Eliza grew impatient. "Did I tell you? They buried Amanda in a shallow grave in Witch's Warts. A dead dog gets more respect. Wonder what they'll tell Sophie Marie. Will she know that they cut her mother's throat like a pig?"

"And you know the worst thing?" Jacob asked. "You could have prevented it."

All at once, Enoch turned pale again. Jacob went to the kitchen to get a pan. Eliza sat on the couch, fuming. Let him throw up. He was a coward and deserved to twitch with guilt. She, for one, wasn't moved by stories of kittens and toads. What was that to the life of her cousin?

As Enoch bent, she caught a glimpse of something at his chest. He wore temple garments beneath his clothing, but beneath that was a necklace with some sort of medallion on the end. Jacob returned. Enoch straightened and took the pan from Jacob, but he put it aside. The green look had faded.

Jacob tried again. "Enoch, it's important that you tell us what you know so we can stop this from happening again. I'll tell Brother Joseph how you helped us. If you truly believe in the gospel, then you'll value the blessing of the prophet. Maybe…"

"Okay, that's thick enough," Enoch said. "I know what you can and cannot promise. Very little, I'd think. But I'll tell you what I know." He paused, ran his tongue over his lower lip. "First, I don't know who killed Amanda. It might be one of several people."

"Names?"

"No, Jacob. That's one thing I can't do. I made covenants, and unless you want to see me with my own throat cut and my tongue ripped out, you won't push me for names. And anyway, I couldn't tell you who did it. Not for sure. You'll have to find that out on your own."

"But suffice it to say that Gideon Kimball is one of those names," Jacob said, to no response. "Would his father, Elder Kimball, be involved? How about Taylor Junior?"

Again, no answer.

Enoch wanted to talk, Eliza could see. The guilt was clear on his face, but he still needed prodding. Eliza was wondering how hard Jacob could push without making Enoch retreat fully when the cordless on the wall just outside the kitchen rang. Enoch started, then rose to his feet.

"Let the machine get it," Jacob urged.

"I can't. It might be work. I left so quickly, someone might be calling to make sure that I'm okay. This is Las Vegas. Things happen."

He picked up the phone. A grim look passed across his face, and then he went into the bedroom and shut the door.

"That's not work," Jacob said.

"You think it's Gideon Kimball?"

"Maybe. I shouldn't have let him take that call. You know, he wants to tell us, you can see that. But he wants to tell us without telling us, if that makes any sense. You notice he's wearing garments? Someone has taken him through the temple."

"Yeah, and what's that thing he's wearing around his neck?" Eliza asked.

"What do you mean?"

"A medallion on a chain. Underneath his shirt. I saw it when he bent over."

Jacob frowned. "A medallion? I didn't see it."

"Silver. About this big." She made a ring with her fingers the size of an old-fashioned silver dollar. "Markings on it, symbols and such."

"Like the zodiac, maybe?"

She thought about it. "Not exactly, no. More like Egyptian hieroglyphs. Maybe it doesn't mean anything."

"No, but it makes me think of Reformed Egyptian. As in the Gold Plates."

The Gold Plates, translated by Joseph Smith into the Book of Mormon, had been written on sheets of gold in a language they had called Reformed Egyptian.

They looked toward the bedroom door and waited. Still no Enoch. It had been perhaps fifteen minutes. At last, they could stand it no more and made their way to the door. Jacob knocked. "Come on, Enoch. It's not going to get any easier." He waited a moment, then tried the door. It was locked. He knocked again.

Eliza felt a twang of alarm. "Open the door, Enoch," she said. "You've got to help us. They killed Amanda, Enoch. They left her daughter without a mother. Enoch?"

"Damn it, Enoch!" Jacob said. "Open this door or I'm going to break it down."

Still no answer. Jacob leaned his shoulder in and rammed the door. It held. He leaned in harder this time, but the door didn't move.

They both joined in now, more worried than anything. "Enoch, open up. Right now. We're not fooling around."

Jacob rammed the door again, first with his shoulder again, harder, then with his shoe. It held. Anxious now, they swept the magazines from the coffee table and hoisted it toward the bedroom door like a battering ram. The first blow was tentative and uncoordinated. The second burst the door open. They shoved aside the coffee table and rushed into the bedroom.

The room was empty.

Jacob threw open the closet doors, thinking, perhaps, that he was hiding, or, following Eliza's thoughts, that he'd hung himself with his belt. It, too, was empty.

She looked around with mounting confusion. "I don't understand. It's like an angel took him."

Jacob snorted before she had a chance to finish this thought. He picked up the cordless phone where Enoch had dropped it on the bed before disappearing, then made his way to the window, where he threw open the curtains. "What's more likely, an angel spirited him away, or he ran like a coward?" The window was open.

Eliza followed her brother to the window and looked down. They were on the second floor, but there were bushes below to break a fall. The exterior of the building was well lit, as was the street and parking lot beyond. No sign of Enoch.

She gave Jacob an embarrassed smile. "I just…well, it caught me off guard. What now?"

"We'll wait. Look at all this stuff. He's got to come back."

They took stock of the bedroom. There was a bookshelf filled with all manner of secular and spiritual books. Enoch had a lava lamp on his nightstand, a curious touch, she thought, and a print of the Angel Moroni appearing to a young Joseph Smith on one wall. On the opposite wall sat a framed photograph of the Blister Creek temple.

"Maybe," she said, "but nothing says he has to come back tonight or anytime soon. How long will we have to wait?"

"He's got a job and a life here, and probably bank accounts, bills, et cetera. He'll get out there, wherever he ran, and start thinking about this stuff, and then he'll come back. I'd give him an hour."

She wasn't so sure. He'd been spooked. Or maybe the phone call had told him to run. Either way, who said he had to come back? She sat down on the bed. Jacob rifled through the nightstand drawers.

The front door to the apartment opened. Jacob looked up with a smile on his lips. "Make that five minutes."

The smile died just as quickly. Two men entered the apartment, shutting the door behind them. They wore black ski masks and carried baseball bats. Jacob pushed Eliza deeper into the bedroom, then moved between her and the intruders. The men crossed the living room toward the bedroom.

The taller of the two men stood on the threshold of the bedroom. The other stood at his back. "By thy deeds thou hast condemned thyself. Jacob Levi Christianson, in the name of the Lamb of Israel, thou shalt be utterly destroyed even this very day. May thy blood atone for thy sins."

The masked men raised their bats and rushed at Jacob.

CHAPTER EIGHT

After fleeing his brother and sister, Enoch had made his way to Gideon's apartment, located just minutes away by foot. Gideon was not there, but he found Elder Kimball waiting. The man wore a suit and tie, as if he'd just come from priesthood meeting. He had a peeling sunburn on his neck and nose, but he'd gelled his gray hair into place, and while the suit no longer fit his heavy frame, his appearance made Enoch acutely aware of the lingering smell of vomit that hung about his own clothes.

Elder Kimball took him by the arm. "Come inside, Brother Christianson. You look like you need a blessing."

Enoch let Elder Kimball lead him into the front room and to a chair. "I shouldn't have talked to him," he said, repeating the apology from his earlier phone call. "I'm sorry. I knew it. I knew there was something wrong."

"Don't worry, Enoch. You did the right thing in the end."

Enoch still wrestled with doubts. "Are you sure?"

"The prophet has looked in Jacob's soul, Enoch. There is a dark countenance resting there. He has been deceived by the Adversary. You did the right thing."

So what? How would they turn Jacob away? Amanda Kimball was dead. Is that what they intended to do to Jacob? Kill him?

Elder Kimball placed his hands on Enoch's head. "Enoch Nephi Christianson," the blessing began, "in the name of Jesus Christ and by the authority of the Holy Melchizedek Priesthood, I lay my hands upon your head."

The power of the priesthood flowed into Enoch's body through Elder Kimball's hands. Enoch had been cursed, excommunicated, and driven from Zion. Now he was restored.

On that night when Father had driven him from Harmony, Enoch had lain down on the train tracks south of Boise, Idaho. The train would come, churn his intestines into soup, pulverize his spine, and rend his spirit from his body. They had withdrawn his blessings and condemned his soul to Outer Darkness.

The night had been cool. The rail ties pushed against his back. The cold metal of the rail pressed into his cheek. The rail hummed with a distant, nervous energy. The vibrations of a train, still too distant to hear.

The depression was a black howling in his ears. A self-loathing so deep that he wanted to punish himself. He wanted to feel the pain, at least for a few seconds, as ten thousand tons of freight train ripped him to shreds. The remains would be unrecognizable, just tattered flesh and scraps of bone and clothing. He hoped the train conductor would not even see him on the tracks, or feel the slight bump as Enoch was caught up in the wheels. A brutal, anonymous death.

But then a single, solitary voice had whispered through the gale in his mind: *It's not your fault.*

"Yes," he said aloud. "It *is* my fault. I'm a worm. Lower than a worm. Stomp me, God. Destroy me. Burn my soul with everlasting fire."

No, the voice said. Was it fear of death that spoke? Or some pinprick of sanity? *You were chosen to fail.*

It was true, wasn't it? He'd stood no chance next to Jacob. His brother was better than him in every way.

Growing up, Jacob had been diplomatic enough not to mention his superiority, but it stared Enoch in the face every day. Jacob listened to his elders. Jacob never needed reminding to do his chores or his homework. He could beat an adult at chess and had a natural gift with the piano. He understood a new mathematical concept the first time and had excellent spelling and handwriting. When Father wanted to show off one of his children, he always chose Jacob; the boy would never let him down. Even the younger children flocked to Jacob to hear his stories, or to follow him on adventures; he would include even the youngest, and they loved him for it. Enoch, coming along just ten months later, could never reach the level of his brother. He had tried.

Enoch had not given conscious voice to these thoughts until that day fishing with Grandpa Griggs. Grandpa Griggs was working on a logging project in northern Utah. He never went anywhere without taking two or three of his grandsons or younger sons. It was Jacob and Enoch's turn.

Jacob and Enoch had explored the forest during the day while Grandpa Griggs spent two hard weeks working at a logging camp. They'd eaten hot dogs and s'mores every night for dinner and slept in Grandpa's Toyota Dolphin motor home.

When the work ended, Grandpa had driven them to Mirror Lake for two days of camping and fishing. It was there that Enoch had broken his thumb. All trying to impress Grandpa Griggs.

Grandpa had brought out his prized collection of flies and taught the boys about each one: woolly buggers, zonkers, humpies, and black spinners. He taught them the different kinds of flies and when to use each: nymphs, dry flies, wet, streamers, and so on. And then, he taught them how to cast. They started with the simple forward cast, how to false cast the fly until it was in the perfect position.

Jacob was a natural. He picked up each technique effortlessly and caught his first fish in about ten minutes. Enoch couldn't get the stroke right. He wet his fly, then snagged it on a rock. He lost two flies and almost a third, and didn't catch a thing. Jacob and Grandpa caught their dinner. Grandpa Griggs told Enoch not to worry, that tomorrow was another day. His muscles would learn during the night.

Yes, Enoch thought, *but not while I sleep.*

Instead, he waited until the others were asleep, then crept out of bed. He took the fishing pole and the box of flies. He picked his way down to the lakeshore, some twenty yards distant, careful to choose a place with no rocks or trees on which to snag the fly. And he practiced. And practiced some more.

He practiced through the night, casting and casting and casting by the light of the moon, and ever so gradually improving. Finally, he dropped the fly exactly where he wanted it. A few minutes later, another good cast. Before long, he was making good casts with regularity.

And at last he had it. A perfect whip, whip, whip, drop. He could duplicate it nine times out of ten.

Enoch was exhausted, his muscles quivering. If he had stopped then, he would have triumphed. The next morning, he would rise nonchalantly and take his place next to Grandpa Griggs and Jacob. He would show them what he'd learned, never mentioning the night's labors. And he would catch fish. Lots and lots and lots of them. Monster trout from the depths of the lake that had never before been tempted by an artificial fly. He would show them.

Just a couple more casts to make sure he had it.

But his legs, tired to the point of trembling, betrayed him. He took a step on a rock to shift his position and his foot slipped. He slid sideways into the water and, in his attempt to hold onto the fishing pole, caught his hand on the rock. There was a twist. A sharp pain.

Enoch did not cry. He did not drop the pole. But his thumb burned as he crawled from the water. Even in the moonlight he could see how it dangled helplessly. His thought, foolish even for a nine-year-old, was that he'd wrap it in a sock and they'd never notice. But he was wet from his fall, and his feet made squishy sounds as he walked back into camp. A light came on inside the motor home. Grandpa Griggs came out a moment later with a flashlight, blinking groggily.

"Hell's bells, Enoch," said Grandpa Griggs as he eyed the fishing tackle and Enoch's bedraggled appearance. "What on earth are you doing at this time of the night? You know the fish won't bite until first light. That's two hours away."

Enoch choked back a sob. "I was trying to practice. I wanted to be better. Like Jacob."

Grandpa had not yet seen his broken thumb. That would be just as bad, in its way, because it would bring their fishing trip to an unceremonious end. Very shortly Grandpa would see the broken thumb and they would drive the rest of the night to the hospital in Provo. Enoch would never have a chance to show how he had learned to cast.

But not yet. Now, Grandpa had one final remark, and it would cause the most serious wound Enoch would suffer on this trip. "It's no big deal, Enoch. Jacob's got a knack for it." He chuckled and said, half to himself, "He's got a knack for everything, that boy."

It was a fumbling, unintentional remark. Grandpa had not meant to be cruel. But at that moment, Enoch understood now what had been devouring him for so many months. Jacob had a knack for everything. Enoch would always be a failure in comparison. *Always.*

It was this memory that had roused Enoch from his stupor that night on the train tracks near Boise. He had been chosen to fail. It wasn't just that he hadn't taken to fly-fishing—he had figured it out through his own dogged determination. No, it was that rock, that fatal step that had brought him low. A chance occurrence. Only there was no chance in the universe, was there? God, yes, God himself was making him fail.

He had grown angry lying there on the tracks and thinking about the night he'd broken his thumb. Anger was not depression. It burned away the blackness, and before he knew it he was on his feet and stepping back from the tracks. The train roared past. Enoch stood a few feet away, swaying in the wind kicked up by the cars.

Enoch had gone south to Las Vegas. He'd gotten a job in a casino, had sex with half a dozen prostitutes, and drank himself stupid. And then Elder Kimball found him.

"Forget those people," Elder Kimball had told him. "They abandoned you. They're not your family anymore. We are."

The goal, Kimball had told him, was the redemption of Israel. The church had grown weak and complacent. The Lord demanded sacrifice, change, striving. Nothing less would bring about the Kingdom of God on earth. The Lord had chosen an imperfect vehicle to bring about this redemption. The Lost Boys. The outcasts.

Gideon Kimball was their leader, but there were young men from every family: Youngs, Kimballs, Griggs, Pratts, Johnsons. And now, a Christianson.

Enoch had gladly shed his apostate lifestyle, so recently adopted, to fellowship with the other outcasts. He had remained skeptical of their goals, not to mention their methods. They kept him working at the casino; it was there that he met the men who helped him launder hundreds of thousands of dollars. One guy would play the gambler, another worked as a surveillance officer, and a third as a cage cashier, and cash could be exchanged for chips, then back to cash, and declared as gambling winnings. Dark hints came of a murder of a gentile. Maybe more than one.

But then he'd seen the angel. A man does not see an angel and remain lukewarm.

The strangest thing about the whole incident with Grandpa Griggs, Enoch thought now as Elder Kimball spoke the words of Enoch's blessing, was that Jacob didn't remember any of it. Enoch had mentioned it once; Jacob had remembered the fishing trip and a trip to the hospital, but not how or why Enoch had broken his thumb. This thing, this coal-black, diamond-hard memory from his childhood, had been so unimportant to Jacob that he had completely forgotten it. Did that speak more to Enoch's failings or to Jacob's?

"Well done, thou good and faithful servant," Elder Kimball continued. "The Lord is pleased with your faith and obedience."

There was no greater feeling than guilt lifting from one's shoulders. It should have been a happy moment. But he kept thinking of Jacob.

As if on cue, Elder Kimball said, "But do not be deceived by the Adversary, my son. Others, even the very elect, have been deceived. They have become his servants. Do not follow their path with doubts and contention. You will fall away. You will become truly lost."

He meant Jacob. His brother, the servant of Satan. The problem was, Enoch didn't believe it.

"*By their fruits, you shall know them,*" Jacob had said.

For all Jacob's skepticism, his brother had a good heart. Enoch had not forgiven Jacob for his role in driving him from Zion, but neither could he fully blame him. It had not been maliciousness on Jacob's part that had led to Enoch's expulsion.

No, he thought. *You cannot doubt. Not the Lord's plan. Not the angel.*

The angel had spoken to Enoch. Elder Kimball had led the outcasts in thirty-six hours of fasting and prayer. When their faith had proved insufficient to show them the angel, the Lord had instructed them to take a sacrament of bread and wine within the very heart of the temple. It was the first time many of them had tasted wine, as Mormons had taken water in its place for over a hundred years. A righteous fervor swept over the men, meeting in the heart of the temple, a place into which these outcasts had never expected to set foot.

After so much fervent effort, the angel had at last appeared. A burning figure of white. Enoch had felt such a fire in his soul that he had sworn to do whatever the angel instructed, no matter how difficult it might be.

And this, this was difficult. It would be the greatest test yet of his faith.

Elder Kimball closed his blessing and removed his hands from Enoch's head. Enoch rose to his feet. He felt almost stunned by the experience and more than a little shaky on his feet. The light was brighter in the room than he remembered, and it took a moment for his eyes to adjust.

Elder Kimball's eyes glowed with the spirit. Kimball was a difficult man to read, dismissed by many for his temper and often petty behavior, yet when the spirit filled him he was a giant among men. He communed with angels and could prophesy the future. The Lord spoke through His prophet, but the actor of God's will was this man, of that Enoch had little doubt.

The man had driven several hours to get to Las Vegas. As the spirit eased its presence, it was replaced with exhaustion and Elder Kimball looked every bit his fifty years, and then some.

Elder Kimball handed him two scraps of paper. "This is it, Brother Christianson. Thy commission from the Lord."

Enoch bowed his head. "Thou sayest."

He handed Enoch a set of car keys. "White van, California plates."

With that, Elder Kimball led him to the door of Gideon's apartment. Enoch rode the elevator down in a haze.

He stepped into the parking lot. Lamps cast puddles of light on the pavement. He found the white van, parked in visitor parking. He clicked open the lock and slid open the door. Before he got in, he unfolded the first of the slips of paper given to him by Elder Kimball.

Deliver the coolers, it read simply.

There were six coolers in the back of the van. He'd looked before, but couldn't resist the urge to open the first cooler. Packed on ice was a tray containing several hundred thumb-sized glass vials, stacked in layers. He lifted a vial and examined its milky, frozen contents by the interior light of the van. Each vial contained some five milliliters of ejaculate, containing hundreds of millions of sperm. How many vials were here? A thousand? Five thousand? Thawed, Enoch imagined a river of sperm, flowing to impregnate hundreds of women.

Enoch replaced the vial and shut the lid. Taped to the top of each cooler was a manila envelope with a name, a phone number, a clinic, and an address. He knew that each envelope was stuffed with hundred dollar bills.

Enoch backed out of the van and shut the door, then climbed into the driver's seat and started the engine. Before he drove off, he looked at the second slip of paper.

It read:

Jennifer and Samuel Gold
7705 East Landover Rd.
Oakland

Below this, in Gideon's spidery hand, the chilling script, "*Let the blood of the wicked be spilled to justify the souls of the righteous.*"

He stared at the paper, reading it again and again. He had made deliveries like the ones now expected of him, but this was new. Death had come to his hands. Enoch had become the Destroying Angel.

* * *

Jacob fought the urge to cower when he saw the two men with baseball bats. Eliza cried out and fell back. If he had allowed it, terror would have doomed him. Fear begat fear. It would drain the blood from his head and leave him weak as an old man.

The first man rushed at him with bat poised to deliver a crushing blow.

Jacob did not submit to fear. False bravado could substitute for the real thing.

He lifted his right arm to the square and said in a commanding voice, "In the name of Jesus Christ, I command you to halt!"

The effect was electric. The two men stopped short. Eliza's cry strangled in her throat. Jacob felt the power of his own words even though they had been said with all cynicism.

Jacob cocked back his fist and punched the first man in the nose. A satisfying crunch. The man lowered his baseball bat, and Jacob grabbed for it. He twisted it from the man's grasp and shoved the end into the man's stomach, driving him backward.

The second man came on the attack now, his bat swinging wildly. Jacob parried his blows easily, but couldn't get back on the offensive. The other man recovered and moved to join the battle, albeit unarmed this time.

Eliza had regained her wits. She snatched the liquid globe from the lava lamp on the nightstand and hurled it at the man with a bat. He lifted the bat to parry the globe. Jacob caught him a blow on the shoulder as the man lifted his guard. Jacob wrenched the man's bat loose and tossed it behind him. Eliza picked it up. She waved it shakily. Nevertheless, they were now armed, and their opponents were not.

"You fool," the first man said. He clutched a hand to his nose. Blood trickled between his fingers. "You are playing with fire."

"Is that you, Gideon?" Jacob asked. It had been too long since he'd seen the man to tell from his voice. "And you?" he said to the other. The other man hadn't spoken, and he wondered if this were deliberate. He would recognize Taylor Junior's hoarse voice in an instant. "Is that Taylor Junior?"

"Consider this your warning," the one he thought of as Gideon said.

"A warning? Were you going to beat me within an inch of my life, is that it? Maybe rape my sister? Is that what you mean by a warning? I don't think so. I think that crap about blood atonement was your way of justifying my murder." No answer from the others. He continued, "But you failed. Maybe you should consider this *your* warning. I'm on the errand of the prophet. The Lord won't permit you to stop me."

The words sounded right when they came out of his mouth, and he could see they had some effect on the men. For the moment, they did not move. They would be torn between fear and their desire to complete the murderous task.

He pushed his advantage. "Who are you?" No answer. "Who sent you? You think you can get away with this, in full view of the world? What is it supposed to look like, a drug deal gone bad? Did you think the police would buy that?"

Without a word, the two men turned to leave. He let them. Moments later, Jacob and Eliza were alone. The entire incident had lasted just minutes.

And now the aftereffects of adrenaline washed over him. His hands shook, and he was so lightheaded that he had to sit down on the bed. He bent over and breathed deeply.

"Wow," Eliza said. She put back the globe from the lava lamp. To his surprise, it had not broken. "Where did that come from?"

"What?" He sat up.

"Your words. It was like God had taken hold of you. I've never heard you talk like that before."

"Ah, I see." How could he tell her? The words had not come from God. They'd been his own, calculated and cynical.

Whatever the source, they had bolstered Eliza's confidence.

"It doesn't matter," he said. "We've got to get out of here. Before they come back to finish the job."

"Can we go back to Utah?"

"Not yet, no. We'll find a place to hang out until we can find Enoch. He's bound to come back soon."

But he didn't. Eliza and Jacob found a cheap hotel room a few blocks away, paid for in cash. In the morning they called Enoch's apartment several times, but there was no answer. Jacob left Eliza in the room while he went to Caesar's Palace. No, Enoch wasn't there. As a matter of fact, he'd called that morning requesting two weeks' leave to take care of urgent family business.

He wasn't returning. Not anytime soon. Jacob shared the news with Eliza when he returned to the hotel.

"What now?"

"We could spin our wheels in Vegas for a long time. I don't have any other addresses or phone numbers. No way we'll find anyone here just wandering around." He shrugged. "So it's back to Blister Creek. There, at least, we have a lead. We know the Kimballs are involved somehow."

She said, "Assuming that one of the Kimballs—say, Gideon or Taylor Junior—killed my cousin, we still haven't answered why. What possible motive do they have?"

"She betrayed them in some fashion," Jacob said. "But it's not so simple as that, because Enoch is mixed up in this, too, except he didn't know anything about Amanda's death. There's something else going on."

* * *

Jacob made Eliza drive back to Blister Creek. It was Tuesday afternoon and five days since they'd arrived in town to examine Amanda's body. Eliza didn't mind the drive. Sitting in the hotel room that morning she had done nothing but stew in her own thoughts. She worried about Enoch, worried about Jacob. And she was afraid for herself.

Once they escaped the snarl of traffic around the city, the freeway stretched straight and empty for mile after mile. They stopped for dinner in Mesquite, a gambling oasis just inside the Nevada border.

Jacob read while Eliza drove. He had pilfered books of Mormon history from Enoch's apartment. As they cut through the top of Arizona and back into Utah via the magnificent Virgin River Gorge, just south of St. George, Jacob stopped to rub his temples. "I hate reading in the car."

"So take a break. Enjoy the scenery."

"Can't," he said. "Enoch is right about one thing, you know."

"That we ignored his troubles?"

"*Ignored* is a neutral word. *Abandoned* is more accurate."

"You didn't. You said you found Enoch one other time?"

He nodded. "Dad told me not to. Enoch had called the house and left a message on the machine. Drunk, I think. He was begging for help and forgiveness. Dad told me it would be a waste of time. But I took the phone number Enoch left and tracked him down. By the time I arrived in Vegas a couple of weeks later, he was no longer asking for help. He was hostile, in fact. But quite sober."

"He'd probably already taken up with the Lost Boys," Eliza said. It was odd, though, that a drunk Enoch had asked for forgiveness. A sober Enoch had decided that no forgiveness was necessary. Not from them, at least.

"Maybe so. At the time I thought Dad was right. It had been a waste of time. Now I think I gave up too easily. I should have pushed him. Should have insisted he get out of Vegas."

"Don't beat yourself up," she told him. "You had no choice. The church teaches us to shun apostates."

"There's always a choice, Liz. Anyway, think how self-serving that injunction is. What's the cardinal sin in the church? The sin against the Holy Ghost. Even the murderer or the adulterer gets some measure of glory in the next world. But turn your back on the church and that's it. God throws you into Outer Darkness when you die. Think about that for a moment."

She already had. "Apostates are dangerous. Someone who has the truth and then decides the gospel is not for him. We've either got to be wrong, or the apostates are enemies of God."

"Quite. It's like the church is a foxhole and shells are raining down on us from all sides. It sucks, but at least we're in it together. Then suddenly one guy puts down his gun and climbs out of the foxhole waving a white flag. Hey! What's that guy doing? He's going over to the other side. Shoot him in the back!" He looked out the window. "We shot Enoch in the back."

Jacob turned back to his book and a few minutes later said, "Here, I found it. Pull over."

She pulled off the freeway just outside St. George and parked at a Chevron station. He handed over the book and pointed to a picture. It showed two sides of a medallion, together with some sort of hieroglyphic or astrological signs. "Is this what Enoch was wearing?"

She studied the picture. She'd only had a glimpse of the one around Enoch's neck, but it looked right. "I think so." She read the inscription. "A Jupiter Medallion. What's that?"

"Joseph Smith wore the Jupiter Medallion against his breast at the time of his martyrdom. It was a totem of divine protection, something like the temple garments, but more exclusive, like a talisman for his inner circle."

"Never heard of it."

"Neither had I. Just reading about it now."

"But where did Enoch get this thing?" Eliza asked. "Do Gideon and the others wear these medallions as well?"

"No idea." He read from the book: "Typically, a person born under Jupiter will have the dignity of a natural ruler. He knows what is due him and expects to receive respect accordingly. In physical appearance the highly developed Jupiterian is strong, personable, and often handsome."

"Handsome? We're not talking any of the Kimballs, then. Taylor Junior is about as handsome as an earthworm. Seriously, though, what does it mean?"

"I don't know. Maybe nothing. But there was a lot of symbolic stuff in the early church. Sunstones, Masonic symbols, that kind of thing. Joseph Smith liked to study hieroglyphs, Hebrew, old esoteric rituals. This is something like that. Like I said, it's probably nothing." He tossed the book into the back seat. "Let's gas up and get back on the road. Want me to drive?"

She welcomed the chance to pass off the driving responsibilities and take a nap. As she drifted off, she heard Jacob mutter, "Only I've seen the Jupiter Medallion somewhere else. But where?"

CHAPTER NINE

Elder Kimball sat in the buffet hall at Circus Circus, eating from a dinner available in quantities that would satisfy the greediest glutton. Several of said gluttons had taken up residence at the next table and made repeated forays to the buffet, returning each time with huge mounds of food. Kimball found the food unimpressive. The breadsticks were stale, the pork chops overcooked. There was soggy pasta, pre-whipped mashed potatoes, and potato wedges that had sat too long under a heat lamp.

Jacob Christianson had died, and Kimball was eating a cheap, never-ending buffet in a casino in the heart of modern-day Gomorrah.

And Kimball had authorized the murder. If his enemies ever learned the truth, there would be hell to pay. Abraham Christianson, and indeed, half the population of Harmony, would come to Blister Creek looking for revenge.

His son arrived at last. Gideon stepped into the restaurant and looked around for his father, not seeing him at first. His son's nose was swollen, perhaps broken, and his eyes were bloodshot. He studied the room with all the intensity of a contract killer before fixing on his father.

But he didn't come directly. Instead, he made his way to the buffet. He took a plate and made his way gradually down the line, scooping up country fried steak, beef tips, fried chicken, pork chops, and buffalo wings.

Elder Kimball was irritated by the time Gideon took his seat across the table. He eyed the plate. "What, no ribs? They were out of hot dogs and chicken nuggets? You'll give yourself a heart attack."

"Love this place. Come here all the time." Gideon stuffed beef tips into his mouth, letting grease and gravy run down his chin before lapping it up lazily with his tongue. "So you've eaten already."

"Yes, and what took you so long? I've been here for forty-five minutes, waiting. And why didn't you call me last night?"

"Too bad I didn't know Jacob Christianson better. I thought he'd be like Enoch."

This was the way it went between them. Kimball would ask questions that received no answers. At one time, Kimball had worked with members of the church, but thanks to Abraham Christianson's interference, that avenue had closed. Instead, Kimball had been forced to seek out Gideon and the other Lost Boys, who sometimes followed their own agendas. That's what came from living in Vegas.

"What happened? Did you take care of things?"

Gideon pushed aside the onions from his sweet and sour Chinese and forked a deep-fried pork ball into his mouth. "Enoch wouldn't have stood up to me like that. Oh, maybe he'd have crept around behind my back, but certainly no open defiance. Jacob fought back. I was unprepared."

Elder Kimball let out his breath. "Dammit. You had a plan. It was simple."

"Sure, simple to someone sitting in my apartment, watching TV. Yes, I had a plan. It failed."

"Jacob is still alive."

"That's what I mean by failure, alright."

What a pathetic, no-good excuse for a son the Lord had seen fit to send him. None of his sons were worth a damn, truth be told. Taylor Junior was a coward and bully in turns, Harold was a chronic masturbator, and he suspected Nephi of being a sodomite, as was Ronald, if he was honest with himself. William was a liar, and Ammon had been caught more than once trying to molest his younger sisters. The older sons were mentally strong but morally weak. The younger boys, mentally weak but morally strong.

His daughters, on the other hand, took after Kimball's mother, a bright, iron-willed woman who had always followed the straight and narrow and demanded the same of others. They outdid their brothers in every way imaginable. It was in his female posterity that any spark currently rested.

Patience, he told himself. *The Lord has promised you a righteous seed, and it will come.* The angel had said that his seed would "number greater than the sands of the earth," if he obeyed the will of the Lord, and his posterity would someday rule the earth in righteous dominion.

But still, he couldn't help but think as he looked at Gideon that he had sent a lesser man to kill a greater man. No matter that the angel had sealed Jacob Christianson unto death. Kimball would have been fiercely proud of a son like Jacob. A son like that could lead the church someday, could be the very prophet and mouthpiece of the Lord.

He shook his head. "And what happened, did someone call the police? Did someone get arrested? Something about the girl?" Maybe a scattershot of questions would yield an answer.

"Does it matter? He escaped." Gideon kept eating.

Kimball leaned forward and glanced to either side to make sure nobody was listening. "But how? The angel promised us."

The angel hadn't just promised. It had quoted scripture. *The Lord giveth no commandments unto the children of men, save he shall prepare a way for them that they may accomplish the thing which he commandeth them.*

But they had failed. How could an angel, imbued with the knowledge of God, have made such a mistake?

The stranger thing was the relief Kimball felt at the news. He hadn't wanted any of this. First Amanda, then Jacob. This one had come by his direct command. The entire plan was in jeopardy, but he did not trust a campaign of murder and intimidation to set it to rights.

So what now? He said, "The Lord has given a command, and we must obey. This is a setback, but nothing more."

"Jacob and Eliza left Vegas this afternoon. I tracked them to a hotel not far from Enoch's house. But they'd already checked out. They've probably returned to Utah."

Elder Kimball nodded. "That will help matters."

Gideon set down his fork and pushed the half-eaten plate of food away. "Jacob's no fool. And he has friends and family in Blister Creek. If we can't get to him here, how do you propose we do the job in Utah?"

Elder Kimball turned the problem over in his head. "Enoch. He's the one to do it. He can get close to his brother."

"You think Jacob still trusts Enoch?"

"No," Elder Kimball said. "Enoch ran from him and obviously told someone, because you guys showed up not long after. Jacob will figure that part out, but Jacob needs his brother. Enoch can call, contrite. Request a meeting. Jacob will be anxious to agree."

Gideon paused and then nodded his head. "Okay. And what about the girl?"

"Eliza Christianson?"

Elder Kimball eyed his son. Gideon wanted the girl, he knew. Not like Taylor Junior and his naked desire, but Gideon, too, was desperate for a wife. He could never lead in the church without one.

And Eliza was a comely child, there was no denying. With Jacob out of the way, Abraham Christianson would be hard-pressed to prevent the marriage of his daughter to one of Elder Kimball's sons. But which one?

"The Lord will reward those who serve him, my son. And Eliza Christianson needs taming if she is to make a good wife and mother. Who better than my son to accomplish that task and collect his heavenly blessings at the same time?"

Gideon smiled, and Kimball knew that his words had done their job. "Then we have work to do, Father. Jacob Christianson must be laid low."

There was a strange glint in Gideon's eye, and Elder Kimball felt a moment of doubt. The sudden fear that Gideon had led *him* to this point instead of the other way around. Taylor Junior, for all his scheming, was less dangerous.

Gideon returned to his plate of meat.

Kimball watched with disgust and wished again for a son like Jacob Christianson.

*   *   *

Eliza woke that night to the rumble of distant thunder. Several seconds passed, and she was drifting back to sleep when she heard another rumble, followed by a third. She went to the window and drew open the curtains.

Tongues of lightning licked from the sky. The storm played far to the south, and in that direction she could see for miles. Most of the thunder didn't reach Blister Creek. The lightning lit the underside of a dark front, coming this way.

Jacob had set out for priesthood meeting that evening almost as soon as they'd returned to Blister Creek. He had men to question. Fathers of some of the Lost Boys.

Meanwhile, Eliza had continued her discreet inquiries. She'd taken aside her sister Fernie and later had spoken to Charity and three of the other wives. What had Amanda been doing the last few days before her murder? Had they seen any Lost Boys around, other than Enoch? Or maybe Taylor Junior? Did he come and go a lot, perhaps to St. George or Las Vegas? She could sense that some of them suspected that Eliza was working with her brother to resolve Amanda's death.

Turns out that neither Elder Kimball nor Taylor Junior were in town. Ostensibly, they'd gone to St. George to settle business with the agricultural co-op. Eliza thought otherwise. As for Gideon Kimball, nobody had seen him. They were surprised that she asked.

The storm hit. The flashes came so quickly that the sky did not darken between strikes. Thunder rumbled, then roared, and then finally cracked like so many whips. The rain fell in sheets.

Water guttered off the edge of the house. It flowed into the street and met a stream growing on the side of the road. Every minute the stream grew bigger, and soon branches and debris joined the water. It soon covered most of the road.

Movement came from the hall outside her room, voices. Someone knocked, hard. A woman's voice said, "Eliza, are you up? Eliza, open the door." Eliza unlocked the door and the deadbolt. Charity Kimball stood in the doorway. "There's flooding at the Jameson Young compound. They need all able hands. Can you come?"

"Of course."

The rain still fell hard when they left the house minutes later. People poured from homes all along the street. They hurried east on foot or climbed into the back of pickup trucks pushing through the flooded street. Eliza caught the spray from a passing truck. Another truck stopped, and she joined several Kimballs in climbing into the back. They reached the Jameson Young farm minutes later. Half the town was already hard at work. Cones of light spread out from tractors and pickup trucks, illuminating faces and the relentless downpour from the skies.

The farmhouse sat on a floodplain, surrounded by farmland, but the family had built up the land at the lip of the creek to hold in the water during floods. A snarl of broken tree limbs had formed a blockage downstream. Dislodged stones ground along audibly at the bottom of the creek and piled against the obstruction. The water poured over and around the tree limbs.

In the meanwhile, the backed-up water streamed over the top of the dike and toward the house. It spilled into the window wells of the basement and lapped against the foundation of the house.

More people arrived every minute. Shovels filled wheelbarrows and buckets. Others hacked at an irrigation ditch to channel water away from the house. Someone came with a truck full of sand, and the Kimballs brought a Bobcat, whose shovel could do the work of twenty. Young children held open sacks while adults and other children filled them with sand.

Eliza took up a shovel. This was Zion. People working with singularity of purpose. Every member of the community had arrived to offer assistance to one of their own.

Two men hooked up a diesel pump, but it strained against the water still pushing over the top of the dike. A growing wall of sandbags topped the dike, but it wasn't enough.

The Bobcat pushed into the water but couldn't get far enough in to reach the obstruction in the river, which was the source of the problems. The water had risen too high, and the prophet—she saw Brother Joseph directing the efforts nearest the river—kept people from getting too close to the river where they might be in danger.

Eliza saw Taylor Junior working with two of his cousins from the Anders family. He didn't look her direction, and she stayed out of his way. She kept an eye on him, ready to move away if he looked her way. And she was not the only one watching Taylor

Junior. There was Eduardo, working near the man and watching him out of the corner of one eye.

That was curious. Were the Mexicans working for the Kimballs? She couldn't remember. She looked for Jacob, thinking she should point this out to him. She couldn't see him.

Whether he'd been gawking or checking her out, she wasn't going to be intimidated. She worked her way to his side before she remembered that he didn't speak English. But he looked up when she came, and she thought he might understand a few words, at least. "Hello, Eduardo. Where are your friends?"

He gave her a brief look. "*Disculpe.* No speak English."

"Friends. Uhm. *Amigos.*"

"*Ya no están.*"

Eliza had no idea what that meant, and he hefted a newly filled sandbag and made for the dike before she had a chance to try again. She thought that was the end of it, but he came back a minute later.

She watched Eduardo as he worked. Unlike the other men, with long sleeves and high collars, he wore only a white tank top, stretched tight over his muscular shoulders.

Maybe he *had* been interested that evening when she'd gone to their trailer with Jacob. Or maybe he'd been gawking, but now he was aggressively *not* noticing her. Either someone had warned him off—unlikely, as only Jacob could have noted the exchange, and that was not her brother's style—or he was feigning disinterest.

While she was watching Eduardo, she found that she'd drawn closer to Taylor Junior than she would have liked. He was talking to Jameson Young. "Look," he said, "you've got to pull it back. The water's too high over there. Goes any higher and it'll kill the engine. We'll never move it."

"We need five minutes," Jameson Young said. His flashlight cut through the raindrops to shine against the foundation of the house, then back to the growing dike. "Five minutes and we'll have the water diverted. But I need that Bobcat to stay where it is."

"We've had that thing for six weeks. Thirty grand. My father will kill me if I lose it."

"Five minutes and you pull it back. And if you lose the Bobcat, I'll pay for a new one. Five minutes."

"Yeah? Alright. Five minutes." He waved to one of his younger brothers who was operating the Bobcat, and the boy kept digging in place.

And then Taylor Junior turned and saw Eliza watching and smiled. "Hey, gorgeous. Can't let me out of your sight?"

She retreated quickly to the shadows, but not before she saw the dark look cross his face and saw him glance at Jameson Young to see if the man had been listening. He had.

What had she been thinking? Why hadn't she just stayed out of his way? And could she have handled that any worse?

"What an asshole."

She turned in surprise to see Eduardo still working next to her even though she'd moved over toward the house. "You speak English." He said nothing, maybe regretting that he'd opened his mouth. "Come on, Eduardo. I'm not an idiot. Why were you pretending not to speak English?"

He looked at her closely for the first time since she'd addressed him. "Why does it matter?" His English was almost perfect, with just a slight accent.

"I don't know. It's just weird." She hesitated. "I couldn't tell if you were checking me out the other night or just wondering whether it's the lack of makeup that makes polygamist girls so ugly."

He laughed, then returned to shoveling as someone moved past. He looked up a minute later. "Some girls don't need makeup. Look, won't your brother cut off my *cajones* if he catches me talking to you?"

"Jacob? Nah, he's not like that. My father, on the other hand... oh, and I've got a number of cousins, uncles, and family friends who would happily do the same." She smiled. "Don't worry. Just play your 'me no understand' routine and you'll fool ninety percent of them. Where are your friends?"

Someone sloshed by, and Eduardo waited until she was out of earshot before answering. "Jaime broke his big toe this afternoon on the jobsite. They took him to the clinic in Cedar City. We've got to pick up some supplies, so they're spending the night and returning in the morning. Guess they missed the excitement." He raised an eyebrow. "To answer your question, yeah, I was checking you out. Not the ugly thing."

"Good answer, since I'm carrying a shovel," she said with a smile.

He glanced over her shoulder and then quickly turned away. She followed his gaze to see Jacob go by with a wheelbarrow filled with sandbags. Even though her brother didn't see her, she turned back to see Eduardo moving away with his shovel. She was more than a little disappointed to see him go, but it occurred to her with a thrill that they'd been flirting.

The rain let up with all the speed of a tap shutting off. One moment downpour, the next, nothing. Blister Creek still overflowed its banks, but they'd diked off the Young house and moved the Kimballs' Bobcat to safety. The pump, at last, worked without opposition. It sent a jet of water back into the creek. And they'd made some headway in digging around the obstruction in Blister Creek as well. The water level outside the dike fell. They had saved the Young house.

The work groups broke up over the next half hour. It was sometime after midnight. Younger children and their mothers left first, followed by anyone without machinery, meaning the rest of the women, Eliza included. She set off for home on foot, following the stream of people. She was exhausted from the backbreaking labor, but with the memories of her conversation with Eduardo running through her mind, she wasn't particularly sleepy.

Why, exactly, did he pretend not to speak English?

She found herself turning from Main Street and away from the bulk of the people returning to their houses. She headed north, onto a darker street, where she was soon alone. The rain had stopped only minutes before, but already toads emerged from holes and croaked for mates, looking to take advantage of the brief rains to breed. A fox or coyote slinked by her on the right, and she heard other animals rustling in the sagebrush or crossing the road.

Ahead, sheltered by cottonwoods and raised on cinderblock above the muddy ground, was the Mexicans' trailer. The porch light was on, and more light streamed through a single window. She made her way toward the trailer.

This was crazy. Eduardo was a gentile, and a Lamanite to boot. What was she thinking? She should let Jacob question the man.

She stepped up to the door and knocked.

CHAPTER TEN

Gideon Kimball stared at the ATM with disgust. He had entered the PIN number three times. The first time, he'd thought he had clumsy fingers. The second, he'd known something was wrong, and the third he'd begun to curse his brother's name.

He was three blocks west of the Strip, in an all-night booth next to a small casino. Perfectly situated to drain a bank account so as to feed a gambling mania. He needed two thousand dollars, but not for gambling. The machine would not cooperate.

Gideon dialed Taylor Junior's number from his cell phone. His younger brother answered in that raspy voice that made Gideon grit his teeth. The saccharine sweet veneer did nothing to improve it. "Yes? What is the matter, my dear brother?"

"You know damn well what's the matter," Gideon said. "This card doesn't work."

Someone rapped on the window. He turned to see a couple of punks, maybe nineteen, twenty, with hoods pulled up and baggy pants. One of them wore sunglasses, even though it was night. Gideon shook his head and motioned them to move on.

"Ah, well, you see," said Taylor Junior, "there was a lot of money coming out of that account. I thought I would change the PIN. In case you'd lost your card."

If Gideon could have reached through the phone to throttle his brother he would have done so. "Father authorized these withdrawals."

"Yes, I know. Most of it, at least. Twenty thousand last Monday. Fifty thousand more on Friday," Taylor Junior said. "But then you took out a thousand yesterday. That was *not* in my instructions. What was that?"

The money had come from one of several fat accounts that his father held, thinly disguised, in gentile banks. He wasn't sure why his father hid the money, probably to avoid paying a full ten percent tithe to the church. But if someone looked hard enough the accounts could be discovered.

As for what he'd taken, Gideon had withdrawn the larger sums via bank teller. No ATM would dispense tens of thousands of dollars, not even in Vegas. He'd gone to the ATM for the smaller amount. But really, what was a thousand dollars next to the earlier seventy grand? No, the problem was that Taylor Junior didn't know where the money was going, and he didn't like it.

One of the guys outside the window knocked again, then cracked the door. "Are you done?" asked the one with the sunglasses. "Or are you in there jacking off?"

"Find another machine," Gideon said over his shoulder. "Listen," he continued, trying to reason with his brother. "What's another couple of thousand? I was short. I needed the money."

"That's for Father to determine."

The guy with the sunglasses wouldn't give up. He sounded pissed now. "You don't get out of there and I'm going to come in and drag you out."

Gideon turned to the men. His nose felt better, but his head still throbbed and he hadn't slept in thirty-six hours. He knew he looked like hell. And was in a mood to match. "You step into this room and you'll never walk out of here alive."

The man eyed him, no doubt wondering. Crazy guy? Mob? Drug dealer? Dangerous types filled Las Vegas. Apparently deciding not to find out for sure, the two moved on.

Wise move.

Gideon still fumed from that humiliation with Jacob Christianson in Enoch's apartment. Jacob had tried to call down some sort of priesthood power on him, and Gideon had actually stopped. Stopped dead, in fact, and he could not forget or forgive the way he'd faltered. A moment of weakness. It had made all the difference in the subsequent fight. One man and his teenage sister had defeated them.

God, how he hated Jacob Christianson. He'd hated the man since childhood. He had never managed to intimidate Jacob. The reverse, actually. How he wanted to crush Jacob, kill him, take his sister and oppress her.

Looking on the bright side, Gideon's failure had reinforced his weakness to Father. That was a carefully cultivated image that

masked an undercurrent of deception. Gideon had his own plans.
They did not always involve Elder Taylor Kimball. And certainly
not his most pathetic of sons, Taylor Junior.

"Trouble?" Taylor Junior asked. Hopeful, it sounded.

"Not anymore. Look, I need that PIN."

"I don't think you do. Look, I just got in. There was flooding
at the Jameson Young farm, and I'm cold and wet. I'm going to
take a shower. Why don't you take it up with Father next time you
see him?"

"Good idea," Gideon said. "Maybe while I'm at it I'll tell him
about the women's panties. Wonder what account paid for those."

He reserved such cards for special occasions. Play them too
often and they would lose their efficacy. Now was one of those
times. The man he was meeting tonight did not accept credit.

Taylor Junior was quiet. No doubt weighing the threat behind
Gideon's words. And wondering how the hell Gideon knew about
the underwear.

The truth was, Gideon didn't know why his brother had
ordered the women's underwear. Maybe it was for a special girlfriend. Perhaps one of Father's younger wives who liked to take
off her long underwear—temple garments—once in a while to feel
sexy.

Or maybe the pervert liked to wear panties while he fondled
himself. Gideon didn't care. Taylor Junior had grown weirder and
weirder about sexual matters over the years. Much of that was
Gideon's fault.

When Gideon was twelve and Taylor Junior eight, the two
brothers had entered an extended period of struggle. Gideon had
recognized the need to dominate his brother—at least that was how

he framed it now, but at the time he wasn't conscious of motives—and set about bending Taylor Junior's will to his own.

Once, when the two boys were swimming at Blister Creek Reservoir, Gideon had asked, "How long can you hold your breath underwater?"

Taylor Junior had eyed him suspiciously, perhaps alerted by the overly casual tone in Gideon's voice. "I don't know. Thirty seconds?"

They'd swam out to a place known simply as Black Rock. It was about fifty feet from shore. Other kids climbed on the rock and dove in, or used it as a point of reference on swimming races. No adults around.

"Because, you know," Gideon said, "the top swimmers can all hold their breath for a long time. Take the Olympics…"

"I don't want to swim in the Olympics. That's a worldly pursuit."

"Come on," Gideon scoffed. "Everyone wants to be in the Olympics."

The truth was, Gideon knew, Taylor Junior had always been a little afraid of the water. He was a good swimmer when he could see Black Rock, or when he stayed in shallow water. Get him into deep water, where your toes kicked at the colder, darker water beneath, and he would lose his nerve. The water was deep around Black Rock.

"Now, I'm going to teach you how to hold your breath." Quickly, he struck. He wrapped his arms and legs around Taylor Junior and used his weight to drag the boy underwater.

Gideon was not so much bigger than Taylor Junior that he didn't have to go under too in order to hold his brother down. But he was not panicking. That made a big difference.

Taylor Junior was crying when Gideon let him up a short while later. He swam for the rock, now some ten feet away. Gideon grabbed him before he reached the stone.

"Help me!" Taylor Junior screamed. But the only person on this side of the rock was Gideon's friend Israel Young. Israel watched with a grin.

"That was pretty good," Gideon said, treading water out of reach of his brother's flailing arms. Whenever Taylor Junior swam for the rock, he would grab the boy's ankle and pull him back. Otherwise, he stayed out of the way. "Let's go for a minute this time. No, two minutes. Oh, and don't scream. Your voice is so annoying it just makes people want to drown you."

The younger boy was weak from the struggles, and it didn't take nearly as much effort to push him under a second time. This time Gideon was able to come up for air while keeping his brother under. When he let the boy loose a couple of minutes later, Taylor Junior burst up screaming and coughing water. He climbed onto Black Rock and sat there trembling and sobbing for a long time. Eventually, Father had to swim out to pry him loose and bring him back to shore.

Taylor Junior had told on Gideon, of course, but adults only listened to the whining of a child with half an ear. Gideon had been scolded and lost his dessert privileges for the night. A worthwhile trade.

It had been a good start. The second opportunity came a couple of weeks later when Gideon and Israel came upon Taylor Junior wandering by himself down a dry wash on the edge of Witch's Warts.

"Hey, TJ," Gideon said. "You want to play bounce with us for a little while?"

"What do you mean, bounce?" Taylor Junior asked with narrowed eyes. He'd already glanced behind him as if wondering whether or not he should run.

"That's where we drop our pants and push our bodies next to each other and all bounce up and down at the same time."

Taylor Junior wrinkled his face. "What? Why would we do that?"

They'd showed him. Taylor Junior, of course, hadn't been the one doing the bouncing. He'd been standing unhappily in line while the other two rubbed their penises against his naked bottom. There hadn't been any penetration; that wasn't the point.

Taylor Junior had submitted to the bouncing, but had looked sullen and unhappy when the two boys grew bored and let him pull up his pants.

Gideon said, "You're a fag, TJ."

"Yeah," Israel had said. "You just got bummed. Homo."

Over the years, Gideon had taken whatever opportunity had presented itself to reinforce this impression. He had made Taylor Junior put on his sister's panties. He had snapped him in the balls with a wet towel when he came across him getting out of the shower. It had worked to the extent that Taylor Junior played the same tricks on his own younger brothers and sisters. Gideon knew of at least two girls and a boy that he'd fondled over the years.

But that game had grown too fun, and Gideon had not been smart enough to leave it alone. Later, when they were teenagers, he had ordered gay porn delivered to the house in Taylor Junior's name. He would collect the magazines from the mail and leave them around his brother's room. Taylor Junior would search his room several times a day in paranoia. He wanted to find them before someone else did.

And someone did discover the magazines. It happened when Gideon was back from college on Christmas break. Charity Kimball walked in while Gideon was thumbing through the magazine to see all the disgusting things that fags did and wondering how long it would take Taylor Junior to turn to faggotry.

Two hours later and Father was pushing Gideon from the car in the 7-Eleven parking lot with sixty bucks and a single change of clothes. A Lost Boy. He was two weeks short of nineteen. Tuition and rent due. No job or employment history. It had taken years to worm his way back into his father's confidence.

But Gideon had never lost the ability to bend Taylor Junior to his will. One of those times was now, and Gideon's brother reluctantly agreed.

"Okay, fine," Taylor Junior said over the phone while Gideon sat in front of the ATM. But instead of giving the number, he recited a verse of scripture. "And with righteousness shall the Lord God judge the poor, and reprove with equity for the meek of the earth. And he shall smite the earth with the rod of his mouth; and with the breath of his lips shall he slay the wicked." A pause. "It's a mnemonic. The PIN is the chapter and verse. You do know the scripture, right?"

There were people who could recite entire chapters of Biblical or Book of Mormon scripture from memory. Most knew hundreds of verses at the very least. Gideon had never been one of those people, and Taylor Junior knew it.

"Give me the damn number."

"Look it up, asshole. You should remember the part about the Lord slaying the wicked. It is especially apropos." The line went dead.

Gideon boiled with rage. He tried to remember the scripture. Something about reproving the meek and the breath of God's lips. And slaying the wicked, of course. It should be easy enough to find from the index. But that meant returning to his apartment for a set of scriptures. He had no choice.

Gideon left the booth. He met the two punks in the street and gave them a ferocious glare as he passed. They stared back, but he could see fear behind their bravado.

His rage toward Taylor Junior only grew as he thumbed through the scriptures back at his apartment. He'd make his brother pay for this.

Here it was. Second Nephi, chapter thirty, verse nine. The PIN would be 2309. The mnemonic still meant nothing to Gideon. But he could remember a four-digit PIN number that guarded an account with half a million dollars easily enough.

And then it came to him. The perfect revenge on his brother. Taylor Junior wanted this girl. Eliza Christianson. His first wife, so very important. And Taylor Junior had half convinced himself that he loved the girl. The fool.

Gideon would take Eliza for himself.

The idea was perfect. It would punish Taylor Junior, while delivering a blow to Jacob Christianson and the whole miserable Christianson family. And Eliza herself was a good catch, pretty and intelligent. Perhaps overly headstrong, but that would be a pleasant challenge. A smile came to his face.

PIN fixed firmly in memory, Gideon left the apartment with his mood completely altered. Time to get that money, and with it buy the LSD for the temple.

* * *

Abraham Christianson called from Canada while Jacob was in the shower. The work at the Jameson Young house had left Jacob wrung out, but a hot shower restored his spirits. It was still night, and he hoped to sleep a few more hours.

He stepped out of the bathroom to see his cell phone blinking that he'd missed a call. He glanced at the clock. It was almost four in the morning. Abraham Christianson was a famous early riser, getting more work done by breakfast than many men accomplished in a day. Still, this was early even by Father's standards.

"Ah, it's you," his father said when he returned the call. "How are things going down there?"

"The first thing I did was examine the body. The throat had been cut and both the carotid artery and the jugular vein severed. Whoever murdered Amanda—"

"Fine, fine," Father interrupted. "I'm sure you've got that under control. Just give me the gist of it."

"The gist? We were right. It wasn't the Mexicans. I have a few leads, but nothing concrete yet."

No need to alarm his father about the attack in Enoch's apartment. Further, he didn't want to overplay the involvement of the Kimball clan until he was certain which of them were involved. He felt the excuses turning in his mind and stopped, recognizing them for justifications. It was hard to pinpoint why, exactly, he was reluctant to discuss the incident with his father.

Instead, he talked about how Fernie and her children were doing, knowing that his father would appreciate details about his adopted daughter and his grandchildren. He talked about the flood; his father hadn't heard. He was friends with Jameson Young and wondered if he should send help. Jacob assured him there were more than enough resources in Blister Creek to clean up the mess.

Jacob stifled several yawns. "I'm sorry, but I'm really tired. Haven't slept much in the last couple of days, and I need a few more hours. Is there anything else?"

"You know there is," Father said. "How is this other business coming?"

"You mean Eliza? My hands are full with the murder investigation, Dad. I don't have time to interview potential husbands."

"Elder Johnson calls almost every day. He's growing insistent."

"Dad, Elder Johnson is seventy-four years old. He had a triple bypass four years ago and a broken hip last year. Surely we can do better."

"He's an elder of Israel and close friend of the prophet. Short of marrying Brother Joseph himself, there are few better matches."

"Politically speaking, sure. But what's his life expectancy? A year? Two? How many children would Eliza give him anyway?"

"So she'd be free to marry again, maybe this time someone of her own choosing."

Jacob considered. A couple of years of unpleasant marriage for the opportunity to arrange her own marriage at a later date. A woman had much greater leeway after her first husband died. She'd already been sealed eternally in the temple to another man, as would be any children born to her by a second husband; it lowered her value.

Father interrupted Jacob's thoughts. "So you're not crazy about Elder Johnson. That's fine. You have two other men to consider. Has Eliza met them yet?"

"She met Taylor Junior."

"And?"

"Not impressed. Neither was I." An understatement.

"I've never cared for the Kimball boys myself," Father said. "Bright enough, but morally weak. I certainly don't relish marrying my daughter to one of them. Didn't even care to see Fernie marry Elder Kimball. But this might be the best choice."

Jacob said, "Why the rush? She's just not ready. If we push her, she might resent it for the rest of her life. And Eliza's still got some growing to do. Maybe college..."

"College? Jacob, we've been through this. It's not a woman's duty to seek self-actualization. Meanwhile, so long as your sister stays unmarried, it's your own growth that remains stunted."

"Meaning, no wife for me."

"Exactly. How can I ask the prophet to sanction taking some other man's daughter without offering my own in return?"

"Oh, a trade. One of ours for one of theirs." He couldn't keep the sarcasm from his voice. "Frankly, it's a tradeoff I'm willing to accept while we wait until she's ready. It won't be forever. Maybe a few years. When Eliza's older. Just not now."

A pause. "Are you a homosexual, Jacob?" his father asked.

Jacob couldn't say that he was surprised by the question, even if the timing was abrupt. His mother had asked a similar question when he was a teenager and had been more interested in books than girls. *You do like girls, don't you, Jacob?*

"No, Father, I'm not a homosexual."

"Because, you know, I'd still love you. Having homosexual feelings is not a sin, only acting on them. We can suppress our desires, even the unnatural ones, in service of the Lord. I know that some are born with this burden, through no choice of their own."

"I'm not gay," he repeated. It must have taken a terrific effort for his father to acknowledge that some men were born homosexual. Most took a harder edge. Few things inspired greater loathing than the sodomite.

"Then what is it?" Father's voice was sterner now. "Men fight for that first wife. You know better than anyone that you won't be a full member of Zion until you take a wife. Every minute you stay single you put yourself at risk. Other men, more aggressive, will look to supplant you. They'll take your wives, your position, your future."

"Yes, I am fully aware of the ramifications of my ongoing bachelorhood. And we've had this conversation before, haven't we? How many times? Ten, twenty?"

"Then what is it?" Abraham Christianson asked. "Why don't you take what's offered? It's yours. Reach out and grab it."

Jacob didn't have an answer. Nothing his father would accept. "I can't, Dad. Not right now. I need to stay focused on this murder. If I don't, there will be more deaths."

"You really believe that?"

"I don't just believe it, I know it. Now, can we give this a rest? Until Eliza and I return from Blister Creek, at least?"

A sigh from the other end. "I'm afraid I can't do that, Jacob. The pressure on both you and Eliza is growing too great to resist. But it's not like you don't have options. There are three acceptable choices. All three men have at least one daughter on the table."

On the table? The talk of trading girls like so much livestock was repellent. "Okay, let's get this out in the open. Pros and cons."

"Good, now you're sounding reasonable," Father said. "First, Taylor Junior. I know what you think about the man. But Elder Kimball has three daughters between the ages of fifteen and seventeen and two more who will turn fifteen within the next few months. They are all good girls, and some are quite pretty."

True enough. But Taylor Junior? Jacob would sooner smuggle his sister to those anti-polygamy crusaders in Salt Lake than condemn her to that marriage.

"Next is Elder Johnson. That would be my choice. He's old enough to be my own father, it's true, but he's a good man. His daughter Dorothea is sixteen and bright. Rather homely, it's true, but you know what they say about first wives. You'll have others. You can look for pretty down the road."

Jacob had no comment. "And finally, Stephen Paul Young."

"Yes. He's from the William Young family. He's thirty-five and my half first cousin, once removed. I'm not crazy about the genetics of the matter. There's too much cousin marriage in the church as it is. You can't ignore the dysgenic effects of too much intrafamilial marriage."

Jacob tried to picture Stephen Paul Young and could only come up with tall. "Don't know the guy."

"Good family. Loyal to the church. On the Quorum, his father and I share certain...understandings. Stephen Paul is a rancher with a side business of fresh vegetables. Shares a co-op with Taylor Kimball's family."

Jacob knew the business. It moved a lot of vegetables and beef and made more than enough to support Elder Kimball's family comfortably. But being in business with the Kimballs wasn't an endorsement as far as Jacob was concerned.

"How many wives did you say?" Jacob asked, trying to remember their conversation in Harmony. "Two?"

"Yes, Eliza would make three. Both William and his brother Jameson are pushing Stephen Paul for a spot on the Quorum of the Twelve. You might end up serving together on the Quorum someday. A brother-in-law would be a nice ally."

"That doesn't enter into the equation."

"Absolutely, it does," Father said. "Someday you'll be the leader of the family. You'd better start thinking about how to advance it."

"Yes, but what's he like? A good man?"

"I don't know. Haven't heard any complaints, but our paths haven't crossed very often. Stephen Paul has two unmarried sisters, but I don't know much about them either. Go, meet the man. Meet his sisters."

Jacob considered. "Okay, I'll look. In fact, I'll take Liz," Jacob said. "I assume that's fine."

"Of course. But don't get her all riled up. You want to avoid emotions in these matters. And it's not Eliza's choice, ultimately."

And somehow Jacob was expected to make a better decision, knowing he could choose whichever girl most suited him as his prize?

"Can I go now?"

"Yes, Jacob. Get some sleep. Find the murderers. But don't procrastinate on settling this other matter. I'll call you in a day or two, and I want your decision. I've got business in Salt Lake early next week. It would be a good time to come to Blister Creek for a wedding if you decide against Elder Johnson. Come to think of it, we'd have two weddings, wouldn't we? Today is what? Tuesday? That gives you a week."

And with that, Abraham Christianson hung up. Jacob dropped the phone on the nightstand, rubbed his eyes, and fell back on the bed with a groan. A week? Both he and his sister would be married next week?

* * *

Eliza stood on the porch of the trailer, her hand frozen in knocking position. The knock still hung in the air, and she wished desperately to take it back. There was movement behind the door, the lock turning, then the knob.

Eduardo stood, blinking at her in surprise. He had changed out of his wet clothes already, and she was conscious of her own bedraggled appearance. Worse, her dress clung to her skin, and without looking down she knew that it revealed far more of her body than she liked.

"Well, hello," he said at last. "I didn't expect you. Come in."

"I can't come inside," was what she meant to say, but it came out as, "I can't...stay very long."

"Of course not."

The inside of the trailer was Spartan, but clean. A few pieces of furniture, a kitchen on the left, and a hallway to bedrooms on the other side of the living room. Eduardo indicated that she should take a seat on the couch, then turned off the television, which had been blaring some Spanish variety show. He went to the bathroom to get her a couple of towels.

It was long enough to reflect on what she was doing. She had to get out of here. At once. And yet she still sat on the couch when he returned. Eliza used the first towel to dry her hair, then wrapped it around her shoulders. It provided cover to her breasts. She sat on the second towel.

Eduardo sat next to her. "I'm sorry about lying to you earlier."

"You mean about the English? Why? I mean, what's the harm in speaking English?"

"Maybe nothing." He shook his head. "I've had bad experiences with gringos. English just complicates things. Better to stay quiet and stupid."

It didn't ring true. Surely there was more to it than that.

"Anyway," he said. "How old are you?"

"Eighteen," she lied. "You?"

"Twenty-two. What was up with that jerk? That was Elder Kimball's son, wasn't it?"

"Taylor Junior, yeah. He thinks he's going to marry me. Not if I have anything to say about it."

Eduardo said, "So we were hanging drywall for this guy and his wife was only sixteen. Pregnant already. Manuel said they all marry young around here. You're lucky, I guess."

"I don't feel lucky." She sighed. "Feels like my time is running out. My father's putting a lot of pressure on me. It might only be a few weeks, in fact."

"Really? Some man in Blister Creek?"

"I don't know. Maybe. There's this old guy in Alberta, too. The other two are here. One of them is Taylor Junior, but like I said, I'm not interested. My brother is going to choose from the other two."

"And that's how women get married in your church? Someone chooses for you? How bizarre."

"No more bizarre," she said, "than choosing a husband based on lust, like gentiles do. I mean, people outside the church. Half the people don't even get married anymore. Children are born without even knowing who their father is. How is that a better system?"

He held up his hands. "You don't have to lecture me. My family is Catholic. Very traditional. My mother would kill me if I got some girl pregnant."

"Is your family in the United States?"

"My dad is. He's been in Atlanta for about twenty years. Only sees my mother for a few weeks a year, but always sends money. My mother and the rest of my family live in Tepíc, Nayarit. North of Guadalajara. It's a long trip from the border. I've done it about twenty times."

None of that meant anything to her. "And that's how you learned English? Working with your father?"

"Yes, I spent summers up here from the time I was about six."

"It must be great to speak two languages fluently."

He shrugged. "Not so great that I'm not still working with illegals for eight or ten bucks an hour. If there was any work in Mexico, I'd go home."

"You don't like the U.S.?"

He hesitated. "It's not my country," he said at last. "I'm a foreigner. People say things. Store owners check the stock when I leave." He shook his head. "And the worst thing? I'm a foreigner in Mexico, too. Even though everybody has a cousin or a brother in the north, they don't like us. I can't blame them, sometimes. Guys come back from the States with flashy trucks and waving big wads of dollars. They speak English to each other just to show off."

"Then they can hardly be surprised if people find them annoying."

"Sure, but most people aren't like that. I prefer a low profile. But it doesn't matter. I'm a Mexican in the United States and a *gringo oscuro*—a dark gringo—in Mexico. And I feel that way sometimes. Torn between two countries. Two cultures. Two languages. Maybe that's why I choose to speak Spanish." Choose to or not, his English was flawless.

"I'm a foreigner too. Canadian."

"That's different, though. Canada and the U.S. are pretty much the same thing."

"First of all, they're not. Second, I'm a lot more foreign than just coming from Canada. Look at me. Look at this place. It's not Denver or Dallas."

"No, I guess not."

"People drive through town sometimes to gawk. They found us on a map after having seen some television program about those crazy polygamists. And they come through and take pictures of the women or the temple. Look at all those wives. And a million kids each. As if we're animals at the zoo."

He laughed and leaned in closer on the couch. "I have to admit I found this place pretty strange when I first came. But I haven't seen any tourists."

"We do a pretty good job of scaring them off. You know, the gentiles can't get gas or buy groceries in town. We won't sell to them. People won't even talk to them. They say we're standoffish. A cult. But we just want to be left alone to live our faith. Is that so bad?"

"I guess not, when you put it like that. But Eliza, what do *you* want? Do you want to be wife number five to one of these old guys?"

Eliza could feel his leg pressing against hers and thought, not for the first time, that he was very cute. And that she shouldn't be here.

"It's not what I want that matters. It's what God wants. And yes, if He wants me to be a plural wife, then I will obey His will."

And here she was, talking about eternal marriage, and suddenly Eduardo's hand was on her shoulder. She froze. "Are you, uhm, are you sure that your friends aren't coming back tonight?"

He must have felt her tense up. He pulled his hand back. "Not till tomorrow. Are you okay? You're shivering. Can I get you a blanket or some dry clothes maybe?"

She wasn't shivering because of the cold. It was plenty warm in here. She was trembling with nervous excitement. It was lust, she realized with equal parts horror and fascination. That's what this was. And she didn't want it to go away. Not yet. Soon, yes, soon she would get up and walk away from this temptation, but not yet.

"No, I'm okay. Maybe just a little cold."

He leaned in close and took her arm. "You feel cold." He put his other hand on her left cheek. She froze in place. Her breath was shallow and rapid in her ears.

"It's not like women don't have value, you know," she continued. They were whispering now. "We're not property." What did she come here to ask? Oh yeah, why was he following Taylor Junior?

"No, of course not. But what do *you* want to do?"

It was the sort of question that she didn't ask herself. She had a role; she had to play it. Her own very small part in the great work that was God's plan. Press too hard against herself and she'd find herself…well, in situations just like this one.

"I want to choose." She nodded. "I want to map my own life. Even if it means I make mistakes. That's not so bad, is it?"

"No, it's not."

Eduardo made no move to replace his hand on her leg. On impulse, Eliza ran her fingers along his arm. The muscles tightened under her touch. She had never touched such dark skin before and—yes, it was foolish—had been half expecting it to feel different. As if skin texture changed with color. What a sheltered, naïve girl she was. Already seventeen, but she might as well be a child.

His face was close now, and he leaned even closer. She closed her eyes, still breathing hard and waiting for him to move.

"This is such a bad idea," Eduardo murmured. His lips were so close to hers that she could feel his breath, but they didn't close those last two inches. "On so many levels."

"Yes, I know." He was giving her the chance to back out now, before things went too far. "But what's stopping you?"

And then he did kiss her. His lips entangled with hers, and she didn't know what she was doing, but let him lead, and then she was lying on her back and his fingers dug into her back and she had her fingers in his hair, her breath coming faster and faster. Warmth spread through her body. She felt his body pressing against her down there, and she was warm there, too. Burning.

He pulled his mouth away. She groped for more, but he was kissing her earlobe now, and then her neck. His hand untied her dress, and his fingers brushed the bare, raw flesh of her shoulder. She drew her breath sharply at the touch. Her throat lay exposed now, and his fingers moved down and brushed the top part of her breast. She lay back, vulnerable, motionless under his touch but for her breathing and a tremble, neither of which she could control.

Eduardo slid a hand down her dress and brushed one nipple with his fingers. She gasped in shock and pleasure.

Eduardo stopped at once. "I'm sorry," he said. "I know you don't want this. It's wrong."

"It's wrong," she agreed, "but don't stop. Not yet."

He was breathing hard, but he pulled away and his expression changed. "No, I shouldn't do this. I shouldn't have. I'm sorry."

Eliza had heard a million stories about gentiles and their insatiable lust. She was surprised that he had pulled back. And she was flushed, unable to think straight.

"I'm so sorry," he said again. There was a firm set to his mouth. "You should go."

She was confused by how cold he'd become suddenly. "Are you angry?"

He looked surprised by the question. "Angry? Of course not. I like you, I really do, but this is just…I don't know, not very smart." He nodded. "You know what I mean, don't you?"

"I won't tell anyone," Eliza said, feeling guilty. Because he was right. She'd put him in danger just by coming here. "You don't have to worry. You're safe. I promise I won't tell anyone."

"And I won't either. Nobody will know, right?"

And there was nothing to do but straighten her dress and make for the door. He put a hand on her back at the door, but she could see him tense as he looked into the shadows outside the trailer, looking to see if someone was watching.

"Take care, Eliza."

"Thank you. And I'm sorry."

"Don't be. Just be careful."

Eliza turned to walk away. She could feel him watching, but she didn't turn around. When she reached the sidewalk, she heard the door of the trailer shut behind her. She stopped for a moment, closing her eyes tightly. A complex stew of emotions simmered within her.

There were no others on the streets. Dawn threatened from the east, and all too soon the town would shake itself to life again. It took about fifteen minutes to reach the Kimball house. She used the back entrance and let herself in with her key and crept up the stairs to her bedroom.

She opened the door, ready to slip out of her dress and change into pajamas before crawling into bed. A movement from the far side of her bedroom drew her up short. There was someone waiting for her, his face illuminated by the reading light by her bed.

"And where have you been, Eliza Christianson?"

It was Taylor Junior.

CHAPTER ELEVEN

Eliza tried to back her way out of the door, but Taylor Junior crossed the room in two steps and blocked her way with one arm. She should have screamed, but she was too caught up in shock and everything that had happened. Instead, she stood frozen.

"What were you doing?" he demanded.

She found her voice. "I was working. There was a flood, if you didn't notice. Rain, mud, and all that."

"Yes, and everyone else came back an hour ago. They've cleaned up and gone back to sleep, and here you're just coming in. So what were you doing?" There was an unpleasant insinuation in his voice, and she felt a twinge of panic. Had he seen her go into Eduardo's trailer?

No, he couldn't know. "None of your business. Get out of my room."

He seized her arm with a painful grip and leaned in close. "By God, it *is* my business. You're going to be my wife, and that makes it my concern. What, they haven't told you yet?" he sneered. "That's right, you're going to be my wife. What do you think your brother is doing here? He could easily be staying with his cousins out by the bluff. He's checking out my sisters, that's what. And you, you will honor and obey and submit to my will as the Lord commands."

In her fear, she found herself halfway believing him. "You're lying. Jacob wouldn't..."

He chuckled. "It's just a question of whether he wants Jessie Lyn or Annabelle. Once he decides, we'll be married, you and me. It might even happen by this weekend. Since it's already done in all but name, maybe we should get an early start."

"Don't do this."

He threw her down on the bed. She struggled, but still couldn't find her voice. He put his mouth on hers and grabbed her breast with one hand.

"Get off me, you son of a bitch."

He laughed. He gave her breast a painful squeeze. The other hand he shoved between her legs.

And all she could think was, *It's my fault. Oh Heavenly Father, I'm sorry. I didn't mean to sin with Eduardo. I'm so sorry. Please, don't punish me like this.*

She found her voice and screamed. Once it came, it would not stop. She only paused to draw in a ragged breath, then screamed again. Once Taylor Junior recovered his initial shock, he tried to clamp his hand over her mouth, but she bit down hard and he drew back, cursing.

And then the door burst open and several women were there and Taylor Junior was pulling away, his hand shoving her away disdainfully as the lights came on and they blinked and Eliza stopped screaming. His sisters and Elder Kimball's wives stood in the doorway of the room.

"Let go of her, you bastard." Her sister, Fernie.

"What are you doing?" Charity, her voice equally scathing.

And then Jacob arrived. Eliza didn't know if someone had called him or if he had heard her screams. She didn't care. She scrambled off the bed and rushed to her brother, throwing himself in his arms and crying.

Taylor Junior started to sputter. "It was her fault. She came on to me. I told her no, but she wouldn't stop tempting me."

Jacob's voice was hard. "'Woe unto the liar,' sayeth the Lord, 'for he shall be thrust down to hell.'" He released Eliza very slowly. As she stepped aside, she could feel the violence in his body.

But Taylor Junior didn't comprehend. "She did," he insisted. "She tried to seduce me." He gave Eliza a look of disgust. "Slut. Whore."

Jacob moved swiftly. He grabbed Taylor Junior by the neck with both hands and hurled him to the floor. Taylor Kimball sprawled out with a cry. He lifted his hand to shield his face from a kick or punch.

But Jacob held back. "You ever touch my sister again and I will kill you." He did not shout and remained perfectly calm, his voice cold enough to draw heat from the air. "I will rip out your lying tongue, and then I will take a knife and un-man you, and then I will cut your throat. Do you understand me?"

Taylor Junior gave Jacob a sniveling look. Had he been a dog, he would have tucked his tail between his legs and whimpered.

"I'm sorry, I'm sorry. It was a mistake. I just, I couldn't help myself. I *love* your sister. I really love her—I want to marry her. I don't know what came over me, I just…it was a mistake. I swear it will never happen again." He hesitated. "It was the devil. Satan tempted me. He wants to stop our marriage. You know it, Jacob. Please."

Eliza snorted in disgust and turned away.

"Be very, very careful," Jacob said. "One more misstep and you will meet your destruction this very night."

Taylor Junior took another look at Jacob's face, then climbed slowly to his feet. He looked at the women, and at the even younger girls and children arriving and standing in the doorway, then back at Eliza. A dark, unreadable look crossed his face. And then he turned and stormed off.

Jacob turned to the women. "Thank you for coming." He looked at Eliza's sister, Fernie, and gave her a separate nod. "Thank you."

The women gathered the children and left Jacob and Eliza alone. He went to the door and shut it.

"I think I prefer the Kimball women to the men, don't you?" he asked. A forced smile came to his lips. A vein throbbed on one temple.

She swallowed, aware of how close she had come to being raped. But not as close as Taylor Junior had come to death. Violence still clouded Jacob's face.

"I'm sorry. About everything."

"You have nothing to apologize for."

But she did. When she'd left Eduardo's home, she'd had no intention of confessing what she'd done to anyone. Now, it weighed on her shoulders. "Jacob, it's my fault this happened."

A frown. "I thought you knew better than that. How can it be a woman's fault when a man assaults her?" He lifted a hand when she started to reply. "It doesn't matter what you said or did, it didn't justify his attacking you."

"It's not that. Believe me, I didn't say anything to encourage that jerk." She hesitated, ashamed. "I think this was God punishing me for something I did."

He raised an eyebrow. "You think so?"

"Yes, what happened was—"

Jacob stopped her for a second time. "Liz, it doesn't matter. Taylor Junior acted through his own aggression and need to dominate. It has nothing to do with you."

She threw her arms around his neck and gave him a hug. "You're the best brother in the world, you know that?"

He pulled away, and a flicker of uncertainty passed over his face. "You might not say that if you knew the conversation I had with Father tonight." He walked to the window and drew open the curtain. Dawn spread in the east. He looked drawn, exhausted.

His words drew her up short. "Is it true, then?" she asked. "Am I really going to marry Taylor Junior?"

He turned with a scowl. "Do I have to dignify that with an answer?"

"Yes," she insisted. "Yes, you do. I know what I think and I know what you're going to tell me, but I need to hear you say it. I need you to tell me that you'd never make me marry that man." She grabbed his sleeve. "Please, Jacob."

Jacob looked her directly in the eyes. "Liz, you will not marry that man. Now or ever. I swear it." He hesitated. "But, well, your time is running short."

"How short?" she asked.

"Father is saying a week."

She was incredulous. "I have a week to choose a husband with whom I will spend time and all eternity?"

"No," he corrected. "We have *two days* to choose your husband. You'll be married in a week."

She was shaken by the news. "And my choices?"

"Apart from Taylor Junior? The first is Elder Johnson, back home."

Yesterday, this would have brought a shudder, but considering the alternatives, she could no longer rule out Elder Johnson.

"And you'd marry Dorothea Johnson?"

"Yes, if necessary. The other choice is Stephen Paul Young, son of William Young and nephew of Jameson Young, whose house we saved tonight."

"I don't know anything about Stephen Paul." She'd heard the name and had the vague impression that he was in his thirties, but she knew little else.

"I don't either, but I'll call in the morning and invite ourselves over." He covered his mouth to stifle a yawn. "Now, Liz, I've got to get some sleep or I'll be dead on my feet later. Lock your door and scream a little sooner next time, will you?"

* * *

Jacob saw Fernie Kimball set down her basket of tomatoes and watch as he approached. He'd slept a couple of hours, then dragged himself out of bed and to the gardens where they'd said he could find Fernie working. Children worked by her side, picking green beans or clearing debris from irrigation channels, left behind after the heavy rains.

"Hello, little brother."

He winced. "After all this time, I'm back to being a brother?"

"Why not? You're my brother in the eyes of God and in the records of the church." Irony tinged her voice.

Fernie's father had apostatized and run off with a gentile woman. Her mother had remarried Abraham Christianson. Later, Fernie's mother had given birth to Eliza. That made Fernie Eliza's half sister but no blood relation to Jacob. A crucial difference.

"Here, make yourself useful." She handed him a basket. "We're taking produce into Cedar City for the farmers' market. I'll pick for the market, you focus on the canning tomatoes." Those would be the misshapen, the sun-burned, and the undersized.

He took the basket and started to pick. The sun had come up, and it grew warm quickly. Mud stuck to the bottom of his shoes, coagulating into thick second soles.

"How is he?" Jacob asked.

"How is who?"

"Your husband, Fernie. Elder Kimball. What kind of man is he? Not like Taylor Junior, I hope."

"No, not like that." She shrugged. "As a father he's indifferent. To be expected when you've got twenty-nine children and counting. As a husband, well, no more domineering than anyone else in these parts. I honor and sustain his priesthood, and he doesn't cause me trouble."

Is that what Fernie aspired for in a husband? he wondered bitterly. Someone who wouldn't cause her trouble? She deserved more.

"And that's what happened to Amanda?" Jacob asked. "She didn't sustain Elder Kimball's priesthood?"

"Eliza already asked these questions. She was persistent."

"Yes, but she didn't get any answers. I kept thinking that you might know something. You and Amanda are both in your mid-twenties. And you're her cousin. Weren't you close?"

"Yes, we were."

"And what was Amanda's relationship with her husband? Did they love each other? Did they argue?"

Fernie plucked a caterpillar from one of the plants and squashed it underfoot. She turned and looked Jacob in the eye. "A woman has to know her place. Isn't that right?"

"So they say." He met her gaze until she turned away. "As does a man. It just happens to be convenient for some that a man's place is to dominate women."

She gave him a hard look. "Such a cynical view, Jacob. You misheard my answer if that's what you think I was saying. Every person has his or her role in the eternal scheme of things. I have found mine. When will you discover yours?"

He sighed. They had once been close, closer even than the relationship that he enjoyed with Eliza, because there had been a frisson, a chemistry between them that went well beyond the bond one enjoyed with one's sister.

Time to focus on the matter at hand. He set down the basket of tomatoes. He took out a sheet of paper cut from the book from Enoch's apartment and showed it to Fernie. "Do you know what this is?"

She looked down at it, but didn't answer.

"It's important, Fernie. Unless what you meant by a woman knowing her place is that Amanda's murderers don't deserve to answer for their crimes."

"You know that's not what I meant."

"Of course I do, but it seems to me that you need reminding," he responded. He was pushing her now, like he had pushed Enoch, like he had rebuked his would-be assassins, and he knew her well enough to know that she would also yield to pressure. It was what separated her from Eliza, and why she had married Elder Kimball, though her desires had been elsewhere.

He fixed her with a stare and didn't let his gaze falter. She met his eyes and didn't pull away this time. He said, "Having been commissioned of the prophet and of the blood of Amanda Kimball, which cries up from the earth for justice, thou shalt not thwart my purpose, Fernie Kimball."

She bowed her head, and Jacob knew he had won. "Thou sayest."

"You know something. Something that you didn't tell Eliza. What?"

When Fernie looked up again, there were tears in her eyes. "Yes, I've seen the Jupiter Medallion before. My husband wears one on a chain against his breast, beneath his temple garments. I've seen it when he comes to me at night."

Jacob pictured Elder Kimball—a man he had once revered as one of the Lord's apostles, but was now convinced was a murderer or a murderer's accomplice—making love to Fernie. Naked and pale, his throat jiggling, his fat belly pinning Fernie to the bed while she closed her eyes and endured his grunting, thrusting desire. Jacob clenched his jaw and flushed the image from his mind.

"You're sure? A medallion just like this?"

She nodded. "Exactly. Silver or silver-plated. About the size of an old silver dollar."

The mark of the conspirators, then. Who else wore one besides Elder Kimball and Enoch? Gideon, certainly, and Taylor Junior. Anyone else? And why?

"Is there anything else that you know?" he asked. "Anything that might shed light on this murder? A motive? An overheard conversation? Anything?"

"I'll tell you what I know. About two weeks ago, late at night, I was walking past Amanda's room when I heard her crying. Sophie Marie was asleep, and Amanda sat at her daughter's bedside. 'What's the matter?' I asked.

"'Nobody could love a child more than I love my daughter,' she said, 'but I just can't do it anymore.'

"I didn't know what she was talking about. Sophie Marie is three and a half, and not very much trouble, truth be told. But maybe she was talking about the next child, not Sophie Marie."

"The next child? How do you mean?"

Fernie said, "You know, Amanda had a hard time getting pregnant. A miscarriage, then nothing. Finally, when she was pregnant with Sophie Marie, she started feeling contractions at six months. Taylor took her to a specialist in Denver, and she stayed there on bed rest until the baby was born. But one child is never enough, you know." She hesitated. "It's not like it was all Amanda's fault."

"Go on," Jacob urged when it looked as though she might stop.

"Taylor, you know, is not one of those men who can sleep with one wife before breakfast, take a quickie at lunch, and finish off with a third woman before bedtime. Most of us see him about once a month. It matters more to some women than others. Tess, I swear, can get pregnant after washing a load of Taylor's underwear. Most of us have to watch our periods and take our opportunities very carefully. Makes it tough for someone like Amanda.

"So anyway, I didn't give much thought to the incident until the funeral. It was Eliza's questions that got me thinking. I remembered how Amanda kept looking at her daughter that night."

"What do you mean?" Jacob asked.

"It's hard to explain, exactly. Like a mother watching her child swimming in the canal, worried he'll drown. Or maybe like she was afraid that if she looked away too long, Sophie Marie would be gone."

"And did you draw a conclusion?"

Fernie looked more uncertain now. "Perhaps that Amanda's inability to have more children led to her death?"

Only that didn't fit with the facts. Some men, it was true, thought it a mark of dishonor when a wife failed to conceive. But Amanda had already done so, albeit only once, and with a difficult pregnancy. That didn't square with a throat cut from ear to ear and a tongue torn out by the roots. Barrenness was not a crime meriting that particular punishment. That would be reserved for betrayal.

Jacob looked back toward the house and then toward the greenhouses and out to the fields. Still none of the Kimball men in view. When he looked back at Fernie, she was watching him, her face beautiful in the early morning sun. A whisper of a breeze came from the direction of the Ghost Cliffs and blew a strand of hair across her face. Impulsively, he reached out to straighten it. His fingers brushed her cheek, lingered a moment too long.

"Fernie," he said, knowing he should keep quiet, but unable to resist. "Are you happy here?"

"Every life has its joys and its sorrows."

"Stop talking like that for a moment, please."

"Why, because I sound too much like you? Always dancing around issues? You're a man with an opinion about everything who doesn't know what he believes about anything."

"What does that have to do with anything?" Jacob asked.

"Because, Jacob, I want to stop you before you get into whatever it is that you're moving toward. Think about it for a moment. Are you trying to get me to say that I would rather be living a different life? And what then? When I have betrayed my faith and my family, at least in words, when you have convinced me to tell you that yes, I do love you, and yes, I would rather live with you and have you love me and me alone, what then?"

Her breath was shallow. He thought about how one step would be enough to have her in his arms.

She said, "Isn't that the point at which you say, 'Ah, Fernie, it's a tough lot we have, being God's chosen people. In a different world, you and I might have been together, Fernie, but alas, we are not in that different world.' And then you will leave, as you must, and I will remain in my life here with its joys and its hardships. Only the joys will suddenly seem dry as dust, and the hardships will weigh on my shoulders with the weight of eternal expectations. So what would be the point of such a conversation?"

Jacob opened his mouth with a glib, self-defensive reply. He only just managed to bite it back. Instead, he only stared at Fernie, his heart aching to see who she had become, realizing he could never breach the wall that her marriage to Elder Kimball had erected between them.

You do like girls, don't you? his mother had asked.

Yes. One, at least. One he liked very, very much.

He turned away. He had nothing more to accomplish here.

CHAPTER TWELVE

Enoch had no trouble until the final fertility clinic. In Las Vegas, Tucson, San Diego, Los Angeles, and Riverside he had handed over the cooler and the envelope of cash. More money would be forthcoming next year, contingent on compliance with the plan. The men and women had accepted the money and the vials of frozen semen with little comment.

Enoch thought about those vials. Sperm from men of the Church of the Anointing.

And how much did it matter where the sperm had come from? Elder Kimball thought a good deal. They had raised a seed, culled it, pruned it, like a farmer seeking greater yields from his crops. Every generation that seed grew stronger and more numerous until someday it would dominate its surroundings. And now Elder Kimball would mix that seed with the gentiles, taking on an especially potent hybrid vigor. There would be thousands of these children. Some girls would be called back to Zion. The boys, left to grow, would remain a force to be called on when the Lord arrived in His glory.

Or so went Elder Kimball's theories. Enoch didn't know precisely how Elder Kimball meant to recall the girls, but wouldn't the boys be like any other gentile, living their lives in spiritual blindness?

After Riverside, he drove north along the California coast. It was beautiful, sunny weather but not hot. The drive offered views of the oceans and coastal hills, and it was quieter than Southern California. He had never seen this part of California and would have enjoyed it immensely under other circumstances. The final clinic was in the foothills above Santa Cruz, a semirural area covered with secondary-growth redwood forest.

It was a small, nondescript building tucked among the trees with a sign that read, "Santa Cruz County Medical Institute." He looked at the clock as he pulled into the parking lot. Ten minutes after three. Just a little bit late. There was a man standing in the lot, waiting. Enoch opened the side of the van and peeled off the envelope with the name Chen on it from its cooler, tucked it under his arm, and then hefted out the cooler itself. It was the last.

The man held out a hand. "Name is Ron Chen. Are you Ishmael?"

Enoch set the cooler at the man's feet, but declined to take the man's hand. "That's right." He didn't know where the name Ishmael came from, but it didn't matter. In Arizona he'd been Hosea, in Los Angeles, Solomon.

"You've got everything?" Chen asked, meaning, presumably, the money, not the cooler of frozen semen.

He took out the envelope. It bulged with cash. He handed it over.

Chen took the envelope, and to Enoch's surprise, he did not immediately open it to count the money as had all the others. Instead, he waved the envelope with an indifferent look. "How much, exactly?"

"Eighty thousand."

"Yeah, that's what I thought. And eighty grand is a nice sum, don't get me wrong. But have you seen the price of real estate around here?" He waved the envelope. "This would barely even make a down payment on a house. And let me tell you, my job pays pretty well already. I'd hate to lose that."

"You make $62,500 per year," Enoch replied, watching as the man blinked in surprise "This is eighty thousand, tax free. All you have to do is throw out a few vials of semen and replace them with these. They're already labeled according to the list you gave us. All we need back from you are the names, addresses, and genders of the children produced by this sperm. Nothing could be easier. Next year, we give you more samples and more money."

"Sounds like a lot of money, sure." A scheming tone had entered Chen's voice that Enoch didn't care for. "But not for the risk I'm taking. You heard about that case a couple of years ago where the doctor was sticking all his own stuff inside his patients, telling them it belonged to Nobel Prize winners and shit? They sent him to jail."

Enoch refused to show anger, just said calmly, "But your DNA isn't involved, Mr. Chen. There's no way to track this back to you. Unlike the doctor in your anecdote, you'll have left no DNA as a clue."

"Yeah, well whose DNA is it anyway? Whatever rich man you work for must be an egomaniac to want his genes spread all through California. We might have a thousand babies inside this cooler, you know that?"

"Take your money, Mr. Chen. Spend it carefully. Your greatest risk is not exchanging the vials of semen, but drawing undue attention to yourself with the money."

"Yes, but that's just it." There was that calculating look again. "I think I sold myself short. It was an initial offer, but carelessly made. You follow?"

Yes, he followed. "You want more money."

"Not a lot. I'm not greedy. An extra forty thousand should cover my risks. I'm sure that would be no great hardship to whoever you work for."

The man was bluffing. He could see it. Just trying to shake down Enoch. They could have paid it, of course. The woman at the big clinic in Los Angeles had taken a hundred and fifty thousand before agreeing to the plan.

But Chen, should he be indulged, would grow ever greedier. Enoch had seen it a million times at Caesar's Palace. A guy takes a gamble, gets lucky, and doesn't know when to stop. Better to nip the gambling impulse in the bud.

"Just one moment, please." He left the man holding the money.

Enoch returned to the van. The briefcase had been tucked in among the coolers for him to use if the need arose. It had not been necessary to use before now. He returned with a second envelope, which he opened in front of Chen.

The envelope held a mélange of information. A résumé with certain sections underlined. A copy of a tax return. A college paper with the plagiarized sections highlighted. And a photo of Chen at a party, snorting a line of coke.

He handed the papers and photos to Chen. "Take a look."

"Where did you get this stuff?" Chen demanded as he thumbed through the papers with a growing frown.

"You don't think we approached you through random chance, do you?" Enoch shook his head. "We found you because we knew you weren't afraid of pushing boundaries."

"This isn't me," he said angrily, coming across the photograph with the cocaine. "You photoshopped this picture."

Enoch didn't know. "Doctored, real, does it matter? There's enough truth in here and enough innuendo to ruin you. And what about this résumé? Does your employer know that it's pure bullshit?"

Chen was quiet.

Enoch said, "This is just research." He held out his hand, and Chen gave the envelope back. "We like to know who we're working with. But nobody needs to see this. Why would they?"

Chen narrowed his eyes. "Just whose semen is in those vials? Yours?"

"Some of it, yes. Does this shock you?"

"And the rest of it? And what's with the Biblical names? Are you some kind of cult?"

"No more questions, Chen. Are you going to take the cooler and the money? There will be more next time if the samples are properly distributed."

And Enoch knew that it was more than just Chen's reputation on the line. Should he back out, someone would come shortly to kill him. But give the man a death threat and he would likely freak out and do something foolish, like go to the police. Blackmail sweetened with a bribe was better.

Ron Chen rolled his tongue in one cheek. At last he nodded. "Okay, yeah, we're good."

Samples delivered, bribes paid, recalcitrant allies brought into line, Enoch continued north, toward the Bay Area. The easy part was behind him.

It was late afternoon when he arrived at the Gold house in Oakland. Enoch parked across the street and waited. He felt light-headed, like he was floating above his body. It was a leafy, mid-dle-class subdivision. The houses were modest, seventies-era ranch houses, but the landscaping had filled in over the years and the neighborhood had a fantastic view down toward the city, as well as a view toward the LDS Oakland temple.

The Oakland temple was one of the more beautiful he had seen, not like those generic, faux-marble things the Salt Lake church built these days. Architecturally, it drew its inspiration from European cathedrals and the Mesoamerican ruins of the Aztec and Maya. Book of Mormon lands. Of course, the Oakland temple practiced a corrupted version of the endowment, administered by men who no longer had the authority to speak on behalf of the Lord.

The temple view was coincidence. The Golds had no connec-tion with Mormonism. Samuel Gold taught at Berkeley. His wife worked for a biotech startup on the other side of the bay. Enoch knew these things not because Elder Kimball had given him the information, but because he had stopped at a library in San Diego last night—Tuesday—to find directions online to the remaining clinics and to the Gold house. Standing at the computer, he hadn't been able to resist the urge to Google the names of the people he was soon to violate.

He waited and watched until he was sure. The street was quiet. He'd had received a text message from Gideon earlier, saying that Samuel Gold's schedule had him teaching a Wednesday night class that didn't end until seven thirty. The woman would be alone inside with the baby.

Enoch opened the glove compartment. He pulled out the gloves and put them on, then removed the gun, checked to see that it was loaded, and then tucked it inside his pants. There was a knife, too. Eight inches long and sharp enough to butterfly fillet a fish. He would return for that later.

He put his hand on the door handle and shut his eyes tight. He had to steady himself, force himself to breathe, try to calm his hammering heart. *Heavenly Father, please forgive me for what I am about to do. I act only to serve Thy will.*

He opened the door and stepped out of the van. Again, that floating feeling, like he was watching someone else. The air was the perfect temperature, with only the slightest breeze to ruffle the leaves on the trees. No cars, and no sound but birds and buzzing insects. He crossed the street, the bulge of the gun at his waist and the leather gloves soft and unfamiliar on his hands. The weight of the Jupiter Medallion seemed to grow with every step as it swung back and forth against his chest.

He thought of the note that had accompanied the family's address. *Let the blood of the wicked be spilled to justify the souls of the righteous.*

A woman answered the door.

She was pregnant, at least eight months, maybe more. Nobody had told him that. The woman was alone inside with the baby, yes, but that hadn't been the whole of the story. The child he was to take had not yet been born. His heart felt like it was slamming against his chest with such force it would rip free and hurl itself to the ground.

Jennifer Gold had opened the door with a friendly smile and the look of someone who is happy to have an unexpected visitor to break the monotony of an evening without her husband. The look soured into mistrust. She looked down at the gun as he pulled it from his waist. Mistrust turned to fear.

Her naked vulnerability almost undid him. He wanted to throw down the weapon and recoil in horror at his own behavior. His covenants to the Lord won him over, but only just.

He pointed the gun at her chest. He told a lie that burned in his throat and on his tongue like so much bile as it came up. "This is a robbery. If you remain silent, you will not be harmed in any way."

A lie. He had come as the Destroying Angel.

* * *

"What's our best-case scenario?" Jacob asked Eliza as the Corolla bumped, scraped, and complained its way up the ranch road toward the Stephen Paul Young house. A cloud of dust spilled behind them. It was early evening. "Let's say we meet Stephen Paul and he's a decent man. Are you prepared to make a decision today?"

Eliza had tried to busy herself with the midweek cleaning at the Kimball household that morning precisely so as not to think about such matters. Let's see, the thirteenth wife of an old man, the first wife of an abusive bully who had tried to rape her, or the mystery man behind door number three. Another choice had crystallized in her mind.

Run like hell.

It had started as a mindless urge, akin, she imagined, to the instincts of a caged animal. And then she realized: She had options. Last night with Eduardo had awakened them.

By lunch, a specific plan had come into focus. She would wait until nightfall. She would sneak out of the house. She would find Eduardo. Together they would drive into the night and flee deep into Mexico where nobody would ever find them.

She sighed. If only it were that easy.

"Liz?"

"Sorry, what?"

"We were talking about Stephen Paul, remember?"

"No, I'm not ready. It's too quick, and I'd rather wait a year or two or five, if that's what it takes, to make the right decision. And I'd prefer to stay in Harmony, not move out to the desert. That is, if staying in Harmony didn't involve marrying Elder Johnson." She looked at him. "Wouldn't it be nice if I had the luxury of making that decision? But here's the way I look at it. Father and the prophet have said that I am to marry. Hence, it is the will of the Lord that I choose one of these three men. So what you're really asking is whether or not I'm prepared to obey God."

Jacob studied her for a moment, and she wondered how much of her thoughts he could read. At last he said, "Plural marriage is easier for some people than for others."

"Really? Who?"

"Women who don't get jealous and have a low sex drive. Men with a high sex drive who can bond to multiple women or to none at all. The obedient. Power hungry men. Subservient women."

"You think there are people who are wired for polygamy?"
she asked.

"Sure. Some of us, on the other hand, are wired for monogamy. A hopeless sort of monogamy at that. You'd think after six
generations that particular gene would have been purged from the
population."

"But I guess it hasn't been."

He shook his head. "No."

The road grew worse. They climbed into the Ghost Cliffs, onto
rutted ranch roads.

According to Jacob, Stephen Paul Young's ranch centered
around one of the few permanent streams in these parts, fed by
snow-capped mountains to the north and augmented by a pair of
natural springs. It flowed east and eventually fed into Lake Powell.
On the paternal side, the Youngs were descended from Brigham
Young's son Henry, who had refused to give up polygamy and been
excommunicated for his troubles. The maternal side, however, was
a family of longtime desert dwellers named Davies. They had first
resisted, then joined the polygamist protestors in the 1920s. That
early group had included a high percentage of daughters, which had
given the few men in the family an unusual amount of influence in
Zion.

That was the history, according to Jacob. Neither of them
knew the current occupant of the ranch.

Two miles west of the Young ranch they stopped for a herd
of cattle in the road. A woman came into view, riding a horse and
driving the cattle across the road. An even greater surprise than seeing a woman herding cattle was that she wore jeans, and not a dress,

although her top with its high collar and long sleeves was common enough, as was the woman's waist-length hair.

"Well, that's something different," Jacob said.

"Yes, if I were into cattle herding." Still, it indicated a certain flexibility in the Young household. Score one for Stephen Paul.

They found another surprise when they reached the sprawling Stephen Paul Young compound. There was another woman on the porch. She rose from her seat as they approached, holding a rifle.

Jacob stopped the car a good distance off. Dust swirled around them, and the engine ticked as it cooled. They didn't get out of the car. "Interesting reception."

"You did call ahead?" Eliza asked. "Maybe they think we're the Jehovah's Witnesses. Or the Mormon missionaries."

"Yes, I called. Told them I had an exciting business proposal to share."

"Ah, Amway. Even better."

They got out of the car. The woman put down the gun and motioned them to approach the porch. "We've got a coyote problem," she said with a smile. "Just so you know we're not shooting strangers in general. One of them has made a den under the porch. A coyote that is, not a stranger. My husband went to get the dog and chase it out."

Her husband appeared on the porch with said dog and came to greet them. He stood three or four inches taller than Jacob. He had strong arms and shoulders, and would have looked the epitome of a hardworking, corn-fed farmer but for the pair of glasses that added a bookish quality to his face.

"I'm Stephen Paul Young. This is my wife Carol." He eyed the gun with a smile. "I've told her a million times not to shoot the guests." He held out his hand. "You must be Brother Christianson. And this is Eliza?" He appraised her. It was neither a lustful glance nor the look of a man checking out stock at the fair. More like a man considering a potential job applicant.

"Here, could you two do me a favor?" he asked. "Stand on either side of the porch. I'm going to send Brigham under the porch. And I want the coyote to run out the far end where it can see an opening."

Brigham was a sheepdog, probably no bigger than the coyote it was meant to chase. But at a word from Stephen Paul, it belly-crawled under the porch. There was a bark, then a snarl. A furry streak flew out from beneath the far end of the porch. A crack from Carol's rifle and the coyote slammed facedown into the dirt.

A moment later and two more shapes broke free. They ran for the desert, Brigham giving furious chase.

"Careful for the dog!" Stephen Paul yelled.

Carol waited until they cleared the sagebrush. Another shot from the rifle, and then a third. Brigham strutted back toward the porch with a pleased look, as if he'd finished off the coyotes himself. Carol, for her part, set the gun down with a casual gesture and only the barest hint of satisfaction on her face, as if picking off moving targets at forty yards was no more an accomplishment of note than baking the daily bread or breastfeeding a baby. Stephen Paul scratched the dog's ears, then went to look at the dead coyotes. The other three followed.

It was a mother and her two pups, nearly grown. Stephen Paul stood over the bodies. "That's too bad. I hate to do that."

"We can't let them camp out under the porch," Carol said. "Not with young children around."

He nodded. "I know, I know. And there's livestock to think about, too. But I still don't like it." Stephen Paul shrugged at Jacob and Eliza. "Maybe if they'd made it another week or two they'd have returned to the desert and we'd have never known they were down there."

"Come on inside," Carol said. "Dinner will be ready in a few minutes."

It was a small family with only two wives and six children, four by the woman they'd seen on the horse, and two by Carol. The woman on the horse was named Sarah, and she returned a few minutes later, dusty and tired. After they'd all cleaned up, Stephen Paul helped the two women set the table and get the children seated.

The family ate together around a massive farm table. Dinner was chicken potpie with corn on the cob and homemade bread. A simple but hearty meal. Eliza watched for hostility from the other women, but picked up none.

Eliza found herself liking Stephen Paul and his wives. Maybe not as future family, but certainly as people.

Dinner consisted of Jacob and Stephen Paul probing each other for their views. Stephen Paul made the first serious advance. "Where exactly is Zion, anyway?"

"Missouri," Jacob said. "Where the saints will gather in the last days as we await the coming of the Lord. That is what they say, at least."

"And you? What do you say?"

"Maybe we'll return to Missouri. Maybe not. My opinion? Zion is where you make it. It's a community of the like-minded. People who pull in one direction. There's no dissension in Zion. Every part works together, like the human body."

"Like the human body," Stephen Paul said. "Not a bad analogy. I tend to think of a machine, myself, only one running with faith as its fuel."

"Completely independent, then?" Jacob asked.

"Connected to the outside world, but in no way dependent upon it."

"What about bleeding the beast?" Jacob asked.

Members of the church saw the U.S. government as a weak, corrupt institution—the manifestation of Babylon—that would someday collapse in the anarchy preceding the Second Coming. The Canadian government was a fawning acolyte of the Americans and would meet a similar fate.

With such knowledge, it was easy to see welfare fraud and tax evasion as a way to speed the inevitable. And if one benefited from the same, why all the better. The methodology was simple with so many women—unmarried mothers in the eyes of the law and thus eligible for welfare and food stamps—and most transactions either cash sales or off-the-books barter.

"Bleeding the beast?" Stephen Paul gave a disgusted shake of the head. "A morally bankrupt tactic. It's all theft, isn't it?"

"Ah, but hasn't the government stolen its wealth anyway?" Jacob asked. "Isn't theft from a corrupt, self-serving organization justified?"

"In a word, no." Stephen Paul dished himself a second helping of the potpie, then served up seconds for two of his children. "No caveats, no equivocating, and no moral relativity in this house. And I thought your father was against that, anyway."

"He is. Although in my father's case, it's practical. It's a stupid way to attract attention from the government, he says. But I've heard the prophet speak, and his reasons are similar to your own. So are mine. Stealing is stealing, as far as I'm concerned. But it seems like there are plenty of saints still bilking the government."

"It's a hard habit to break. So, how well do you know my sisters?" Stephen Paul asked, changing directions abruptly. "Is there one in particular you're interested in?"

"I don't know them at all, yet."

"Not at all?"

"No," Jacob said.

"Haven't even seen a picture?" Stephen Paul asked.

"I might have met one of your sisters several years ago, but she was a child at the time. I couldn't even tell you the color of her hair. But look, there's plenty of time to meet your sisters later. First, I have to make sure that my sister will be happy here."

"Fair enough." He looked at Eliza. "Your brother's a decent man, thinking of you first."

"Yes, I know," she agreed. "It's a lot for my future husband to live up to."

Stephen Paul smiled at this. "Normally at this point in the conversation I would excuse you from the room. My wives and children, too. Then, I'd have a heart-to-heart with my future brother-in-law to see where we stood. But I have to ask you a question first, and I need an honest answer."

Eliza nodded. "I'll give you the best answer I can."

"Do you want to marry me?"

She blinked in surprise. "Does that matter?"

"To me it does."

Eliza said, "And your other wives, this is why they married you? Because they wanted to? Not because they thought that's what God wanted or because their fathers made them?"

"Liz," Jacob said.

"No, it's okay," Stephen Paul said. "Let me explain, Eliza. I'm not asking if you want to marry me because you find me handsome, or are drawn to my animal magnetism. I'm not so self-absorbed as all that. And so-called chemistry is not important in the grand scheme of things. Husbands and wives gain affection for each other through the natural course of childbirth, parenting, and shared lives.

"What I mean by wanting to marry me is that you have weighed *all* the factors. Your belief that I'm a decent man. Your belief that I'll be a good father and a righteous husband who will obey the will of the Lord. Your desire to form something larger than yourself. Zion. A community of people pulling in the same direction for a holy purpose. In that light, Eliza Christianson, do you want to marry me?"

The explanation and the question itself was more than she had expected and entirely fair. She looked around the room at the Young family. They looked happy enough. The women remained in the room. Partners. Maybe not equals, but not servants either.

Yes, it was a fair question, and it deserved a fair answer. "No, I don't. You seem like a good man, and goodness knows you're a better catch than my other choices. But I've known you—what?—an hour? And I'm supposed to decide in an hour whether or not to marry you, not just here, but in the next world, too? It's too soon."

"Okay then," Stephen Paul said. "That's all I need to know."

"Not yet," she corrected. "You asked if I wanted to marry you, and I gave you my honest answer. But that's not my decision. I *will* marry you, because it is the Lord's will that I marry and you are a man I can respect. I could live here. Maybe even be happy someday."

But in the back of her mind she couldn't help but think those same rebellious thoughts that had stirred in her mind since she'd left Eduardo's trailer. She was now suffering the kind of doubts that Jacob regularly entertained. Would it be so bad if she waited a few years before getting married? Would it upset some eternal scheme if she chose her own husband?

Stephen Paul shook his head. "I have complete respect for your position, but that isn't enough. My own family has to be Zion within Zion. Every member has to pull in the same direction with no doubts."

"Unfortunately, no doubts doesn't describe my personality. Not now and probably not ever. There are always doubts."

"I'm sorry then."

Eliza looked at Jacob. She could see him struggling, not knowing whether he should intervene, and if so, how. When it became clear that he wouldn't help her in this, she said, "You know who my other choices are, don't you? One is Elder Johnson. The other is Taylor Kimball, Junior."

He frowned at this news. "I would recommend Elder Johnson. He's a good man. Taylor Junior...I know him well. He's got all of his father's bad characteristics and none of the good." He shook his head. "And he holds only disdain for women."

"I'm painfully aware of that," Eliza said.

"Then you're capable of drawing your own conclusions." He pushed himself back from the table. "It's getting late. Would you like to spend the night here rather than fight your way down the mountain in the dark?" He directed this question to Jacob.

"Yes, thank you," said Jacob.

Later, Eliza and Jacob stood on the porch watching the June beetles batter themselves into the lamp. Eliza had helped the women clean up the kitchen, then retreated to the porch to gather

her thoughts. She had watched the bugs and wondered what it was about lights that bedazzled the insects and sent them swirling in helpless circles.

Jacob had found her on the porch and said nothing for several minutes. "It makes you wonder, doesn't it? The insects are out, doing whatever it is they do—breeding, feeding, avoiding bats— when suddenly they see the porch light. They forget everything else to get closer to the light bulb."

Eliza said, "There's an analogy to humans in there somewhere, I'm sure." She turned to look at her brother. "I think I made a mistake. Now I'm stuck with Elder Johnson. Not exactly every girl's dream to marry a man with a walker and dentures."

"Stephen Paul gave me these." Jacob held up a folder with several papers inside. "Father had faxed him some of your old school papers, IQ tests, and such. Assure good breeding and all that. Looks like Stephen Paul is a eugenicist. Or at least, Father thinks he is."

"So what's my IQ?"

"Is this the point where I'm supposed to say that of course I didn't look?" He smiled as he handed over the folder. "One hundred thirty-eight. No wonder everyone wants to bed my little sister. A good opportunity to improve the breeding stock."

She snorted. "A couple more generations and one hundred thirty-eight won't even warrant a second glance. Of course, everyone will be so pious by then that there will no longer be time to reproduce between all the fasting and praying." She stopped. "Why the rush? Why can't I have a couple of months to get to know Stephen Paul?"

"Liz, let's be honest here. If what Stephen Paul Young wants is one hundred percent certainty on your part, he's not going to get it. Not in a couple of months, not in a couple of years. On the plus side, it looks like my decision is made too. They say Dorothea Johnson has a sweet spirit."

"E.g., ugly," Eliza broke in.

His phone rang, and Jacob retrieved it from his front pocket. "But she's a good person. That's more important than looks or chemistry." He sounded like he was trying to convince himself and not Eliza. "Hello?"

Jacob plugged his right ear with his finger. "I don't have a good signal out here. What was that? Oh, hi, Dad. Yes, we're out here right now. What? I didn't catch that. Oh, really? Is he okay?" He paused and a frown spread across his face, then deepened. "I see. What? No, I'll tell her. Bye." He hung up.

Eliza didn't like the look on his face. "What is it?"

"Elder Johnson suffered a stroke this afternoon. He's in the hospital, in a coma. They don't think he'll survive."

It was the man she would have married in just a few days, but she felt no sorrow. He was an older man, she didn't know him well, and, well, it might have been cold to say, but old people died now and then. What she did feel was a growing sense of alarm. Her choices, so recently reduced to two men with the withdrawal of Stephen Paul Young's interest, had suddenly become very narrow indeed.

Only Taylor Junior remained.

CHAPTER THIRTEEN

Jacob saw the worry in Eliza's face and cut it off at once. "Don't be stupid, Liz. You're not marrying Taylor Junior."

"Then what, Jacob?" she asked with desperation in her voice. "Do I go inside and beg Stephen Paul to have me? Do I run away?"

His mind had already set itself to the problem, but he had the uncomfortable position of a chess player who has realized that a superior opponent has taken control of the middle of the board and is forcing the surrender of any piece that stands in his way.

"First things first. Elder Johnson isn't dead yet."

Eliza gave an exaggerated shrug. "Dead or not, he's in a coma."

"Sure, but his family will believe that he's going to pull out of it. That's what families do, even if the rest of the world knows the guy is already gone. I'll call the Johnsons. Give them my well-wishes, but also make them think we're still interested."

"And if Elder Johnson dies tonight?" she asked. "The Kimballs won't sit around, especially if they know that Stephen Paul is out of the picture."

"Okay, so maybe we'll talk to Stephen Paul. You heard him. He doesn't like Taylor Junior. At the very least he can feign interest for a week or two while we sort things out."

"Didn't you hear the spiel about moral relevancy, equivocating, et cetera? He's not the sort to pretend or lie, not on his behalf, and certainly not on mine." She turned to watch the insects in their mad battering against the porch light. Her face was despondent.

"You're missing the upside of this," Jacob said. "Really. Dad is not going to marry you off to Taylor Junior. The man assaulted you. In front of witnesses. Yes, there are fathers who would force their daughters into marriages under such conditions. Ours isn't one of them and you know it. Elder Johnson is down, Stephen Paul has declined. What does that mean?"

She said nothing.

"I'll tell you what it means. You're off the hook. There'll be no marriage. At least not until Father comes up with some new names."

"Come on, Jacob. I'm not a fool. The news is always a shock to the girl. And sometimes her mother or father gives her one name and then another man comes and maybe just because the prophet made an offhand remark to someone, she's married to someone else. It takes about five minutes for everything to go bad." She shook her head. "All I know is that Father insists I should get married and that two of the three choices are no longer available. What does that mean?"

He didn't know why she wasn't buying it, why she insisted on this fatalism. Jacob took her shoulders and turned her to look at him. "Fine, you don't trust your own father? You want to know who will stand up for you? I will. That's who. Now stop it, Liz. It's not going to happen."

Jacob turned it over in his mind. It was the uncertainty that was getting to her, mixed with the knowledge that other people were making the decisions. Had news already reached the Kimball family? A call to Fernie might let Eliza know he was serious. He took out his phone.

"Who are you calling?"

"Your sister."

It rang several times, and he tried to think what he would do if one of the Kimball men picked up. Ask for Fernie? Hang up? It was a woman.

"Hi, this is Jacob Christianson. Is this Charity?"

"Hello, Brother Christianson. Yes, it is. I'm sorry, but Elder Kimball is out at the moment. Or are you looking for Taylor Junior? He's got his own line, if you need the number."

"Actually, I wanted to talk to...uhm, my sister Fernie." He hoped he hadn't put too much emphasis on sister and thus reminded Charity that Fernie was not actually his sister in any meaningful sense of the word.

"Sure, let me get her."

She put the phone down, and he heard screaming, laughter, and banging from children. It would be bedtime in the Kimball household. Fernie picked up a minute later.

"Hello, Fernie. Can I talk to you?"

Again? he imagined her thinking. *Didn't we already rehash this?*

Instead, she said in a low, muffled voice. "Actually, I need to talk to you, too. I learned something that might help."

"What is it?"

"Not now."

"Ah, got it. If I look for you in the gardens at, say, nine o'clock tomorrow morning, will I find you?"

"That will work. Why did you call?"

"First, have you heard the news of Elder Johnson?" he asked.

"They said he was in the hospital. Taylor Junior was here earlier and mentioned it."

Jacob looked to Eliza, who chewed on a lip. He shook his head for her to stop worrying. To Fernie, he said, "And you know that Taylor Junior and Elder Johnson both wanted to marry Liz?"

"Yes, I know." Still not talking freely. Voice stiff. Whatever she wanted to share, it had her spooked.

"Fernie, the Kimballs are going to be all over this. But Taylor Junior isn't marrying Liz."

"Of course not."

"Well I'm having a hard time convincing her." This was for Eliza's benefit, not Fernie's. "But just to be safe, can you give me a heads-up if you catch a whiff of any scheming?"

"Yes, right away. No problem."

"Good. Thanks. I'll talk to you soon."

"Take care, Jacob."

When he hung up the phone, Eliza had fixed him with a thoughtful look. "I wasn't aware you knew Fernie that well."

He forced a shrug. "Sure, we were friendly. Of course, she got married at seventeen, so it's been several years. In any event, I spoke to her this morning about the Jupiter Medallion. And I think she's got something new."

"That's good."

"Listen, you look tired and a little shaken. Go lie down. Pray if you think that will help. You'll come back with some perspective. I'll talk to Stephen Paul. I'm sure you can stay here tomorrow, at least. Everything will be fine. You'll see."

She nodded, but without conviction. He could almost read her mind. She was thinking about running. Other girls had done it. She could escape where they had not. He wanted to order her to put it out of her mind, but he didn't want to plant that seed if he'd misread her. If the time came to run, he could help; on her own, she'd never make it. He tried to mentally drill it into her as she turned and went inside.

Don't run.

* * *

Jacob didn't find Fernie in the tomato garden the next morning, or among the squash. Instead, she worked in a far corner of the greenhouse, alone. The greenhouse lay empty but for flats of withered squash starts that had never taken, drip irrigation systems rolled up and waiting for next year, plastic flats stacked in corners with wheelbarrows, trowels, and rusting garden rakes. The air was stifling. Fernie swept the floor, an unnecessary and suspiciously solitary task.

She looked up when he opened the door and urgently motioned him over. He didn't like the look on her face. Terrified, almost.

"They can't see me talking to you."

"Who?"

"I don't know." She looked to the door on the far end of the greenhouse, as if worried someone would come inside suddenly. "I've got children, you know. I have to think of them. I didn't want to get mixed up in this. I don't know why she told me. Why not Charity? How about calling her own mother or telling one of her brothers?"

He drew closer. "Fernie, what are you talking about? Tell me." He put his hands on her shoulders. "Calm down. It's okay."

She breathed out slowly. "I'm scared. I never thought..." She reached into the pocket of her dress and pulled out a folded piece of paper. "I found this in Amanda's Book of Mormon."

Jacob took the paper. It was a half-written letter in a woman's cursive. The writing was shaky, as if the writer had been under stress.

Fernie,

If you read this, then I'm already dead. My blood has atoned for my sins.

Dear God, why am I so alone? I don't know where to turn. I will tell the prophet, but maybe he already knows. That is what they say. You are my cousin, my sister wife, and my friend. And you are a good woman. Maybe I'm making a mistake. Maybe someday we'll laugh about this together. But if you discover this letter in your dresser and something has happened to me, you will know why I died and by whose hand.

First, go to my room and get the manila envelope under my mattress. It will help you understand the rest of this letter.

That was all. Jacob turned it over, but the other side was blank.

"I don't understand either," Fernie said. "Amanda didn't finish, and the letter wasn't in my drawer. Something made me open her Book of Mormon. Well, I know what it was. Amanda would some-times jot notes or journal entries and stow them in her scriptures to look at later. I thought I might find some clue as to what she was thinking before she died."

"Good thinking." It occurred to Jacob that Amanda had guessed Fernie would check her Book of Mormon. "And the manila envelope? Was it under her mattress?"

"I haven't looked, Jacob. I'm afraid. What if someone sees me?"

"In a house as full as yours," Jacob said, "they'll appropriate that space soon enough. We have to get that envelope before someone moves the bed and sees it."

"I know, I just couldn't do it," Fernie said. "I kept telling myself that you were chasing your own tail, Jacob. I couldn't believe it was one of us. It had to be one of the Mexicans, and the sooner you figured that out, the better. I was safe in my own house."

"Fernie, they cut Amanda's throat and tore her tongue out by the roots." She looked blank, so he added, "Think about the temple."

Light dawned in her eyes. "Oh no. Jacob..."

He took her in his arms. She lay against his chest, trembling, and he thought of that day almost ten years ago when he had last held her. She had found him in the west fields, shoveling hay. The cold had brought color to her cheeks, and her breath came out in puffs.

He'd smiled to see her, but that smile had faded when he saw the look on her face. Taylor Kimball had sent for her. Fernie had never met the man, but he had several wives already, and a dozen children. She would leave that afternoon. They had shared one last embrace, and Jacob had wept when she'd torn herself away.

Theirs had been a chaste love, for all its flavor of forbidden fruit. They had shared gentle caresses and a few kisses. Jacob had never touched another woman. He had never wanted to.

He'd been a fool. He should have gone to his father, confessed his feelings for Fernie, begged Father not to send Fernie away. He'd been too young to marry, but she would have waited for him, he was sure.

But it was "the will of the Lord." That's what they always said. God had chosen her husband, and the prophet had relayed His will. Right. Jacob was no longer so naïve. The so-called "will of the Lord" was the wishful thinking of a bunch of old men to justify treating their daughters and wives like chattel.

And now, angry with himself for being such a fool, angry with Elder Kimball for taking Fernie from him, he was tempted. She was weak now, vulnerable. And lonely. What polygamist wife wouldn't be consumed with loneliness? Now was his chance to break the bonds that tied her to her husband.

Yes, and tear her from her family.

Jacob pushed her away with some effort. "Fernie, whoever did this will kill anyone who threatens to expose his secret." He didn't say that this someone was most likely her own husband and his sons. "We have to get that envelope."

"But how? There are people in the house. Two of the boys are painting the hallway in that wing. I've seen Taylor Junior coming and going, and my husband is supposed to be back within the hour."

"The prophet sent me to investigate Amanda's death. I don't need permission to inspect the dead woman's room."

"Sounds great, Jacob. I'm sure they'll be happy to see you waltz into Amanda's room and dig around. And when they see you with that envelope, they'll be sure to give you a pat on the back for a job well done."

"I'll be careful."

* * *

"You don't have the baby." It was not a question, but a statement of fact. It dangled in the air, like the axe of an executioner over the neck of the condemned.

Enoch swallowed hard. He held the phone to his ear and wondered how Elder Kimball would look on the other end. Angry? Disappointed? Vengeful?

"How did you know?"

"The angel told me, Brother Christianson."

Maybe true. Maybe a lie.

Enoch had stood at the doorway of the Gold house, fully intending to follow through with the plan. And then Jennifer Gold had answered the door. A young woman with curly hair and glasses and pregnant. He had tied the hands of the terrified woman with her own shoelaces, then returned from the car with the filleting knife. He'd forced her to the ground and stood over her with the knife in hand.

Enoch had been a premed student too, like his older brother, and knew how to sever the unborn child from its mother's living uterus. It would be a butcher's job, but the child would survive. Ten minutes to do the job, ten more to leave evidence to throw the police off the trail.

A baby. A girl. The daughter of scientists. She would be brought to Blister Creek and raised in the Church of the Anointing.

Jennifer Gold gasped for mercy when she could get words out through her terror. Self-loathing washed over Enoch. Only a monster could do what he'd intended.

And so instead, he had kept his promise to Jennifer Gold, meant as a lie, and robbed the house. It was a halfhearted attempt, and he'd ditched the watches, costume jewelry, and petty cash as he fled east. He'd left the pregnant woman unharmed.

Enoch entered Nevada via Reno. He would call Jacob, then return to Blister Creek. He had to unburden himself, no matter what punishment awaited. He was driving east on I-80 when the call came from Elder Kimball.

"I'm sorry, Elder Kimball," Enoch spoke into the phone. "I couldn't do it. Nobody told me that Jennifer Gold hadn't yet—"

Elder Kimball cut him off. "No details. I don't know and I don't care. If you have questions, talk to my son. You know that. Enoch, what's important is that you covenanted to obey my counsel. By rights, your life is forfeit."

Your counsel, old man? Or Gideon's?

And if Elder Kimball refused to involve himself in the details of his plans, how could he expect Enoch to follow them blindly?

"However, the Lord is merciful, is he not?" Elder Kimball continued. "You are young, you succumbed to cowardice. We all make mistakes, and with righteous contrition, the Lord has promised that He will forgive us. I will plead with Him on your behalf."

The only mistake he had made, Enoch decided, was to listen to Elder Kimball in the first place. Whatever return to glory awaited him in this life or the next, it would not erase the memory of Jennifer Gold lying on the floor, begging for her life.

And yet he had covenanted. Elder Kimball had taken him through the endowment where he had covenanted to obey the Law of Sacrifice. To sacrifice all that he possessed, even his own life, if necessary, to defend the Kingdom of God. To obey Elder Kimball as the emissary of the Lord.

A man could lose more than his life by breaking a covenant. His soul could be cast into Outer Darkness. There was only one way to undo this, and that was to return to the temple where he had made his covenants, and that meant buying time.

"What should I do?"

"Your botched attempt means the police will be watching the Gold house. Probably the woman's work as well. But what about her shopping habits? Does she visit her parents on weekends? What other habits does she have? Gideon will know. Go back to Oakland and wait. I'll have more information by morning."

"Thou sayest."

He hung up but did not get off the freeway to turn around. Instead of returning to California, he continued east, toward Utah. At Winnemucca, Enoch stopped at a McDonald's for lunch. He picked up the phone and dialed Jacob's number.

CHAPTER FOURTEEN

Eliza had remained at the Stephen Paul Young house on Thursday morning and happened to be looking out the window when Manuel and Eduardo pulled up in their Ford F-150. Stephen Paul had set up a bed in the children's wing, but the two children sharing her room suffered from colds, and between the hacking and fussing, his wife Carol decided Eliza would be more comfortable in the office above the barn. The two women dragged over a futon, linens, and a quilt.

The Young ranch sat on a swelling of sandstone in the midst of the wilderness, and she could see for miles from her second-story room. A furnace-red landscape stretched beyond, with buttes rising above the desert floor, framed by a blue sky without a single cloud.

The entirety of the Colorado Plateau, an area roughly the size of Maine, had a population of about thirty thousand people, and the bulk of them clustered in towns on the region's periphery. There was no better place for God's chosen people to gather and build His kingdom than its desolate center.

Eliza had not been happy to remain at the Young house. She wrestled with an unexpected feeling of humiliation. Stephen Paul had rejected her. Affection, or lack thereof, aside, he had been her salvation from the other two suitors. Make that one, now that Elder Johnson was out of the picture.

It was Eliza's duty to pitch in with the chores, but she otherwise avoided Carol and Sarah. Instead, she retreated to the makeshift bedroom in the office above the barn. It was quiet, and apart from a hint of bovine smell in the air at all times, she found it a pleasant respite from the constant company of women and children. If her goal had been to gain the Young women as allies, she had no doubt failed.

The truck looked like a dust devil approaching across the desert floor as it followed the road snaking its way toward the house. The road followed dry washes and skirted eroded sandstone bluffs. She only recognized the truck when it was within a hundred yards of the house.

What would draw the Mexicans so far from town? A little side work for the Youngs?

A spur led from the road to the house, and then to a poured concrete slab of a driveway just below Eliza's window next to the barn. The truck pulled up and stopped. A haze of dust hung in the air around the truck and all the way down the road for miles. The doors opened. Two men stepped out.

Eduardo and Manuel. They were dressed like Mexican laborers, in long sleeves now to protect against the sun, and with hats to shield their faces. Shovels, toolboxes, and other tools sat in the back of the truck, and the two men had gloves tucked into their front breast pockets.

And yet there was something about the way that they held themselves that wasn't right. They had a certain confidence and certainty of purpose. They did not carry themselves like illegal aliens.

They stood chatting right below her window. She flipped the latch and eased it open, wincing at the squeak.

To her further surprise, Eduardo and Manuel spoke in English, even though they were by themselves. "So this guy is good?" Eduardo asked.

"Depends on what you mean by good. I wouldn't trust any of them. However, given the circumstances—"

The front door opened on the house, and Manuel stopped mid-sentence. Stephen Paul crossed the space between the two buildings. She pulled back from the window so he couldn't see her. "Good morning."

"Have you got it?" Manuel asked.

"I do, but let's be clear. My participation is contingent upon the conditions we agreed upon earlier. Contingent and limited in scope."

Eliza held her breath. Stephen Paul didn't know she was up here, either. He thought she was sleeping in the house, near the children.

"Understood," Manuel said. He took something from Stephen Paul, then passed it along to Eduardo, who returned to the truck. Eduardo's body shielded whatever it was that Stephen Paul had given them. Eliza shrank back from the window as Eduardo tossed the object into the truck's cab and turned around.

"That's all we need," Manuel said. "But we'll have to kick around here for a few hours so the others will think we've been working. We're supposedly up here on a side job."

"I've got a guest back at the house," Stephen Paul said. "So it might be better if you were actually seen working rather than sipping lemonade on the porch. You up for that?"

"Yeah, I guess." No enthusiasm in the voice. "What have you got?"

Stephen Paul said something about a fence in need of repair, and the three men walked around the side of the house.

Eliza watched them leave with some confusion. At first glance of Eduardo she had felt an aftershock of the desire that had gripped her the other night. But there was no question now. He was involved in something underhanded.

She was angry with herself for not following up on what she had learned earlier. Eduardo had spoken perfect English. His excuse had not rung true. She should have known that he was not in Blister Creek to work. Neither was Manuel. Could they be involved in the murder after all? And what did that say about Stephen Paul?

Eliza looked at the truck. What had Stephen Paul given them?

She made the sudden decision to get that envelope and have a look before they came back. She shut the window and hurried from the bedroom.

* * *

Fernie left the greenhouse from the far end. She would go to the house and cycle through as if on meaningless errands. In reality, she would keep vigil while Jacob searched Amanda's room. If she spotted either her husband or Taylor Junior, she would call Jacob on his cell.

Jacob left through the opposite side. The air was cooler outside, and drier. Sweat was streaming down his sides and plastered his hair to his forehead. He made straight for the house.

He reached the wing where Fernie had directed him. A different hallway than where Eliza had slept. Two boys, maybe ten and eleven, painted the railing leading up the stairs.

"Hot out there," he said as he maneuvered past them. "You're lucky to be working inside where there's AC."

They stopped their painting and watched him go up the stairs. The boys might tell their father that they'd seen him, but by then he'd have what he needed.

Jacob hurried down the hallway to Amanda's old room. It was the second door on the left, according to Fernie. He stood outside the closed door for a moment, listening for sounds. He heard nothing.

He could have sent Fernie to search Amanda's room. She would have aroused less suspicion. But Fernie was terrified. And he feared for her safety. They had butchered Amanda; they would do the same to Fernie.

He opened the door and let out his breath when he saw the room was empty.

Children had already moved in to bunk with Sophie Marie now that the girl's mother was gone. One wall held a framed picture of Jesus with children, another a poster of math facts next to a world map. A cork board held drawings, spelling work, and math worksheets. Two bunk beds sat in one corner, but a queen-sized bed still sat in the middle of the room, with an adult-sized dresser to one side. That had to be Amanda's.

He put his hand between the mattress of the queen-sized bed and the box springs and ran it along the side of the bed from the headboard down to the foot. Nothing on this side. He went to the other side and did the same. He felt nothing unusual.

Frowning, he lifted the mattress as far as he could before it started to fold over on itself. Something caught his eye near the middle. He pushed the mattress halfway off the bed and stretched out his free hand. It came back with a manila envelope. Inside, what felt like papers.

His first inclination was to shove the envelope down his pants, then lock himself in the bathroom and examine the papers there. But he didn't know what it contained, and it occurred to him that he might have to come back and shove it back under the mattress. And take another risk that someone would spot him coming or going. He opened the envelope.

It held clippings from newspapers and magazines. He looked at the first, a photocopy of the *San Francisco Chronicle* with a four-year-old date. It was about the murder in San Francisco that had drawn the nation's attention—the one to which they were comparing the more recent kidnapping in New Mexico. The second was a similar article from the *Los Angeles Times*, together with a grainy photo of the murder scene. He glanced at the articles with some impatience. What did this have to do with anything? And then he came to the third and final clip. Amanda had cut it neatly from a glossy magazine like *Time* or *Newsweek*. The headline read, "A Satanic Cult Stalks California's Intellectual Elite."

The picture was color, not newsprint, and large enough to see details. A bedroom, with a body on the floor. An editor had blurred the body, deeming the details too horrific to print. But not the wall behind the body.

Occult-like symbols, written in blood, streaked and coagulated against the wall.

Jacob read the article. The body was that of a top scientist at a Silicon Valley firm. They'd found her husband—himself an academic at Stanford—dumped in San Francisco Bay, strangled. They'd killed the woman and painted the walls with her blood. There was no sign of the couple's baby.

Two days after the murder, the killer had sent a letter to the *San Francisco Chronicle*. Referencing details known only to the killer, he had claimed to belong to a Satanic cult. The cult had taken the baby as a sacrifice for Lucifer. They had consumed its flesh in a black mass in a convent near Santa Rosa that had burned down a few years earlier. Police had found fresh blood in the ruins and similar occult-like markings, but no body. The blood had been contaminated with some other chemical, and tests came back inconclusive.

It was the second crime claimed by the cult. In the first, the cult had stolen a baby from the neonatal unit of a hospital in Los Angeles. That baby's father had been a world-class brain researcher at UCLA. Authorities now believed the first baby had met the same grisly fate.

Jacob had to stop reading. He put the articles down and shut his eyes. He had recognized the symbols written in blood at once. He had studied them several times over the previous few days. They were not the marks of a Satanic cult as the letter writer would have the police believe. They had been taken from the Jupiter Medallion.

Amanda had collected these articles. Perhaps she had threatened to share the information about the symbols with the police, along with her suspicions about who had left them at the scene. Maybe she'd kept quiet but had been discovered. Either way, someone had killed her to assure her silence.

The rest, he simply could not wrap his mind around. The church had no connection to these academics and scientists as far as he knew. Had they written something hostile to the church? Unlikely.

And the bit about the Satanic cult, surely that was meant to throw off the investigation. But why use symbols from the Jupiter Medallion? Was that intentional, or someone being careless? And what had motivated Amanda to get involved?

He returned to the clips. Nobody in Blister Creek would subscribe to these newspapers or magazines. The most likely source was the library at Southern Utah State University in Cedar City. Amanda would have passed by the place with her sister wives while they were selling vegetables for the co-op, and she'd found a way to get inside by herself.

Is that how they caught you? He imagined them coming upon her, questioning her, maybe even torturing the information from her. She had confessed, and they had exacted their vengeance. Did they cut her tongue from her mouth first? What had she thought as they'd taken the knife to her throat?

But her secret had remained, both here and tucked into the pages of Amanda's Book of Mormon. And now he knew.

Bastards.

His phone vibrated in his pocket. Two rings, then it stopped. The signal from Fernie. One of the Kimball men had come home. Time to get out.

He folded up the articles and stuffed them in his pocket, then pushed the mattress back into place. It looked rumpled, so he fiddled with the bedspread. Not quite right, but it would have to do. He turned to go.

Footsteps sounded in the doorway outside the room. He froze with his hand on the doorknob.

"Jacob!" Fernie whispered from the other side of the door.

He opened the door in relief. She stood in the hallway looking anxious. He said, "I told you not to come up. I got the call."

"But you didn't answer and I thought…never mind. It's Taylor Junior. He's asking about you. I told him I'd seen you out by the greenhouses. He went to look, but it won't keep him long, I'm sure."

They made their way outside without running into the prick. Possibly murderous prick, Jacob thought.

"Did you get what you were looking for?" Fernie asked as she followed him back to his car.

"Yes, do you want to know?"

She studied his face. "I don't know. Do I?"

He thought of Amanda, throat cut, buried in the sand. "No, you don't. And I don't want you any more involved. It could have been you. So unless you feel you must know, I'd rather not tell you. But thanks, Fernie. This helps a lot."

Jacob wanted to stay and talk, to comfort her at least. Fernie was scared. But he'd already put her life at risk. He said goodbye and climbed into the Corolla.

The phone rang as he pulled away from the Kimball house. He picked it up and answered.

A familiar voice spoke on the other end. "Hello, Jacob. It's Enoch."

CHAPTER FIFTEEN

It was too good an opportunity to pass up. Stephen Paul had given something to Manuel and Eduardo, and they had put it into their unlocked truck. Jacob would have been down there at once to rifle through the papers and see if it had anything to do with their investigation. Eliza must do the same.

Deep breath. Must move quickly.

Eliza stepped outside to a gust of hot air off the desert. She stood in the shade of the barn and looked around, but saw no one. Voices came from the far side of the house. The men would be in the shed now.

The F-150 sat on the concrete slab. Its engine ticked as it cooled. They'd rolled down the windows so as not to turn the cab into an oven. It would be easy enough to step up and grab the folder without opening the door.

She walked to the truck, so nervous that she almost opened the door without remembering her earlier observation. She froze a second time with her hand poised outside the window. If she stopped now, she could still deny everything. She'd noticed the truck and came outside, curious.

What would Jacob do?

He wouldn't freeze in place like an idiot, for one. Quickly now, she reached in and grabbed the folder. She undid the clasp and pulled out the stack of papers.

At first she didn't understand what she was looking at. All business stuff. There was a balance sheet and a bank statement. There were expense reports, credit card statements, and the like. Eliza didn't know what she'd been expecting—photographs of Taylor Junior murdering Amanda, perhaps?—but it hadn't been this. She'd overheard their conversation and mistaken it for a part of the conspiracy.

And then she did catch the Kimball name, first Taylor Junior and Elder Kimball, and then Gideon Kimball. There was a list of salaries paid, $125,000 in the case of Elder Kimball and $65,000 apiece in the case of his two sons. Looking further, she saw that these papers pertained to the Blister Creek Co-Op, which was the company run by the Kimballs and the Youngs to sell everything from fruits and vegetables to pies and beef jerky in farmers' markets and small grocery stores in Southern Utah. Her own family belonged to a similar operation in Harmony.

There was nothing suspicious about the papers, except for the bit about Gideon. He was an outcast. Why would he draw a salary? And then she saw something that surprised her even more: someone with the initials E.N.C., also drawing a salary of $65,000.

She recognized those initials at once, being as they belonged to her brother. Enoch Nephi Christianson. That he would draw a salary was even more surprising.

A voice came from behind her. "What are you doing, Eliza?"

She turned with a startled gasp and dropped the papers. They scattered and the breeze turned them over. It was Eduardo.

He bent to grab at the papers now blowing across the driveway. "Don't just stand there. Give me a hand."

His words startled her into action, and she bent to help. Eduardo put the papers back in the envelope. He returned the envelope to the truck, then turned with a sharp look.

"What the hell were you doing?"

"I could ask you the same thing," she said. "You're no day laborer. And what was all that crap the other night about not wanting to speak English?" She was growing angry. "Yeah, what *are* you doing?"

He didn't answer. "Frankly, it's none of your business. I just can't believe you grabbed a bunch of papers out of my truck."

"Why are you trying to make this about me? You're the one spying on us. I saw those papers. Talk about none of your business." She was growing angrier now. "And the other night, what was that about? Some kind of game? Seduce the polygamist girl?"

"Hey," he said. He looked angry. "That's bullshit and you know it. I didn't seduce you. You came over to my house. You found *me*. You practically threw yourself at me."

That part was true enough, she thought guiltily. "Well, you could have said no. I was in way over my head. And I thought you liked me."

"I do like you, Eliza. Maybe I shouldn't have done anything, but believe me, it wasn't an act. And I *did* say no, remember?"

Eliza softened. "Well, it was stupid."

"Probably. But I didn't do anything that you didn't want."

"Eduardo, what are you mixed up in? Do you have any idea how serious this is?" He didn't reply. She glanced over his shoulder. Still no sign of Manuel and Stephen Paul. "Why did you come back to the truck, anyway?"

"Stephen Paul said he had a guest. Had no idea it was you. I thought it might be a good idea to lock the truck. You know, in case someone got nosy." He gave her a pointed look.

She snorted. "Well, go ahead and lock up. But I'm serious that you'd better have a good explanation for what's going on here. I already told my brother you were here," she lied. "He'll go straight to the prophet if he thinks you're up to something weird, or if anything happens to me."

Eduardo took her by the wrist, but it was not an aggressive gesture. "Eliza, you can't tell anyone else. That goes for Jacob, too."

"Eduardo, the more people who know, the better."

He shook his head. "Then it must not be what you think."

"Well?" She stared at him, willing him to tell her something to allay her fears.

"Listen, I'll talk to Manuel. Can you be patient for a few more hours? Please, Eliza."

She considered. What she needed was to talk to Jacob. In the meanwhile, she must be confident. "You can talk to Manuel. We'll come by the trailer this evening. If you don't give us a good explanation, we'll go to Brother Joseph."

He nodded. "Fair enough."

* * *

"I don't know what this is all about," Jacob told Eliza as they drove
to the Mexicans' trailer that evening, "but whatever you do, don't
mention the murders."

"You're assuming they don't know already."

"Right, I am. But if they're here for something else, we'll be
causing ourselves a lot of trouble by mentioning Amanda."

"You think they could be cops?" Eliza asked.

"I thought of that. But why are they here?" He thought about
the clippings he'd found beneath Amanda's mattress. He'd already
shared the details with his sister. "Did they follow the trail of the
murdered scientists? Then why all this undercover stuff? Why not
get search warrants and be done with it?"

He was proud of his sister for keeping her eyes and her ears
open. The information about the murder in California had left him
stunned and unsure where to turn. And then Enoch had called, and
that, combined with this business with the Mexicans, might be the
key to unraveling the whole mystery.

They'd driven west as if leaving town, then circled back around
on a ranch road so as to conceal their movements. He didn't want
anyone to know that they were talking to the Mexicans.

Elder Johnson had died in the middle of the night. First word
had come to Blister Creek by afternoon. Shortly, a flurry of mes-
sages from Canada. One had been a text message from Dorothea
Johnson, telling him to be patient and she would find another man
from the Johnson family to marry his sister. Her father's death was a
blow, but she assured him that Jacob and Dorothea could still marry
if they were patient.

Jacob had reread the text message three times before coming to the conclusion that yes, she was serious. Someone had convinced Dorothea that he wanted nothing more than to marry her. This, apparently, had been the reason for Eliza to marry Elder Johnson, and not the other way around.

He had written back, expressing condolences for her father's death, and telling her that it was inappropriate to discuss marriage during this time of grief. Eliza was quite broken up over the death of her would-be fiancé and did not want to talk about marriage at the moment, not to the Johnsons or anyone else for that matter.

There'd been a message from their father, asking about Stephen Paul. Did they like the man? And if not, was he willing to reconsider Taylor Junior?

Jacob had been tempted to keep this information from Eliza, but he needed her to trust that he was fighting for her. That meant full disclosure. "Dad doesn't know what Taylor Junior did the other night," he assured her, "or he wouldn't have sent that message."

They parked the car in the deep shadows between a farmhouse and the Mexicans' trailer. It was partially obscured by a cottonwood tree. As they stepped outside, Jacob said, "There's something else you should know."

"You mean, besides the fact that Father wants me to marry a would-be rapist? Or that Enoch might be mixed up with a Satanic cult?"

"Yeah, besides that." He considered how best to approach this. "Enoch called me this morning."

She dropped the ironic tone. "He did? Is he okay?"

"I don't think so," Jacob admitted. "He sounded afraid and—I don't know—unbalanced. Said something about an angel with a sword."

"Really?"

"Yeah. I didn't press him. Maybe I was afraid he was losing his mind. He said he was ready to unburden his soul. Whatever that means. Confess? Rat out his co-conspirators? I don't know, because he wouldn't tell me anything over the phone."

"Does he want us to go back to Las Vegas?" she asked.

"No. He's coming here."

"But that's good news, right? If he tells us everything, we'll be able to put all the pieces together."

"Right, if it were that straightforward. Enoch said he can only tell me in the temple. It's the only way to be sure."

"The temple?" she asked.

"The Celestial Room, to be specific." It was the most sacred space in the temple with the possible exception of the Holy of Holies. Eliza may not have been through the temple yet, but she would understand that much.

"But he can't get inside, can he? He's been excommunicated."

Jacob said, "Right. And he'd never even been through the temple before he was ex-ed. Father never gave him the Melchizedek Priesthood. Only we saw that he was wearing temple garments, didn't we? If there was any doubt, it's gone now. He said he'd meet us at the veil. He knew what he was talking about, that's for sure. This isn't his first time."

Eliza looked uncomfortable. It was an unbreakable taboo, entering the temple without authorization. "I don't understand. How did he get in?"

"No idea," Jacob said. "But somehow he's been through and knows he can get back in. Maybe the Lost Boys have been taking out unauthorized endowments?"

"And why the temple?" she asked again. "Why not meet us in Cedar City or St. George if he doesn't think Las Vegas is safe?"

It was a good question. "First, Enoch doesn't think the others will look for him there. Maybe. Second theory. Enoch saw an angel, or thought he saw an angel. He might be wondering now if it's an evil spirit. If it's an evil spirit, it can't follow him into the temple."

Eliza stopped short. They'd reached the last bit of shadow before stepping into the porch light of the Mexicans' trailer. "But what if it *was* an angel?"

"Come on, Liz. No angel told these guys to murder a young woman and consume her infant in a black mass. It's either an evil spirit or a delusion. I vote delusion."

She shuddered, clearly fixing on the evil spirit. "Maybe Enoch thinks he'll be safe in the Celestial Room. From the other Lost Boys, I mean. They wouldn't dare attack him there."

"You think a man who'd tear out a woman's tongue would respect the temple?"

"Well, no." She looked more troubled still.

Jacob put a hand on her shoulder to comfort her. "Me neither. In any event," he added, "Friday morning is the day when you will go through the temple for the first time."

"Tomorrow?" She drew back. "Really? Are you sure?"

"Quite. I called Father back, but he was out, so I left a message. Told him my plans. Told him it was the best time to take out your endowment so you'd be ready to get married."

"But that's not it?"

"I want you with me when I meet Enoch. I don't know what his mental state is. Not good. He might listen to you. I don't know."

Eliza still looked stunned. "But I'm going through the temple? Really?"

Nothing could prepare you for the temple. The details were never discussed on the outside. And there were warnings as you started and then the signs and tokens. And someone playing the role of Satan in the endowment and a reference to Satan's own "priesthoods," which threw some people. Oh, and stripping your clothes off for the initiatory while strange hands anointed your body with oil.

"Only we can't do it alone," Jacob said. "We can double up some of the roles, but we'll need some help. I'm thinking Fernie and Charity Kimball and Stephen Paul and his brother, Aaron Young. Plus Enoch, who will draw us through the veil and into the Celestial Room."

"Stephen Paul won't be happy to meet an apostate in the temple," Eliza said. "And what about Charity? What if she tells her husband?"

"It's just an endowment, as far as they're concerned. By the time Stephen Paul sees Enoch, we'll be in the Celestial Room. And Enoch will tell us everything about the murder. My white lie to Stephen Paul will pale in comparison."

"And it has to be in the temple?" Eliza asked.

Jacob nodded. "You know what Enoch said when he called? 'We must have an endowment. Then I'll tell you everything. There shall the veil be taken from thy mind and the eyes of thy understanding opened.'"

Eliza blinked. "What does that have to do with the endowment? Isn't that where you learn what you need to enter the Lord's presence after you die?"

"Yes, symbolically," Jacob said. "You learn the signs and tokens to give to the angels that stand as sentinels to the Celestial Kingdom. But that's about ten minutes of the endowment ceremony. The rest is instruction and covenant to obey certain commandments. The thing is, we only take out our endowment once. Every time we go back after the first time, it's to stand as proxy for someone who is dead."

The outside world mocked the saints for performing ordinances for the dead in their temples, including celestial marriage and baptism. But if the Lord required these things for salvation, then temple work for the dead made perfect sense. Billions of people would die without ever knowing the truth. You either believed God excluded people from heaven for nothing more than being born in the wrong family, or you allowed a way for the dead to gain salvation.

"Yes, I know that," Eliza said. And yet she'd never heard it articulated quite like that and felt a twinge of guilt that Jacob was speaking so openly. She'd always been told that one only discussed these things within the walls of the temple.

"So why not skip to the good stuff? Why repeat all the parts meant for living people? The covenants and oaths? Dead people don't apostatize. Look, I've gone through the endowment about fifty times. I know it word for word. Ninety percent of it is for the living members of the church."

He waited patiently while she thought it over. At last she said, "Because it's not about redeeming the dead, is it?"

"No, it's not. It's about reconfirming your loyalty. And taking on a mantle of divine protection. When we enter the Celestial Kingdom, we will be endowed with the power of the Lord. Enoch, too. Nobody will be able to touch us there. Or so Enoch tells himself. Now," Jacob added as he turned his thoughts to the matter at hand. "Let's find out what these Mexicans are up to."

* * *

Eduardo and Manuel were alone. The others—the two *real* Mexican laborers—had taken the truck to St. George. Manuel and Eduardo welcomed them inside and offered them seats on the couch. Eduardo offered them first an iced tea, and then a Coke. Those drinks were against the Word of Wisdom, so they declined.

The two men remained standing. It was meant to make them feel uncomfortable, or at least assert their dominance. Jacob relaxed on the couch, and Eliza tried to adopt his posture.

"You know, then," Manuel said, "why we're here. Or, I assume, you have a pretty good guess after your sister rifled through my papers."

"Yes, of course," said Jacob, which Eliza knew was a bluff. "Maybe we can help."

Manuel nodded. "Of course. It's not up to us, but it might be possible to arrange a deal in return for your cooperation. That depends of course, Mr. Christianson, on your level of involvement."

"Please, call me Jacob. Or Brother Christianson, if you prefer." He shook his head. "But my involvement is zero. I've done nothing illegal. Neither has my sister. I thought you'd know that."

"Even better. Then you'll have no second thoughts. Now, Mr. Young—who is cooperating fully, you must know—told us that you are an honorable man and no friend of the Kimballs. Is this true?"

"We have our differences with the Kimballs," Jacob said. "That's true enough. But before we go any further, can I respectfully ask what you'd like us to do?"

Manuel nodded. "Of course. The two of you are staying at the Kimball house, aren't you?"

"Yes, that's right."

Well, Eliza thought, *not anymore.* It was no longer safe for them there. All their stuff was in the back of the Corolla. They'd sleep somewhere else tonight.

"We need surveillance of the Kimball house. Stephen Paul, for all the information he shared, doesn't have that kind of access." Manuel reached behind the couch for a briefcase. "I have some bugs here. I need you to plant these in several places throughout the house. Bedrooms, living room, the telephone."

Jacob looked wary. "That's quite a risk. The house is never empty."

"Which is precisely why we can't enter ourselves. We've been trying for weeks to get work at the Kimball house itself. No dice."

"But what are you hoping to hear?" Eliza asked. "You think they'll just talk about things in the open?"

"Of course," Eduardo said. He looked right at Eliza. "That's the beauty of our disguise. There are no outsiders in your community. Just a few Mexican laborers with limited English. They won't expect anyone to be listening."

Eliza nodded. Every word from the Mexicans left her more convinced that they were talking about something else, and not the murders. But what?

"I hope you'll excuse me, but may I please see your badge?" Jacob asked abruptly. "Are you state police? Federal?"

Manuel reached into his shirt pocket and retrieved a badge. "FBI. We're the ones charged with investigating this type of fraud."

The word fraud brought everything into focus. Eliza had seen the salaries on the printouts from Stephen Paul. Evidence of salary, and evidence of profit from the co-op. What had been the discussion about "bleeding the beast"?

Eliza watched Jacob for his reaction. He just nodded as he took the badge, examined it, and then handed it back. "Thank you, Mr. Cardoza. I guessed FBI. But I thought it might be the state. Or even the IRS. I thought they had their own investigative unit."

"The IRS will come in after we're done and perform a full audit. They're the ones who tipped us off. Seems Mr. Kimball was careless with a few of his bank accounts. But we're the main guys. Given the scope of the fraud, it will be big. Money laundering, tax evasion, welfare fraud, illegal transfer of funds, you name it."

"How much are we talking about here?" Jacob asked.

"Well, I can't give numbers, but you've seen their house," Manuel said. "New wing, new vehicles. All those greenhouses and the farm. New tractors, irrigation equipment, that grain silo. None of that comes cheap."

"Sure, but Elder Kimball sells produce all throughout the Southwest," Jacob said. "My family runs a similar business, albeit smaller. There's a lot of money in agriculture, if you know what you're doing."

"Yes, but that's not what Kimball claims," Manuel said. "According to his taxes, he's just struggling to get by. But like I said, we're not the IRS. We're looking mainly at fraud and money laundering. All those wives file as single mothers with lots of dependents and very little income. And where does all the money go, anyway?"

"Well then, Mr. Cardoza. You'd better explain your bugs."

Manuel opened the briefcase to reveal what looked like the bargain bin at Radio Shack. He spent a few minutes going through each kind of bug and where it should be placed. The most important, he said, was the phone bug, followed by the bug in Kimball's office. Jacob listened and asked a few pointed questions.

"The Mexicans—the ones from south of the border, that is," Manuel added with a half smile, "are bringing back a van loaded with carpet and linoleum. We've got some work at the Jameson Young house tomorrow, but after that, I'm going to send them to Kanab for a week to work on a job there. Get them out of the way. Meanwhile, Eduardo and I will equip the van with some additional gear. We'll be ready to go by tomorrow night. Think you can get the place bugged by then?"

"I'll give it a start," Jacob said. "It might take a couple of days to get everything placed. As I said, the house is never empty." He nodded at Eliza. "My sister can help, of course."

* * *

"Now we're in a bind," Jacob said as he and Eliza made their way back to the car. He held the briefcase in both hands, away from his body, as if he wanted nothing more than to fling it into the darkness. "We can't plant these bugs."

"It won't just turn up fraud."

"No, not if we're right about the Kimballs. Much as I'd like to plant those bugs and listen in myself, if we're right, everything will go to pieces. This murder, together with what happened in California, will be like the Lafferty murders, Elizabeth Smart, and Jon Benet Ramsey all wrapped up in one. There will be so many media people descending on this place...well, let's not go there. It can't happen."

"They'd have to move the whole community to Harmony."

He shook his head. "The days are long gone when you can run to the other side of the border."

"But why did you agree?" Eliza asked. "Why not just say sorry, but we're not getting involved?"

They reached the car, and Jacob unlocked the door for her. He fixed her with a sideways glance. "It's too late for that, Liz. They know we're snooping around already. And the last thing we need is them checking up on *us*."

"So what's the deal with those papers I found in their truck?" Eliza asked.

"Guess they're trying to track money. Elder Kimball claims he's barely in the black, but then why all these salaries? Stephen Paul does business with the Kimballs from time to time. He must have got hold of some sensitive files and passed them on to Manuel and Eduardo. In any event, the fact that Elder Kimball is paying salaries to Gideon and Enoch is pretty good evidence for us that he's involved with whatever the Lost Boys are up to."

It made sense. "But what are we going to do about the FBI?"

"I don't know, stall for time?"

"How are we going to manage that?" she asked.

"Surely we can put off a couple of FBI agents for a day or two. We meet with Enoch at the temple tomorrow. After that, everything will resolve itself in a hurry. One way or another."

CHAPTER SIXTEEN

The conspirators met in the Holy of Holies, deep in the bowels of the temple. This room, where the prophet was said to commune with the Lord, was off-limits to all but the Quorum of the Twelve and the prophet, but Elder Kimball owned a complete set of temple keys. It was easy enough to gain entry. Almost as simple to smuggle in the others.

The Holy of Holies was a windowless room with a lofty ceiling, built beneath the temple's spire. A brass chandelier hung overhead; it was said to have been taken from the temple built by Joseph Smith in Nauvoo, Illinois, and later burned by a mob when the saints were driven west. Wooden benches ringed the room. Varnished wainscoting covered the lower half of the wall.

In the center of the room sat an aged cedar chest some four feet high. Winged cherubim perched on both ends of the chest, wood overlaid with gold. The chest itself was carved with all manner of symbols: all-seeing eyes, the sign of the compass and square, a moon with a face. In the chest, it was said, lay the Urim and Thummim—used by Joseph Smith to translate the Book of Mormon from the Gold Plates—and the sword and breastplate of Laban. The chest was not locked, but Gideon had never seen anyone touch it.

Gideon had shivered with terror the first time he'd entered the room. He'd come as a fugitive. Excommunicated, banned from the temple. To enter the Holy of Holies was sacrilege of the highest order. The Lord would strike him down. His father had assured him otherwise. Some of the Lost Boys had been through the temple before their excommunication, and Elder Kimball had refellow-shipped these men first before employing them to initiate the others during secret, late-night endowment sessions. They had taken oaths and covenants and repeated the ceremony until every man knew the endowment by heart.

Later, as Gideon had come to know the secrets of the Holy of Holies and turn them to his own purpose, he had come alone with the intent of opening the chest. Inside he had found a white stone of a curious, polished appearance. And the Jupiter Medallion. He had taken to wearing it and later had hired a metalworker in Las Vegas to make copies.

Elder Kimball had not yet arrived. Gideon assessed the other men in the room. Some were allies, others strivers who would stab him in the back if they got the chance. Several shared Enoch's temperament. Weak in the mind. Cowards.

Most were outcasts. The others, younger brothers and unloved sons, could already see that their futures would play out in the same way.

Won't it be a delicious revenge, Gideon thought, *when we become the rulers.* And he, the biggest outsider of all, would rule them all. He thought of the role of Satan in the temple endowment—and wasn't that the only interesting character?—when he had been expelled by the power of the priesthood. *Now is the great day of my power,* Satan had railed against his oppressors. *I reign from the rivers to the ends of the earth. There is none who dares to molest or make afraid.*

Satan, Gideon decided, was the true hero of the Lord's plan. Jesus suffered in Gethsemane and on the cross. They said his suffering was eternal. But it had ended after three days, after which God lifted Jesus to his right hand, where He ruled over the universe and shared in Heavenly Father's glory. How was that eternal?

But what of Lucifer, the younger brother of Jesus? What of *his* sacrifice? To be despised, driven from God's presence. There must be opposition in all things, the scriptures taught. And in the end, when all men had received their judgment, what would become of this hated brother? They would cast him into Outer Darkness.

And that was a fate with which Gideon could sympathize. Only he had been supplanted by a *younger,* more beloved brother. Worse, by the memory of a brother. The boy had never reached adulthood, and it was the memory, the thought of what he might have become, that was Gideon's true enemy. Taylor Junior could be fought. Not so Joel, who was forever two years old.

Gideon hadn't meant to kill his younger brother. Gideon had been too young to swim after Joel, or even be responsible enough to fetch grownups. He hadn't even pushed the little shit into the water, though goodness knows he'd had the opportunity.

There had been a heavy rainfall. The irrigation canals ran deep and swift. Gideon had been only four years old. But he remembered seeing Crafton Peterson's apple tree ripped from the ground and deposited on a raft of tree limbs. It had floated past the Kimball house, upright, apples red and ready to pick, and looking for all the world as if it had grown on that island of sticks.

The weather had been unseasonably dry in the weeks leading up to the flood, and this enabled the farmers to open the gates on their irrigation ditches and flood the fields. It dropped the river just enough to prevent widespread devastation. Gideon went to the fields when it had stopped raining, fascinated by the water surging through normally placid irrigation ditches.

All sorts of interesting things floated by: a dead cat, a bicycle tire, a ski glove (odd, that, in the desert), and a child's doll. Gideon hooked the dead cat with a stick and was hauling it onto shore when his younger brother found him.

Joel was two, still in diapers, and shadowed the older boy. Gideon hated his brother. He could not remember when his brother had been born. But he remembered how Aunt Charity—his mother's sister wife—would pick up Joel when he would cry, even if it meant putting Gideon on the ground. He saw Father praise Joel, how he lifted the boy into his arms to share a laugh at Joel's delighted smile. He saw how they gave Joel more ice cream, more juice, more crackers, more everything than they gave Gideon. He saw how his grandfather preferred Joel, how his own mother fed the boy his bedtime bottle as Aunt Charity grew pregnant with her second child, instead of singing Gideon to sleep as she had once done.

Joel had squatted and leaned to look into the water. He still had the body of an overgrown baby, all bulging stomach and oversized head, and little balance. It would take just a nudge to send him into the water. The water would carry him away, and maybe he would never come back. The thought gave Gideon a thrill.

But that would be wrong. He knew that. And no matter how close Joel leaned, even as he reached out for something shiny floating by, the boy kept his balance. Why wouldn't he just fall and be done with it?

And then Gideon looked upstream and saw how it would be done.

The limb of a tree drifted down the irrigation ditch. It was too big for the channel, and it caught on the edge before the water dislodged it again. One branch jutted several feet out of the water, and as it approached, the tree limb rotated just so to where the branch would hit Joel. Gideon watched with fascination.

At the last moment Joel stood and looked upstream, and Gideon thought that he would move out of the way. But he just stared at the drifting branch, as if uncomprehending that something moving so slowly could be so dangerous. The branch gave Joel a nudge that knocked the boy from his feet.

Joel fell without a cry. Just a plop and he was underwater. He stayed down for several seconds. But then his head bobbed to the surface and he grabbed hold of the branch, which had lodged itself against the side of the channel. Water rushed over and around the smaller boy, who somehow managed to hold on. And then, to Gideon's surprise, his brother began to crawl hand over hand along the branch to the edge of the irrigation ditch. In a moment he would reach the side, and Gideon would have no choice but to pull him from the water.

The tree limb held, even as the water piled behind it, pushing, urging it to float downstream. One tiny twig at the edge of one small branch had snagged the dirt at Gideon's feet and it was this fingerhold that made the difference.

Gideon never made the decision. He just moved as if his hands had decided for themselves what to do. He bent and snapped off the edge of the twig. The rest of the branch sprang back, and the limb pulled free of the culvert. The limb began to move. Joel clung to his branch as it floated down the river.

They came to Gideon that afternoon, reading a book in his room. Adults, frantic with worry. Had he seen Joel? No, he said. He didn't look up from his book. They had left.

They had found Joel's body only after the floodwaters had subsided and the irrigation canals drained. The branches had pinned him in an underground culvert. Gideon had not felt bad. Why should he? He had not pushed Joel into the water. The tree limb had knocked him in. It had been an accident. And anyway, Gideon couldn't swim. What could he have done?

It was an odd memory to bubble to the surface. And why? Perhaps because if things had turned out a little different and Joel had not drowned so tragically all those years ago, Gideon would still be in Las Vegas, a Lost Boy, railing against the misfortunes of the world. Because Joel had been perfect, and no doubt that perfection would have stuck to him until he was an adult. Taylor Junior, on the other hand, anointed though he may have been, was an idiot. Taylor Junior was an adult, he'd been chosen by his father, an important member of the Quorum of the Twelve, yet he still had not managed to find a wife.

Gideon would take better advantage of the opportunities that presented themselves. He told himself that as his father entered the Holy of Holies. Elder Kimball looked angry. Six other men, including Gideon, had arrived before him.

Elder Kimball turned to Gideon. "Let's get one thing straight. I call these meetings, not you."

Gideon forced a smile. "Yes, of course, Father." Soon, very soon. For now, however, the illusion must continue. "But I couldn't reach you," he lied. "It was critical that we gather at once in light of Enoch's defection."

The other men had taken their seats around the edges of the room, and only Gideon stood. He rested his hand against one of the gold cherubim. He could see that this act in particular made the others squirm. He enjoyed the look on their faces and the relief when he finally removed his hand.

"We don't know that Enoch defected," Elder Kimball said.

"Then where is he?" Gideon asked. "If he's truly repentant, as you claim, then why isn't he here?"

"He'll come around. Just a little more persuading…"

That's what you said last time, old man, Gideon thought. He said, "Why are we waiting? Let's forget him and move on."

"Don't underestimate Enoch's importance," Elder Kimball said. "We must have an ally among the Christiansons if we're to succeed."

It was why, Gideon noted, looking around the room, the others in the room represented the most powerful families within the church: Kimballs, Johnsons, Youngs, someone from the Wesley family, and a Pratt. Mostly Lost Boys salted with a couple of ambitious younger sons who had not yet been given their first wives. All of them eager. Gideon had groomed each young man to step in for a brother or father.

Even so, taking over the Quorum would be messy. They were old men, yes, but some would fight. The rest could be bullied. The old man himself, Brother Joseph, would remain as a figurehead. Gideon's father would stay on as senior member of the Quorum, but not for long.

"As of now there's no ally from the Christiansons," Gideon said. "What's more, you've made an enemy of Jacob Christianson and alienated his daughter, thus assuring the hostile opposition of Elder Christianson himself."

"Which was assured from the beginning, I promise you," Elder Kimball said. "Elder Christianson has stood in opposition for years." He shook his head. "Jacob is an even more certain adversary. Enoch is our best hope."

"Then what do you propose?" Gideon asked. The others stared, and he wondered if now wasn't the time to make his ascendance certain. No, not yet.

"We call him back to Zion. When he comes, we chasten him. Perhaps severely. We'll give him a second chance. Once he brings us the child, he'll never doubt again."

Gideon listened with disgust. If Enoch had betrayed them before, he would betray them again. He had panicked when he had heard about the necessary killing of Amanda Kimball. He had balked when the moment had come to complete his assigned task in Oakland. And now, he was not communicating.

"What does the angel say?" one of the other men asked. It was David Johnson, nephew of the recently deceased Elder Johnson.

"Yes," someone else said. "Call the angel."

"We must speak to the angel."

Only Elder Kimball himself looked uncertain, but they had come to rely on the angel for advice, and the man said nothing.

"Yes, we must," Gideon said, as if with great reluctance. "Let us call him."

In the early days it had taken great effort to call the angel. They would fast until weak, then pray fervently, then take a sacrament of wine—several times if necessary.

Gideon had lived in Babylon. He knew more than one way to call an angel. A group of fasting men with wine was a good start. Better still was the powdered LSD that he mixed into the wine. He took only a small measure himself, just enough to join the spirit of the meeting but not so much as to dull his wits.

He always gave the largest dosage to his father. Perhaps that explained the old man's increasingly erratic behavior. It might also explain why the angel appeared to Elder Kimball at other, random moments. Flashbacks.

Gideon had been a junior at the University of Utah, studying electrical engineering, when he'd been expelled from Zion. With no money, he'd drifted to St. George, where he'd found a job as an electrician's apprentice. The knowledge gained on that job had come in handy when the time had come to rewire the lights in the Holy of Holies.

He bent behind the cedar chest in the middle of the floor and retrieved a pre-opened bottle of wine and a silver communion cup pilfered from an Episcopal church in Salt Lake. The cup already held a few micrograms of LSD.

Gideon poured wine into the cup, then held it up and prayed. "Oh God, the Eternal Father, we ask thee in the name of thy son,

Jesus Christ, to bless and sanctify this wine for the souls of all those who partake of it."

As he finished the prayer, he lifted the wine to his lips. He tilted it back, as if taking a large swallow, but just let a little bit stay in his mouth. The rest washed back into the cup. He passed it to his father, who took a sip. It passed to the end of the line and returned empty to Gideon's hands.

As the cup had passed from one man to the next, Gideon nudged the dimmer switch on the floor with his toe. The light from the chandelier grew faint. He refilled the wine cup behind the chest. He added more LSD. He took a sip and passed it to his father again.

This time he started to pray. His father had once performed this role, but had grown more hesitant with every angelic visitation.

"Oh Lord, hear the words of my mouth. Thin the veil and show us Thy servant that we may know Thy will."

He prayed in this manner for several minutes. As he did, his voice grew more insistent. Pleading, begging the Lord for guidance. Others joined with their own cries. The goblet made another pass through the group. William Johnson began to speak in tongues, a wild gibberish that sounded like no language, or all of them at once. Men wept, flooded by the spirit. When the emotions reached a fevered pitch, Gideon flipped the second switch on the floor.

He'd installed three 1,500-watt quartz floodlights in the ceiling far above the chandelier. The light burned like the sun within the small confines of the previously darkened room. The men, now drugged and semi-drunk, lifted their hands to their eyes. After five seconds, smaller, 300-watt floodlights joined in, or replaced the main lights at random intervals. Gideon saw halos and sunbursts. Some only saw lights, while others saw a figure of burning fire. One man said he saw a fire salamander in the light and others the heavenly face of the angel. Sometimes, they would all see the angel; other times just the lights and the voice.

Gideon looked to his father, who wore a look of perfect ecstasy and terror jumbled together. Every face in the room gazed toward to the ceiling and the heat and light radiating downward.

Gideon pulled a remote control from his pocket, which he hid in his hands. He'd recorded a message earlier that he'd passed through a distorter to deepen and disguise his voice. Speakers hidden behind panels overhead would send down the voice of an angel. Gideon had rehearsed a dialogue with himself.

"Speak to us," Gideon called as he thumbed the remote. "We will listen and obey."

The voice rumbled down from the lights above. "Well done thou good and faithful servants."

Ecstatic cries. Tears flowed down one man's cheeks.

"We have obeyed," Gideon said. "What more shall we do?"

"The time has come for the winnowing," the voice spoke. "The Lord shall guide thee, shall fortify thee in the terrible task that awaits."

"Mercy!" Elder Kimball cried. "They are good men, all of them. And they mean well."

Weak, pitiful fool. Didn't his father see what danger this so-called mercy would bring? Sweep them aside. Crush them underfoot. And Gideon couldn't afford doubts. If his father harbored them, so would others.

"Yes, Father," Gideon said. His father had deviated from the script, and he had to get it back on track so the recorded voice could give its commands. "Mercy for those who beg forgiveness. But God's way is never the easy way. We must do what is commanded. What the angel tells us."

He thumbed the remote again, and the voice continued, "Some saints will refuse to obey the Lord. Others will join the apostate church in Salt Lake or flee with their wives. After the winnowing, there will be a shortage of men to carry on the work. This is when the Lord's servants shall take their rightful place among the Lord's elect."

This meant the Lost Boys. Their day had arrived. They would replace those who had expelled them. They would have their wives, their priesthoods, their endowments, and their glory. It was what had brought them to this room.

Gideon had recorded the next part knowing it would be a risk. "The Lord is most pleased with his servant, Gideon Smith Kimball. It is he who shall lead these events. Accept his counsel. Obey his word as thou would obey the word of the Lord. For God sayeth, 'By mine own voice or the voice of my servants, it is the same.'"

And with that, the angel departed. Gideon pocketed the remote. He turned off the lights with his foot. The dreary light of the chandelier replaced it. The men sighed as one.

The meeting broke up quickly. The men would leave at intervals, via the back entrance where they would not be seen. In the past, they had left town at once when these meetings had ended. Not today. The time for leaving town had ended. They would find their way to safe houses, wherein lived allies, secret girlfriends, sympathetic older brothers or uncles. And here they would wait for Gideon to direct their final actions.

Soon, only Gideon and his father remained, and they too prepared to leave. "Courage, Father. We will do what must be done."

"And Jacob Christianson?" Elder Kimball asked. His hands trembled. "He's getting too close."

"We have to kill him."

"Kill him? Is there no other way?"

"There is no other way."

"I don't like this killing. Gentiles is one thing. But killing saints?"

"You heard the angel. And doesn't the Book of Mormon say, 'It is better for one man to perish than a nation to dwindle in unbelief'?"

"True." An elder of Israel could not argue with the Book of Mormon. "Okay, Jacob Christianson. But then it stops."

"And then it stops," Gideon agreed. He needed to placate the old man. Elder Kimball was fooling himself if he thought that men like Abraham Christianson or William Young would step aside without a fight. They too would go. And Elder Griggs, who had the ear of the prophet.

His father nodded. "Do what needs to be done. But get it over with quickly."

"Of course."

CHAPTER SEVENTEEN

It had been six years since a gathering of the Quorum of the Twelve. It was never safe to have the entire Quorum in one location. The church had enemies. Foremost was the government. Both Canada and the United States staged periodic anti-polygamy crackdowns. Having everyone in one spot made a tempting target. Worse still were the apostates and heretics.

In 1962, an apostate had kidnapped the prophet and the entire Quorum at gunpoint as they emerged from the temple. Brother Heber had refused to accede to the man's demands that he be anointed the prophet. The gunman had killed two members of the Quorum and injured a third before a church member with a deer rifle had shot him in the head from sixty yards.

The outside authorities had never known about the incident.

But it had shaken the church and Brother Heber and his successors now gathered in one spot only to appoint a new member of the Quorum. That is what they faced now. Elder Johnson lay dead, and the Quorum moved quickly to fill vacancies. The Lord's house was a house of order.

The remaining eleven members gathered from Harmony, Blister Creek, and the smaller settlement in White Valley, Montana. It took less than twenty-four hours to bring them together in Southern Utah, no mean feat when the average age of the members was over sixty-five, with Elders Pinnager and Finn pushing ninety.

Elder Abraham Christianson, father of Jacob and Eliza and thirty-one other children, had chartered a plane from Cardston and landed in St. George two hours earlier.

The first Jacob learned of his father's arrival had been when Abraham Christianson called him from Blister Creek. They had a few hours before the temple endowment that afternoon and were halfway to Panguitch when the call came.

They could no longer stay at Stephen Paul Young's house, nor would Jacob risk leaving Eliza with the Kimballs. He'd found a motel near the Panguitch library where he could get Internet access. He hoped to spend some time online, searching for information about the murders in California.

Jacob pulled over to take the call. He frowned when he saw the number. The last thing he could take right now was more pressure about Eliza's marriage.

"Who is it?" Eliza had asked. Her face fell when he told her. "Don't answer it. Let him leave a message."

"You know I have to."

"Where are you?" Abraham Christianson asked when he picked up.

"We're in the Ghost Cliffs. Why?"

He needed only delay Father a few more hours. Meet with Enoch and solve the murders. Present his findings to the prophet. Discredit the Kimball family and the issue with Taylor Junior would resolve itself.

"Can you please be specific? Where in the Ghost Cliffs?"

"Past the reservoir, on my way to Panguitch. Why?"

"Because I'm in town."

The news left him off-balance. "In town? You mean here? Blister Creek?"

"Yes, of course," Father said. "I want you to meet me at the chapel. Can you get here in half an hour?"

"Maybe forty minutes."

"Then hurry. The entire Quorum will be here."

"And I'm going to meet with the entire Quorum of the Twelve?" Jacob asked, off-balance yet again.

"Isn't that what I just said? We're meeting with the prophet to choose Elder Johnson's replacement. They want an update on the Amanda Kimball matter. I'll tell them you'll be here in forty minutes." He hung up.

Jacob turned the car around at once.

"No mention of your marriage," he said to Eliza. "Looks like you've dodged that bullet."

She was watching him with a curious expression, no doubt drawing her own conclusions from what she'd heard. "You sure? They're not calling you back to talk about the weather."

"He said they wanted an update on the murder investigation. Sounds reasonable. I'm going to take it at face value."

He drove quickly, even across the stretches of dirt road. Even so, it was almost forty-five minutes before they pulled into the chapel parking lot. Other cars had gathered, some with Alberta or Montana plates. Young men milled outside, together with a few wives and their children. Jacob saw several relatives from Harmony. The newcomers mingled with the residents, catching up with people they saw only rarely. Children ran and played, making friends with seldom-seen cousins. Other people came walking down the street to join the impromptu reunion now growing on the chapel grounds.

Jacob left Eliza with the gathering; Fernie and Charity had come, and there was their sister Grace from White Valley, who had married just two years earlier to Elder Pinnager of the Quorum; she must have accompanied him. Probably even drove him the entire way, as Elder Pinnager was nearly ninety and half blind. It hadn't stopped him from fathering a child by Grace, though; from the looks of it, she was about eight months pregnant.

Inside, the halls of the church sat empty except for two of the prophet's sons who stood watch outside the bishop's meeting room. Jacob walked to where they stood in their dark suits, expecting to be challenged. But they just nodded, and one of them opened the door for him.

The bishop's meeting room was a simple room, with a big, boardroom-style table in the middle. Here the bishop organized the ward for weekly services, met with members to discuss building projects or tithing, and interviewed members for worthiness to attend the temple. It was also the room where the bishop directed church courts—adjudicated by a member of the Quorum of the Twelve—to disfellowship or excommunicate wayward members.

The bishop was not present now, but the prophet and the Quorum of the Twelve sat in chairs around the table. There was Brother Joseph, with his beehive-handled cane, and Jacob's Grandpa Griggs—make that *Elder* Griggs, in this room, at least—along with Jacob's father and the other members. Allies, longtime rivals. Everyone.

Men had loosened their ties, and empty or half-empty water cups sat around the table. Some men had notebooks, others open scriptures, as if they had been consulting specific verses.

And here came Jacob into the middle of their meeting. He felt like a boy, and a dirty, underdressed one at that. The other men wore suits and ties while he wore jeans and a gray button-down shirt. His boots were dirty and scuffed.

Abraham Christianson rose first, extended his hand, and clapped him in a hug. As he did, he whispered, "Be sharp."

The other men rose, and they shook his hand one by one. Some, mainly his father's friends, but also the prophet, greeted him warmly and by his first name. Others, with a terse, "Brother Christianson." To his surprise, there was little hostility from Elder Kimball, though the man sat as far from Abraham Christianson as possible.

His father directed Jacob to the empty seat. Jacob sat, uncomfortable. The men settled down, and the prophet addressed him.

"Let me get right to the point. Do you know the identity of the murderer?" Brother Joseph asked.

"Not yet, but I think I'm drawing close." He arranged details in his mind as he considered how to reveal what he'd learned without giving away too much. Especially since a prime suspect sat in this very room.

"And your preliminary analysis?"

"The killer himself was most likely one of the Lost Boys," he said. "He might have had inside help." He watched Elder Kimball from the corner of his eye. The man looked uncomfortable.

"I'm going to be blunt, Jacob," Brother Joseph said. He clasped his hands in front of him and leaned forward. "Your work in this matter has been invaluable. And I think you should move forward until you've found the killer and he can be brought to justice." He hesitated. "But not now."

The news drew him up short. "Not now? You want me to drop everything?"

"Not permanently. Maybe later we can take a fresh look. Now, if you say a Lost Boy did it, then fine, we'll tell the saints to be on the lookout for anyone who doesn't belong in Blister Creek."

Right, except the Lost Boys had shown their ability to move about town with impunity. Someone was harboring these men. And for all their beliefs in the Kingdom of God on earth, what would they do if they found a Lost Boy in town? This was America, after all, and you couldn't ban someone from a public street. The only tool was shunning, and what good was that with murderers?

Jacob looked at his father, surprised by his silence. He'd thought that Father, at least, would insist that the investigation continue. And Elder Pratt, Amanda's father. Not to mention Brother Joseph, her uncle, and the spiritual father of every man, woman, and child in Zion. Few looked pleased at this turn of events, but not a single man voiced disagreement.

"The problem is," the prophet continued, "your arrival stirred things up in Blister Creek."

"It wasn't my arrival that stirred things up. It was the murder of Amanda Kimball."

"Jacob," his father warned.

"It's okay, Elder Christianson," Brother Joseph said. He turned back to Jacob. "You're right. It's not your fault. And we're not stopping you forever, just for now. Later, when we've resolved other matters, you can continue your investigation."

He still couldn't believe it. "And you're serious?"

"I'm afraid so, Jacob," Brother Joseph said.

Jacob stared for a long moment, then unclenched his teeth long enough to say, "Thou sayest."

He said the words, but he didn't mean them. He would defy them in private. They left him no choice. And then, when he had his evidence, he would present it. It would be too late to stop him. He glanced at Elder Kimball. The man looked troubled rather than smug or triumphant, or any other emotion that Jacob might have expected.

"Good," said the prophet. "Now we can move on to the business of confirming Elder Johnson's replacement." His voice wavered, and Jacob thought he sounded tired. "As we are all agreed on a course of action, can we now agree to heal the rift that has developed between us?"

Jacob took his cue. He had been dismissed without the bother of a dismissal. He rose to his feet, growing angrier by the second.

The prophet motioned for him to sit back down. "This concerns you, Jacob."

Another surprise. "Me? How so?" He returned to his seat.

Brother Joseph said, "You will be the newest member of the Quorum of the Twelve, Jacob Christianson."

Jacob gaped at him. "How is that possible? I'm twenty-six. I'm not even married."

"Not yet," his father put in.

"Not yet, fine. But there are others more worthy than I am, who have more experience and stronger testimonies. Men who are spiritual giants compared to me."

"All of which may be true," Brother Joseph said. "Nevertheless, you are my choice and the choice of the Quorum. Will you accept this calling?"

Someone else—Taylor Junior, certainly—would have grabbed the prize. Jacob knew it for the burden that it was. A man didn't gain strength by gaining power, though that seemed a contradiction. Look at the prophet. What man carried a heavier burden than Brother Joseph? He was responsible for the souls of four thousand men, women, and children. Lead them astray and God's condemnation would fall upon his head.

Jacob spoke slowly. "There's something else happening here, isn't there? Some other arrangement." He looked from one man to another around the room and stopped when he reached Abraham Christianson. "Dad, what is it?"

His father sighed. "These are difficult times, Jacob. There has been discord among our ranks. It's come to the point of tearing apart Zion. This is the solution to which we have consented."

"This sounds like *part* of the solution," Jacob said. "But nothing comes without cost. You've promised something in return, haven't you? If I'm going to join the Quorum, I have to know what."

His father said, "You will take this position and Elder Kimball's son the next opening in the Quorum. Elder Young's son will take the next opening after that." He didn't need to mention the age of several members of the quorum, including the two nonagenarians. Those next openings would not be long in arriving.

Taylor Junior as a member of the Quorum of the Twelve? Appalling. Stephen Paul Young? He was a good man. So Father would take a son and an ally in trade for one treacherous son of his enemy. A devil's bargain.

"I see."

"There is one other thing," Father said. "You will marry Elder Kimball's daughter. Taylor Junior will marry your sister. The weddings will take place tomorrow morning."

"Eliza." The single word came out of his mouth.

Father nodded. "Yes, Eliza. I'm sorry, Jacob."

The men at the table watched Jacob, waiting. One word, one nod from him and a sigh of relief would ripple through the room. What struggles had brought them to this point, what crisis threatened to tear apart the church? He could dissolve that crisis with a single word of consent.

"I can't do that. I won't."

"Jacob—" his father began.

Brother Joseph cut in then. "I understand this is difficult for you. I've seen that you love your sister and would shield her from harm. You would choose a different man for her. But this solution, agreed upon by all parties, would bring healing to the Quorum. It is the Lord's will that we resolve the spirit of contention in this body."

"And you're telling me this is the Lord's will?" Jacob shook his head. "I don't believe it. Why would the Lord force me to sacrifice my sister and her happiness? Did you know that Taylor Junior attacked Eliza?" Jacob looked around the room, now speaking to all of them. "He broke into her room, waited till she came back, and then groped her. Probably would have raped her if I hadn't intervened. And you want her to marry this man?"

Men shifted in their seats, and he saw their discomfort. No surprise, however. They knew already what Taylor Junior was or was not. Oh, but don't look too closely or it might disturb the convenient solution to their problems. And why should this surprise him? They had already abandoned Amanda Kimball.

Brother Joseph broke the silence. "I sympathize with your position, and I'll counsel Elder Kimball's son before the marriage. He must learn how to manage his passions."

Jacob shook his head. "That's not enough. Maybe Taylor Junior can reform himself. Maybe not. But I still won't trust him with my sister. Eliza holds only contempt for Taylor Junior. Contempt and fear. What kind of a brother would sell out his sister like you're suggesting?

"And isn't a woman also a child of God?" he continued. "Doesn't she deserve happiness? Or is she a brood mare, to be sold, traded, and bred with whatever stallion her owners have chosen?"

The prophet said, "Jacob, we are none of us our own masters. This is the hard truth. We are servants of the Lord, and we belong to Him. The Lord has commanded that we build His kingdom. This means that our personal desires must be subsumed for the good of Zion. Our reward comes not in this life, but in the world to come. It is there that we will receive our glory, that the Lord will embrace each of us and say, 'Well done, thou good and faithful servant.' In the meanwhile, our path is sometimes difficult."

"The world to come?" Jacob couldn't help himself. "Why should we expect to treat each other any better in the next world? Somehow we're going to value individuals in the next world when we can't manage to do so here?"

Grandpa Griggs leaned to Jacob's father and whispered something. Abraham Christianson nodded. He rose to his feet, looking troubled. *Good,* Jacob thought, *let him twist on a skewer of his own guilt.*

His father said, "I'm going to excuse myself to the hall to have a word with my son."

Jacob turned on his father as soon as they reached the hall. "You sold out your own daughter. What's more, you betrayed Amanda Kimball. Her blood cries from the grave, and you made a bargain to silence that cry." He stared at his father with white-hot fury and a dawning realization. "You never sent me to Blister Creek to resolve her murder, did you? You knew all along he'd try to cover up the crime, and you wanted to take advantage of that, undermine his position in the community. You sent me forward, like a pawn on a chess set, to get behind Elder Kimball's defenses."

His father slapped him. An open hand, hard across the cheek. Jacob drew back and stared at his father with disdain, daring him to strike him again. His cheek throbbed.

Father said, "Get a grip on yourself. You are a man who can control his emotions, Jacob. I expect you to do so now. Now, I want you to listen, and listen well."

His anger roared in his ears, but he didn't give it voice. Instead, he sat for a long moment until it receded. "I'm listening."

"Ready? Good, that's better. First, there will be time to find Amanda's murderer. Later, when the dust has settled. More important is to cut off the men who are maneuvering for power. If they gain mastery over our side, then Amanda will *never* receive justice."

"But what about the prophet? Isn't *he* the leader of the church?"

"Yes, of course. But he's a peacemaker. Harmony and a singularity of purpose are of supreme importance. The people who stand in open conflict will always lose. We must match our enemies' tactics step for step. Our enemies are subtle, and so must we be."

His father took him by the arm and led him a few paces away from Brother Joseph's sons standing vigil outside the door to the bishop's office. When he spoke again, his voice was low. "Do you know why they want Eliza so badly? There are other women available."

Jacob shrugged. "To gain leverage in our family?" They already had one such with Fernie, although she wasn't a blood relative of Abraham Christianson.

"More elemental than that."

"She's young, attractive. Intelligent."

"Intelligent. Yes. IQ of one hundred and thirty-eight. Very high for a woman. Now, I don't mean anything sexist by that, but most of the time we can only work one end of the gene pool."

Jacob said, "Meaning it's easier to select for intelligence in our men. We kick out the dumb ones, but every woman stays, intelligent or not."

"Exactly. So think how valuable that makes Eliza. The Lord has chosen us to rule the world someday. To do so, we need two things that we do not yet have. First, we must multiply our numbers. We are doubling in population every twenty years, but is that fast enough? And the second thing we need is the mental and spiritual

faculties to rule. When the Lord first told Joseph Smith to imple-
ment the principle of plural marriage, He said that it was to raise up
a righteous seed. A seed is cultivated, selected for its vigor. We must
do the same thing within the ranks of our people."

It was a straight-out admission of what Jacob had confirmed
with his own observation. That it was so direct came as a surprise.
"We're breeders of people."

Father continued, "Now, here's where we reach the conflict
within the Quorum. There are some who say, 'Faster, faster.' They
want to see improvement within their own lifetimes. The Second
Coming might be just around the corner. Selecting for intelligence within our men isn't sufficient. And it fosters competition
for the intelligent young women within the church. Like Eliza.
There is another factor, too. That is the dysgenic effect of inbred
communities."

Jacob nodded. In churches such as the Fundamentalist Latter-
day Saints or the Kingston Clan, it was common to force women
into marriage with first cousins, or even uncles. They even *looked*
inbred.

He'd never heard it spoken, though. The saints considered
themselves a chosen people, and there was a tendency for all chosen people to consider their blood and their kin to be superior to
others. The ancient Israelites, the royal families of Europe, the pha-
raohs, the ruling classes of Imperial Japan. All purposefully inbred.

"Of course we're not inbred like *some* polygamist clans," Father
said, "but don't forget that we're all descended from a handful of
families. By your generation, everyone is a second cousin, usually
by several different lines. We need fresh blood."

"And what's the solution to that? Proselytize? Send missionaries door to door like the Salt Lake Mormons?"

"Some people explored adoption about twenty years ago. It was a hard sell. Let us adopt children—girls only, mind you—and raise them in our polygamist community. Then we'll marry them to our sons at the age of sixteen." Father smiled. "Then there's the small matter that the genetic heritage of adoptees is not strong. Whatever we'd gain from hybrid vigor would be lost by mixing our genes with the daughters of drug addicts and prostitutes."

"That's a little harsh."

"I'm just laying out the argument, Jacob."

"Fine, so then what?"

"I say nothing. I say we keep a lookout for likeminded individuals who are open to joining Zion. And we guard against cousin marriage. Over time, as Zion grows and we add a small number of converts, the dysgenic effects will fade. I'm not expecting the Second Coming to arrive within my lifetime, you see. There are too many prophesies yet to come true, and we are too small to form the foundation of Christ's kingdom on the earth."

Father shook his head. "But here's the heart of the matter. There's a small, but influential and growing group within the church—let's call them super-eugenicists—who don't accept the slower pace."

"And this group is led by Elder Kimball?" Jacob asked.

"That's right. Some of them took their wives to fertility clinics to bring in outside genetic material. Have you noticed how many twins have been born in the last ten years?"

"I just thought that was normal fertility treatment stuff."

"Some of it might be. Maybe even one of the twins would be their own, the other from a purchased embryo."

"It's all rather slimy."

"I was outraged when I found out," Father said. "And Brother Joseph put a stop to it. But Elder Kimball keeps pushing and pushing. What does it mean for Zion if we become nothing more than a program of scientific breeding? We can't let those people win."

Jacob felt a helpless despair. "But, Father..."

Father fixed him with a hard look. "This is bigger than you, bigger than Eliza. Bigger than me. It is nothing less than a struggle between God and Satan."

Why does Satan have to be involved? Jacob wondered. *Aren't our enemies perfectly capable of evil behavior on their own?*

Father drew a breath. "So you see why I need you on the Quorum. And you know what that means for Eliza."

Jacob let out a groan that had been building in him. He balled his fists and put them to his temples in frustration. "Father, I can't."

"Think about the practical ramifications of your opposition. First, Taylor Junior will take your place in the Quorum of the Twelve. The super-eugenicists will keep taking their wives to the fertility clinics. Amanda's murderer, you can rest assured, will never be punished. What's more, you won't even stop Eliza's marriage into the Kimball family."

His face hardened. "Jacob, there can be no argument. Either you will come along with me, or I will dismiss you now and make the same arrangement, but with your younger brother Joshua."

"Joshua is only eighteen."

"Yes, I know. A good boy, but not ready to move into a leadership position."

"And I am?" Jacob asked. "I'm only twenty-six."

"Is that your answer? No?"

He had made a promise to his sister, but this, this burden his father had placed upon him would force him to break that promise. Jacob bowed his head and didn't lift it for a long moment. It felt as though a millstone hung about his neck. A millstone of guilt and shame and weighty expectations that he could not hope to fulfill.

At last he lifted his head and said, "Okay, I'll do it."

They returned to the room where they had kept the prophet and the other elders waiting. Jacob took his seat. He would not look at Elder Kimball. If he did, he would lose his resolve. He'd rather climb over the table and rip out the man's throat than betray Eliza.

He looked straight at the prophet. "Okay, Brother Joseph. I'm in agreement. Let there be harmony among the servants of the Lord."

"Let us form a circle then, and ordain you to your office," Brother Joseph said.

They pulled a chair aside, and Jacob took his seat. The men gathered around him, apostles of the Lord with the keys to bind on heaven and earth. Each man placed his right hand on Jacob's head and his left on the shoulder of the man to his left. Jacob didn't belong here; he wanted to throw off their hands and break from the circle.

Brother Joseph spoke. "Jacob Levi Christianson, in the name of Jesus Christ and by the power of the Holy Melchizedek Priesthood we ordain you to the office of apostle…"

Jacob left the room as the junior member of the Quorum of the Twelve Apostles. They had blessed him with the spiritual keys to the kingdom. The ability to converse with angels. An elder of Israel.

He was engaged to marry one of Elder Kimball's daughters, a girl named Jessie Lynn. There had been three to choose from. It made no difference to him, so he chose the oldest. Almost eighteen. They would marry Thursday evening. Tomorrow.

As he stepped outside, he found Eliza talking to Fernie and Jessie Lynn Kimball. The irony drew him up short. The sister he had betrayed, the woman he loved, and the girl he would marry. All three looked his way as he came. They were laughing.

He had entered the church building with two goals. Continue his investigation, and protect his sister from a marriage to the treacherous Taylor Kimball Jr. He had failed on both accounts.

CHAPTER EIGHTEEN

Elder Kimball was the second person to slip away from the meeting. Others saw him go, and perhaps thought that he was hurrying after Jacob to have a word with the boy. Perhaps he would play the part of peacemaker, now that his needs had been met. Maybe welcome Jacob to the family.

Instead, he walked to the other side of the chapel until his phone had service, then dialed his eldest son. Gideon picked up on the second ring. "We're ready, Father. Jacob just left the church house. We haven't found Enoch yet, but that's only a matter of time."

Gideon must be somewhere within sight of the church, then, as Jacob couldn't have left the building more than a minute earlier.

Kimball said, "Stop. Don't move another inch forward." A long silence on the other end. "Did you hear me? We're not going through with the plan."

"I heard you." What was that in Gideon's voice? Defiance?

A nervous tickle grew in Elder Kimball's stomach. The growing feeling that he had misjudged Gideon now flowered into full-blown fear. "We're not going through with it, Gideon. I'm serious. There's no need. Jacob has capitulated completely."

"Has he?" Gideon asked in a flat tone. There was not even skepticism in his voice. It was worse than that. He didn't care what Jacob did or didn't do.

"Yes. He'll marry Jessie Lynn, and we get Eliza Christianson in return."

"Taylor Junior gets Eliza, you mean."

"But that doesn't matter. Our status just climbed two notches. People owe us favors. You'll be next. I promise. First, your refellowshipping into the church. Then, your own wife. And look, the Christiansons might still be persuaded. We have persuaded them to this point—why shouldn't we keep trying? Surely they'll see that ours is the wisest course to better God's people. The Lord works through gentle persuasion, not by violence."

A chuckle now. "Ah, Father. You don't understand at all. The wheel has turned. The old order no longer applies. The time for gentle persuasion has passed. It's time for the Lord's wrath. We've seen an angel. He won't have us hesitate or delay because of the machinations of twelve old men. Fools, all of them. And you, you are the biggest fool of all."

Kimball could no longer contain his rage and frustration. "Don't ever speak to me like that again, boy. You are nothing. Do you hear me? Nothing! Excommunicated. Apostate. A sinner." His voice sounded shrill, even in his own ears, but he couldn't stop. "You have been cast from the Lord's presence. It was I who took you through the temple, gave you your endowment, you and all the other Lost Boys. And only I hold the key to your return, do you understand?"

"Are you finished?" Gideon's voice remained even. "Good. Now *you* listen to *me*. It is *you* who are nothing. The winnowing has begun. Enoch has been sealed unto death. Jacob too. Will you join their number? Will the Lord take your wives and your children and seal them unto another? Will you lose your kingdom? Will your soul be cast into Outer Darkness?"

Kimball screamed into the phone, "They'll never follow you! Not the Lost Boys, not the people of the church. And the prophet will condemn you when he finds out. As will I. You are a murderer! You murdered my wife! You didn't have to do that. Murderer! I'll tell them. I'll tell the prophet. And Elder Christianson. And Jacob. All of them."

"No, Father," Gideon said, his voice calm. "You won't. Now go home and await my next command. It will come very soon. And remember, we do not treat gently those who break their covenants."

The words chilled him. Throat cut from ear to ear. Disemboweled. Organs fed to wild animals. "You could do that to your own father?" he asked, his voice small when it came out of his mouth. "But…but…I brought you back, son. I showed compassion. I brought you back."

There was no reply. Kimball held the phone in his trembling hand as the line went dead.

He could not believe what had happened. The enormity of it howled about his ears. He leaned against the wall to steady himself.

"Are you alright, Taylor?"

Elder Kimball turned to see the prophet approaching, watching him. Brother Joseph stopped a pace away and leaned against his cane. There was love in that face, and the gentleness of a father toward his child. And worry. That look made Kimball want to weep.

Elder Kimball swallowed hard. Now was the time. Now was when he would tell the prophet all that had happened. He'd made mistakes. He had never meant for it to come to this. He would fall to his knees at Brother Joseph's feet and beg for forgiveness. There was still time to stop the horrible sequence of events set in motion by his son. Brother Joseph would know what to do.

Instead, he said, "Yes, yes, I'm fine. I just...conflict with one of my sons. You know how they get."

"Ah, yes. It is difficult." Brother Joseph put a hand on his shoulder. "I understand Abraham's fear of doing wrong by his daughter, but it is the sons who break my heart. So much potential. So often thrown away. Come. There will be time enough to worry about that later. For now, lift your spirits. We've once again found harmony in the Quorum. Let your heart be glad."

Brother Joseph carried something under his arm, wrapped in brown paper. He handed it to Elder Kimball. "This is for you."

Kimball took the package, and his fingers fumbled at the paper. A stained glass window. In the picture, a woman with a dark, curly-haired child in her arms. Even in cut glass, the resemblance was unmistakable. Amanda and Sophie Marie.

Brother Joseph was old; he must have worked his arthritic fingers to paralysis to finish the window so quickly. Kimball held the window with trembling hands. He'd have sooner opened his veins

with those shards of glass than to see them assembled into a portrait
of his daughter and his murdered wife.

"To remember your dear, departed wife and the poor child
who is bereft of a mother."

"Thank you," Elder Kimball managed.

* * *

Eliza turned toward Jacob with a smile on her lips, but it died at
once. She had been talking to Fernie and Jessie Lynn. Fernie had
been telling a funny story about her four-year-old son's sudden
interest in the origin of babies.

Formerly oblivious to all such thing, Daniel had asked one day
why one of his "aunts"—Fernie's sister wife—had grown so big.
She was pregnant, Fernie had explained. What's that? How did she
get that way? What is sperm? Yes, but *how* does the sperm get into
the woman?

But the thing that had drawn the most curiosity was the
physical transformation a woman underwent. He was especially
delighted to discover that one especially large woman at church was
pregnant with twins. The day after the twin discovery, Fernie had
taken Daniel to Cedar City to sell vegetables at the farmers' market. An obese woman had presented herself to buy cucumbers, and
Fernie had noted with horror that her son was watching the woman
with slack-jawed wonderment. She could read his thoughts. If the
woman at church had been pregnant with twins, then what on
earth was this woman carrying? Fernie had silently begged her son
to stay quiet. To her relief, he said nothing, but then the woman
turned to go and presented a view of her rear end.

"Look, Mom," Daniel had said in an exaggerated stage whisper, "she's got a baby in her butt!"

Eliza laughed so hard that tears came to her eyes. She had spotted Jacob and motioned for him to come over so she could make Fernie retell the story, when she saw the gray look on his face.

Her laugh died on her lips. The sun seemed to dim overhead. His face darkened further when he saw her own reaction.

Jacob looked to Fernie and then to Jessie Lynn. His face grew progressively more stricken. "Eliza, I need to talk to you alone."

She nodded and followed. They picked their way through the clumps of women and the playing children. Jacob shook the hands of two men he knew from Harmony, but quickly excused himself. At last they stood alone beneath the eaves of the church building.

"You will forever remember this conversation as the moment you came to hate me. Please remember that at least I told you in person."

"Jacob, you're scaring me."

And then he told her. He spared no details, sharing how Father and the others had cornered him. But he did not gloss over his own role in the bargain, exposing himself as a coward. The upshot, of course, was that she would shortly marry her would-be rapist.

And she found, through her fear of Taylor Junior, that she didn't hate Jacob. No, it was the whole damnable situation that had pushed him down this path. Mostly, what she felt was a great loss, and the knowledge that her ally had fallen away during her time of great need. No matter the reason, he had left her and now she stood alone.

"But Jacob," she said. "Jacob, you promised."

He turned away, stricken. She picked up her dress and ran. Fernie and Jessie Lynn called to her as she passed, but she ignored them, as she ignored the stares from others. She ran down the street with only one thought on her mind.

Run.

* * *

Jacob watched his sister running. Betrayed, heartbroken. Terrified. *Oh God. Why? Why?* It was half prayer, half fist-shaking curse.

Fernie and Jessie Lynn came to his side. Fernie had her baby on her hip, and Jessie Lynn held the hand of her half sister, Sophie Marie, now motherless. The girl didn't play with all of the children running around, screaming and laughing, but watched intently, with a look both curious and cautious.

"What's the matter with Eliza?" Fernie asked. Their sister was halfway down the street now, still running with her skirts gathered.

"Eliza just learned the identity of her husband-to-be. As you can see, she was quite pleased with the news." Jacob looked at Fernie with a bitter, ironic smile. "Wonder what kind of a husband Taylor Junior will make."

Fernie put a hand to her mouth. "Oh Jacob. And you? You agreed to this?"

"They didn't give me much of a choice. But yes, coward that I am. Fool that I am. I agreed." He let out a bitter laugh. "Oh, and I get rewarded for my efforts. I can choose one of your husband's daughters."

Jessie Lynn's eyes widened slightly. Jacob looked at her closely for the first time. She had round cheeks and slightly crooked teeth and was certainly not pretty in the traditional sense. But she had lively, dark eyes and a pleasant mouth that would look more so if she were smiling, which she was not at the moment. Cute, at least.

He cleared his throat as he appraised her. "And this is the point, I suppose, where I should ask you to marry me."

Jessie Lynn, to her credit, did not look overjoyed, nor disgusted, nor any of a dozen easy emotions. She said, "Better here than in Eliza's shoes. And I'd heard rumors, so it's not a complete surprise. Can you tell me why you chose me instead of one of my sisters?"

He grimaced. "Honestly? Girls should wait until they're eighteen before marrying. Let them choose as adults. You're not eighteen, but you're the closest of the three."

Jacob glanced at Fernie. She watched, her face unreadable. Would she be upset to have him so close now, a relative by marriage for the second time? Indifferent? Jealous, somewhere in her heart, even though she'd been married for many years now and belonged to another man?

And then he remembered Eliza, and his thoughts turned elsewhere. "Fernie, can you help me find Eliza?"

"And what should we do when we find her?" Fernie asked. "Tie her down?"

Jacob massaged his temples. "I don't know, Fernie. I don't know."

He glanced at his watch. An hour before they were supposed to be at the temple for the endowment. Stephen Paul Young's uncle was the temple president and had opened the building for them and raised the veil for the endowment. Stephen Paul himself would already be there.

"What about the endowment?" Jacob asked.

Fernie nodded. "Yes."

That's how they would get Eliza back. Bring her to the endowment, as planned. Meet Enoch in the Celestial Room at the end. And yes, he thought, grasping for hope, if they could implicate Taylor Junior in Amanda's murder, they might slip from the trap springing around them.

Fernie handed Jessie Lynn her baby. "Can you watch Oscar?" The girl now had a baby at her hip and Sophie Marie holding her hand. Jacob saw her as she would be a few years down the road, perhaps even pregnant with a third.

He should say something to her. The girl would be awash with emotions. He didn't want her to spend the rest of her life thinking that Jacob had never wanted her in the first place.

Jacob put a hand on her wrist. "We never know what life will bring. Sometimes, the Lord knows best what we need." He hesitated, not liking how that had come out. A trial. That's what he'd just told her their marriage would be. Something to be endured. He tried again. "I'm not perfect, but I'll do my best to be a decent husband."

"What he means to say," Fernie said, "is that he's better than your brother, at least."

"I'll have to remember that for when they ask," Jessie Lynn said. "My husband? He's not the worst man in the church."

"You shouldn't marry her," Fernie said as she and Jacob went after Eliza. "Not that there's anything wrong with Jessie Lynn. You'd like her, I think. But you can't let Eliza go through with this. She's my sister too, you know. What about Stephen Paul? Wasn't he interested? Can't you talk to him again?"

They had drawn away from the crowd at the church and walked down the street in the direction Eliza had run. She couldn't have gone far. "There are no other choices, Fernie."

"There has to be something."

"The only hope is to pin Amanda's murder on Taylor Junior. That's it."

Fernie put a hand on his wrist and pulled him around. When she spoke, her voice was fierce and there was fire in her eyes. "Then you be damn sure to implicate him, do you hear me? I don't care who else was involved, it had better implicate Taylor Junior."

"You don't know how badly I'd like to do that," Jacob said. "But I can only implicate him if he's guilty. Anything else would be wrong."

"And selling out your sister? That's okay, is it?" She turned away. "No, I didn't think so."

CHAPTER NINETEEN

Neither Eduardo nor Manuel were at their trailer. Eliza found the FBI agents on the Jameson Young compound, where they shoveled wet cement into the framing for a new concrete patio to replace the one destroyed by the flood. The cement had a reddish tint, like the sand from the desert, and they'd stamped the earlier part with a pattern to make it look like cut stone.

Sweat streaked down bodies and straining muscles. Eduardo worked with a bandana around his forehead and his chest bare and bronzed. In spite of everything, in spite of the forced marriage from which she fled and the heartbreak she felt over Jacob's betrayal, she could not look at Eduardo without a stirring. She imagined him in the shower at the end of a long day, dirty hands and sweat-streaked, and the soapy water as it ran down his body.

And it reminded her.

I have options.

She was a girl with little knowledge of the outside world. But she knew how to work. She wasn't just smart; she had common sense. And if the time came to find someone, it wouldn't have to be a polygamist.

Eduardo saw her and put down his shovel. He picked up his tank top where it lay over the handle of a wheelbarrow and used it to wipe the sweat from his face.

"You shouldn't come here like this," he said. "Someone will see you and start to ask questions. It could compromise the investigation."

Ah, yes. The investigation. She had forgotten about that. Today was the day they were supposed to bug Elder Kimball's house.

"Did you get everything in place?" he asked.

She shook her head. "No, not yet. I've got bigger worries, Eduardo. I need your help."

He frowned. Manuel looked up as if to come over, but Eduardo shook his head and the older man returned to work. "What kind of help?"

"They're forcing me to marry against my will."

"What do you mean, against your will?"

"Surely you don't think women choose their own husbands around here."

"No, I didn't think that. But if you're dead set against it, why not put your foot down? Nobody can force you. You're eighteen, you're an adult."

Well no, she wasn't. She was seventeen, but she remembered now that she had lied to Eduardo that night after the flood.

"Doesn't matter. They're making me do it. But I can't marry him. I really can't."

"Is he your uncle or something?"

Eliza gave a disgusted shake of the head. "We don't do that sort of thing. You're thinking of the Kingston Clan."

"But he's married already, is that it?"

Eliza gave an irritated sigh. "No, he's not. But what does that have to do with anything?"

"Everything. I'm looking for illegal behavior. How am I supposed to help you if there's nothing illegal going on?"

"They're forcing me to marry against my will. How is that not illegal?"

"It *will* be illegal, once they've actually done it. But for now... well, what do you want me to do? Put you in protective custody?"

"Yes, that's exactly what I want you to do." She clenched her teeth, growing angrier. Though why she should hold Eduardo to a higher standard than her own brother, she couldn't say. "Barring that, how about just give me a ride to St. George?"

Eduardo breathed out. He glanced over her shoulder, then back at Manuel, who still watched with a quizzical expression. "Eliza, I can't do that," he said at last. "Not yet. Maybe in a few days, if everything goes well with the investigation. But for now, I can't get involved. It'll blow our cover."

"I don't have a few days. I'm going to the temple this afternoon for my endowment. They'll probably marry me off tomorrow. Maybe tonight. I don't know." She put a hand on his arm, but he flinched away. "Please, for the love of God, help me. This man, he tried to rape me. And now he's going to be my husband."

He just looked at her and she could tell that he didn't believe the attempted rape bit. It was something that she had added for his benefit, he was thinking. Finally, though, he said, "I'll talk to Manuel. There might be something."

He went back to the other men and pulled Manuel aside. They spoke in low voices, and then the two men returned together.

Manuel said, "Eduardo told me what's going on. Okay, we can't get directly involved. But there might be something we can do."

Eliza was desperate. "Please, tell me more."

* * *

Jacob and Fernie found Eliza walking slowly toward the Kimball house with her head down. Jacob hung back while Fernie came and took her arm. Eliza did not pull away. He took a deep breath and approached. She glanced up, briefly, reproach in her eyes.

"I'm so sorry, Liz," he said. "I never thought it would turn out like this."

"But it did. You promised, and it happened anyway."

They walked down the street, Fernie on one side and Jacob on the other, holding Eliza's arms. Were they comforting her or restraining her?

"It hasn't happened yet," Jacob said. "And I've got a couple of ideas."

"I'm listening."

"First, I'm almost certain that Taylor Junior is involved in Amanda's murder. The prophet will never allow a murderer to take a wife."

"That's what you said about would-be rapists."

"Fine. But this is different. Our first step is to keep our appointment with Enoch. It's almost time for your washings and anointings."

"Jacob, Enoch could tell us everything he knows and it might not resolve the situation in time. So what, you'll see me married while you wrap up the loose ends? I'd rather die than spend five minutes married to that man."

"I have an answer for that." He reached into his pocket and took out his wallet. He took out all the cash he had, plus his ATM card. "Three hundred and sixty dollars. The PIN to the card is 0107. My mnemonic is Proverbs 1:7."

Eliza repeated the verse. "The fear of the Lord is the beginning of knowledge, but fools despise wisdom and instruction."

"Yes, exactly. There's more than five grand in that account. It's Father's card, so be careful. Soon as you use it, he'll figure out where you are."

"So I'll run?"

"Isn't that what you were thinking anyway?" he asked.

She chewed on her lip, but said nothing.

"If you have to leave Blister Creek," Fernie said, "go stay somewhere quiet until things blow over. Then give me a call. I won't tell them where you are."

"But let's hope it doesn't come to that," Jacob said. "Come on, it's time to go to the temple."

* * *

It was the first time Eliza had set foot in the temple. From the outside, it was half cathedral, half fortress. Inside, she had the odd impression of standing in the lobby of a posh hotel. The temple boasted carved wooden railings, marble floors with thick, hand-woven rugs, elegant fixtures, and stained glass windows. There was an entrance which wrapped around an atrium, and then rooms and hallways beyond.

Jacob disappeared, and Fernie led her to the women's changing room. She handed Eliza what amounted to a sheet with a hole in it. "Leave your clothing inside. Put on this sheet. You will see a door to your left. Go through that door and walk down the hallway until you come to the end."

She eyed the sheet dubiously. "This is all I'll be wearing?"

"Don't worry. You won't see anyone but Charity and me."

Eliza had a moment of doubt when Fernie left her alone. She didn't want to take off her clothes and put on the sheet. She had no idea what to expect. Would she eventually come back here, or find herself in some room, nearly naked, to discover Taylor Junior waiting for her? No, that was paranoia.

Reluctantly, she stripped. She emerged wearing nothing but the sheet. Fernie waited on the far side of the hallway. The two women stood in front of a screened paper wall, like in a traditional Japanese house.

Fernie slid aside the wall and gestured for her to enter. "Are you ready?"

Naked, vulnerable, and confused, she shook her head. "Are you kidding?"

Fernie smiled. "This is the easy part. Only women help other women with the initiatory."

That was somewhat reassuring. She stepped inside and found herself in a small room—no bigger than an oversized closet, really—with a chair, a washbasin, and a shelf holding a bottle of consecrated oil. Fernie indicated that Eliza take her seat in the chair.

Fernie dipped her finger in the basin of water and touched it to Eliza's forehead. "Sister Eliza, having authority, I wash you preparatory to you receiving your anointings, that you may become clean from the blood and sins of this generation. I wash your head, that your brain and your intellect may be clear and active; your ears, that you may hear the word of the Lord."

Fernie returned her finger to the water and then to Eliza's face. "Your eyes, that you may see clearly and discern between truth and error; your nose, that you may smell; your lips, that you may never speak guile; your neck, that it may bear up your head properly; your shoulders, that they may bear the burdens that shall be placed thereon."

She continued her touch down Eliza's body through the open sides of the sheet. "Your back, that there may be marrow in the bones and in the spine; your breast, that it may be the receptacle of pure and virtuous principles; your vitals and bowels, that they may be healthy and strong and perform their proper functions; your arms and hands, that they may be strong and wield the sword of justice in defense of truth and virtue."

And here, and most strangely, Fernie reached beneath the sheet to below her navel. If it had been anyone but her sister she'd have been seriously creeped out. "Your loins, that you may be fruitful and multiply and replenish the earth, that you might have joy in your posterity." Fernie touched her legs. "Your legs and feet, that you might run and not be weary, and walk and not faint."

Fernie helped her to her feet and led her to a sliding door in the wall, opposite of where she had entered. Charity Kimball waited on the other side. Fernie's sister wife gave Eliza a comforting smile.

The second paper-walled room was much like the first, and as Fernie retreated, Charity helped Eliza take a seat. Charity put her hands on Eliza's head.

"Sister Eliza, having authority, I lay my hands upon your head and confirm upon you this anointing, wherewith you have been anointed in the temple of our God, preparatory to becoming a queen and a priestess unto the Most High God, hereafter to rule and reign in the House of Israel forever; and seal upon you all the blessings hereunto appertaining, through your faithfulness, in the name of Jesus Christ. Amen."

Charity helped her up and slid open a doorway to a third room, also identical to the first, except that there was a pair of new, neatly folded temple garments on the shelf next to the anointing oil. Fernie had come around to this third room and waited for her. Charity retreated into the second room.

Fernie now removed the sheet from Eliza's shoulders and helped her into the temple garments.

"Sister Eliza, the garment placed upon you is to be worn throughout your life. It represents the garment given to Adam when he was found naked in the Garden of Eden, and is called the Garment of the Holy Priesthood. Inasmuch as you do not defile it, but are true and faithful to your covenants, it will be a shield and a protection to you against the power of the destroyer until you have finished your work on the earth."

Fernie instructed Eliza to return to her locker and put on the white dress that she would find there. She was to collect the packet of robes and sashes from the locker, then return to this spot.

Eliza did as she was told, walking back to the locker in her underwear, having left the final paper-walled room through another sliding door. She felt as though she were sleepwalking. The most interesting thing was having women anoint and bless her. Only men gave blessings outside the temple; that was the province of the priesthood.

She looked through her clothes, saw that they were undisturbed, and then put on the white dress and returned carrying the robes and sashes. Fernie gave her a new name, which she was instructed to only repeat at a certain point in the endowment, that point to be shown her later. The new name was Eve.

"And now," Fernie said. Charity stood with her. "You are ready to receive your endowment. The others will meet us in the Creation Room."

And at that moment Eliza remembered the horrid black thing Jacob had pulled from Amanda's mouth, and how he wouldn't tell her what he knew. Something from the endowment.

At last she would know why they had cut out Amanda's tongue and slit her throat.

CHAPTER TWENTY

Enoch Christianson was a hunted man. Gideon would have his men watching every approach to Blister Creek. Lost Boys would watch in St. George and Cedar City. Enoch knew what would happen if they caught him.

So he dressed like a gentile. He wore a cap to cover his red hair. He changed vehicles in Wendover and again in Beaver, Utah, buying junker cars with cash and abandoning the previous vehicles in supermarket parking lots. He took back roads from Cedar City.

Enoch had arrived late Thursday night and left the car two miles east of Blister Creek, next to the rusted-out hulk of a station wagon and the derelict wreck of a school bus, among other assorted car parts. It was one of the ad-hoc junkyards that dotted the West, and he added his own heap to the mix. The '82 Chrysler K had been on its last legs anyway, with body and bumper damage, but he added to the effect. He positioned the car behind the bus, then jacked it up and removed the tires, which he tossed into the trunk. Then he rolled down the windows. The car looked as though it had been abandoned years earlier.

From there he had walked to the temple. Carefully, very carefully. The best approach was through Witch's Warts. It was dark in the shadow of the sandstone fins, traveling, as he was, only by moonlight, and the wind made moaning sounds as it found its way through cracks and fissures in the stone. The moans became voices.

"Enoch. Where are you, Enoch?"

He pushed his hands to his ears, but the voices burrowed deeper.

"Why are you hiding?"

"You know what we've come for."

On and on. God, why hadn't he thrown himself in front of the train that day in Boise? Better than to go mad, to be tormented by angels or demons.

"You're not real," he whispered. "None of you."

And then the wind died and with it the voices. He opened his eyes to discover that he was squatting on the ground with his hands clamped over his ears. Aftershocks, he told himself. Not insanity. Triggered by what he had seen in the Holy of Holies. There was something about the wine, and the lights. Something that lingered in the system and came back at vulnerable moments. He rose to his feet, took a few deep breaths, and continued.

The temple was a sentinel on the edge of the desert. A fortress. A sanctuary.

He knew where Gideon hid the spare key. For all that the temple was the most expensive, opulent building in Zion, it sat empty most of the time. Normal church meetings took place in the chapel. Only marriages and the higher ordinances took place in the temple.

It would be a simple thing to hide himself until the time came to meet his brother in the Celestial Room. He would tell Jacob everything.

*   *   *

Gideon Kimball had never killed an old man before. Elder Griggs of the Quorum of the Twelve would be the first.

Killing was tricky business. He chose his accomplice carefully. There were several outcasts to choose from: Eric Froud, sprung from a group home for troubled teens. Jeremy Pratt, who'd been a friend of Enoch's as a boy. Jeremy's brother Will, who was loyal to Gideon, but dumb as a post. Phillip Cobb, Ernest Anders.

No, it would be Israel Young. Gideon didn't trust him, exactly, but he'd known the man since they were boys. They'd explored Witch's Warts together and later rode bikes around town, harassing younger children, stealing candy from the store, and looking into people's windows late at night. Israel had been with him that night with Amanda Kimball; Gideon had used the pliers, but Israel had cut her throat. It was this bond of blood between them that made his decision.

Gideon and Israel waited in a van in the chapel parking lot. The van had darkened windows, which allowed them to watch the people waiting outside the church building without being seen. First, Jacob Christianson had come through the front door. He had said something to Eliza, and the girl had run away, soon to be followed by Jacob and Fernie. Gideon had resisted the urge to follow them in the van.

Soon, the members of the Quorum of the Twelve came out of
the building, together with the prophet. A bunch of tired old men.
And here came his quarry. Elder Griggs walked with the slump of
a man who had relied on a cane for many years. Two boys, aged
about nine or ten, joined the old man as he walked toward the
parking lot. The three of them climbed into a late-model Lincoln
Town Car, which Griggs pulled out of the lot and onto the road.
To Gideon's surprise, he headed out of town toward the Ghost
Cliffs.

"Follow him," he told Israel.

Elder Griggs didn't stop until he reached Blister Creek
Reservoir. There was a picnic spot and a place for fishing. Gideon
and Israel pulled in behind the car and turned off the van's engine.
The doors opened on the Lincoln.

Gideon's heart pounded. Watching Elder Griggs climb out of
his car was like watching a mouse approach a trap. If the mouse
could smell the steel spring, he could run away. Elder Griggs's
Lincoln would quickly outclass the van should he flee.

Gideon thought about Enoch Christianson, still out there, alive.
He had searched in Las Vegas. Others had watched the safe houses
in St. George and Salt Lake. Nobody had seen him. Thinking perhaps that Enoch would try to meet Jacob in Blister Creek, he had
watched every approach to the town.

Nothing.

Enoch had disappeared. That particular mouse had sensed the
trap.

The two boys got out first, retrieving a pair of fishing poles
and a tackle box from the trunk. Probably grandsons; Elder Griggs
didn't look to be fathering children these days. The old man himself

got out and leaned against the side of the car when he saw Gideon and Israel get out of the van and approach.

"Hello there," Elder Griggs said. "Coming up for some fishing?" His voice trembled with age. "They tell me the bass are biting."

"I came to look for you, Elder Griggs."

"Excuse me. My eyesight is not so good these days. You are...?"

"I'm Elder Kimball's son."

Elder Griggs squinted. "Ah, Taylor Junior. I didn't recognize you. It's been a while. And who is this other young man?"

"I'm not Taylor Junior. I'm *Gideon* Kimball."

Elder Griggs glanced toward his boys, already down by the lake, fiddling with tackle in their eagerness to get their lines into the water as soon as possible. "What do you want?" Voice tense.

"It was I who killed Amanda Kimball. Her blood spilled at my feet." He could see Amanda's face in his mind, frozen in terror and pain.

"You? But why?" An extra tremble in his voice. His face grayed.

"Never mind my motives, Elder Griggs. I'm telling you so that you'll know how ruthless I can be."

"What are you saying?"

He changed his voice. "Elder Griggs, thy time has come. Today, thou shalt meet thy maker." Gideon looked deliberately at the man's grandsons. One cast his line into the water, while the other threaded a worm onto a hook. "Will thou stand at the judgment bar alone or with these two boys?"

He used the executioner's voice to render helpless those who heard it. But to Gideon's surprise, Elder Griggs straightened his back and looked him in the eyes. "I will come quietly, then, if that is what it will take to spare my grandsons. But know you this, that my blood will cry for vengeance."

Gideon put a hand on the old man's arm to steady him as he followed them back to the van. Israel opened the door of the van and stood aside.

Elder Griggs reached his hand into the pocket of his suit coat. It was an innocent, absentminded gesture, and Gideon almost missed it. He reached around and grabbed the man's wrist. The man winced in pain, and his bones creaked as Gideon pulled his hand out. There was a cell phone, and a number halfway dialed. Gideon pried loose the phone and turned it off.

And when Israel and Gideon pushed Elder Griggs into the van, he suddenly stopped cooperating. He struggled against the duct tape that Israel produced and bit the man on the hand. He was still struggling when Gideon climbed into the driver's side and started the van.

Israel punched the old man in the face. Elder Griggs let out a moan and fell back, but his legs kept kicking as the man duct-taped them together. Israel hit him again with a look of pleasure, almost like the carnal look of a man about to sate his lust with a woman.

"Stop," Gideon said. "Don't hit the old man. He's not a traitor and doesn't deserve a traitor's death."

Israel subdued the man's legs and then his wrists. Taped his mouth. Elder Griggs moaned and lay on the floor of the van.

They took a ranch road until they reached Witch's Warts. The land here had once been a sandstone plateau. Over tens of thousands of years, wind and water had eroded the landscape into fins and pillars and natural arches.

Gideon and Israel had discovered Elder Griggs's grave almost fifteen years earlier. You had to climb along a fissure that opened between two sandstone fins, then push past a juniper tree that had grown up in the sand-filled space where the water would run down and pool. Beyond that was the sinkhole. Eroded into a rotten place in the sandstone, it sank some dozen feet straight down along the fissure between the two fins, like a cavity between two molars. Sandstone bowed around the sinkhole, keeping it hidden from view.

"This would be a good place to put a body," Israel had remarked casually, as if he regularly watched for such things. Gideon had dismissed the comment from his mind, only to have it resurface many years later.

Age had sapped the weight from Elder Griggs's bones and muscles, and the two had no problem carrying him from the road and toward the sinkhole. Water from the recent rains had poured off the sandstone fins and filled the sinkhole. The water would grow murky and thick with mosquito larvae as it evaporated, but for now it was clear enough to see to the bottom.

They placed Elder Griggs in a sitting position, and then Israel lifted a flat piece of sandstone and set it against the man's chest. Israel wrapped duct tape around the stone and Elder Griggs's chest to hold it in place.

Gideon removed the tape from around the old man's mouth. To his credit, the old man didn't scream for help or beg for mercy.

"You probably wonder why we are going to kill you."

The old man stared at Gideon without blinking. "No, not really. Some evil purpose or other. The Lord will judge you in due time."

The answer surprised him. "You're not afraid to die?"

Elder Griggs shook his head. "I've lived a good life. I have faith in the Lord. He will give me my inheritance in the Celestial Kingdom. This is not how I would choose to go, but I don't fear death."

"No, I don't think you do." It was an interesting attitude. So many of these old men, those who proclaimed absolute faith in God, left the world clinging by their fingernails. How could they actually believe what they taught? If they were so certain of their reward, why not leave their frail, battered bodies and embrace death?

"It does seem pointless to kill me, Gideon. I'm a used-up vessel of no use to anyone but my grandchildren."

"That, and whispering in the ear of the prophet," Gideon corrected. "He listens to you like he listens to no other man. And your son-in-law, Abraham Christianson, too. If you tell them to oppose me, they will. And you said yourself you have little to lose." He smiled. "Not everyone who remains will step into line, of course, but most aren't so brave as you, Elder Griggs. Brother Joseph will come face to face with the desperate need to hold Zion together. And that's why you must die."

Elder Griggs chuckled in a way Gideon would not have thought possible for a man about to die. "You're a fool if you think my son-in-law will follow you. A Son of Perdition, that's what you are. An excommunicate. I have never prophesied before, boy, but I feel a prophesy coming. You will be dead before the end of the week, Gideon Kimball." He glanced at Israel. "And your henchman, too. They will be ugly deaths, I think. Your name will become a hiss and a byword among the people of Zion. No, you won't be leading anyone, Gideon Kimball."

"Tape his mouth," Israel Young urged.

Gideon saw the uneasiness on his companion's face. Yes, Israel was right. He re-taped the old man's mouth.

Gideon raised his hands above his head and lifted his voice. "Elder Griggs, we now seal thee unto death. May the Lord have mercy upon thy soul."

And now, the old liar gave one last twitch. There was real fear in those watery eyes. Griggs struggled and kicked. Israel looked pleased.

They pushed. Elder Griggs tumbled forward. A single plop and the man sank. It was like the day his brother Joel had drowned in the canal, the same quiet sound, the body slipping below the surface like a stone, swirling down. The old man settled on the bottom. And there, visibly, he thrashed. A single bubble rose to the surface. The ripples stilled. The movement stopped.

It was hard business, this killing. Some couldn't stomach it. Enoch, for one. He had stood in front of Jennifer Gold, having been commanded to sever the woman's unborn child from her body. He had balked.

Enoch's violation of his covenants called for a blood atonement. It would be a mercy, really. Enoch's own blood would allow forgiveness from the Lord.

They left Witch's Warts by a circuitous route. In the desert, protected by the sandstone fins, some of these footprints might last for weeks. Better not to leave a direct path to where they had dumped Elder Griggs's body.

It was because he was thinking about such things that Gideon noticed the extra set of footprints. A pair of tennis shoes tracked through the sandstone maze, pressing hard into the sand and lighter in the gravelly places. Kids often came into Witch's Warts, but rarely adults. And almost never this far in.

"What do you make of this?" he asked. "How old?"

Israel bent and poked at one of the footprints. "The footprints are fresh, but they've formed a crust from the dew. Maybe last night."

A good observation. Gideon followed the footprints for a stretch. They came from the south and headed northwest toward town. Enoch wore tennis shoes. Gideon tried to think of the pattern on the man's shoes, but couldn't. They could easily have been someone else's.

Except that they weren't.

He looked toward Blister Creek. The temple spire lifted above the sandstone fins that otherwise blocked view of the town. Continue in that direction and one would emerge from the desert practically in the back lot of the temple. He used Witch's Warts himself to come and go from the temple without being seen.

Gideon had taken a call from Eric Froud a couple of hours ago, alerting him that Jacob and Eliza would be doing an endowment in the temple that afternoon. It was another sign that Eliza would soon marry. It was useful information, and he'd set it aside for later consideration. But now it occurred to him that maybe this was more than a simple endowment. And maybe there would be another participant, the owner of those footprints, coming off the desert, to meet Jacob in the temple.

The day was pregnant with killing, the anticipation, the promise of something dreaded, desired, and necessary. Before the day was over, he knew that he would kill several more times. He had known that from the moment he'd risen this morning. The difference was, he now knew the identity of his next victim.

Gideon turned to Israel. "Come on. We have an appointment to keep at the temple."

* * *

Jacob watched his sister as she sat at the front of the Telestial Room, which represented the "Lone and Dreary World" into which Adam and Eve had been driven after having eaten the forbidden fruit. The room held seating for roughly thirty people, but was mostly empty now. Chandeliers lit the room in a comforting, incandescent glow. The walls were painted with scenes of Noah's Ark and the flooding of the earth. The first time through, Jacob had fixed on the scene of people drowning as the flood waters climbed. He saw Eliza studying it now.

People climbed upon each other, wild-eyed with fear. A woman held her child above her head as the waters licked her face. Another woman tried to keep her children above water while two men used their heads as stepping stools to reach higher ground. Bodies floated facedown. The serenity on the faces of the chosen and their animals, loading onto the ark, presented a sharp contrast to the terror of those God would drown.

God is merciful. He is also terrible.

Later, they would move to the Terrestial Room, and finally to the Celestial Room where the endowment ended as the initiate passed through the veil and into the presence of the Lord.

Jacob, playing Adam, prayed, "Oh God, hear the words of my mouth."

Stephen Paul came on stage as Lucifer. "I hear you. What is it you want?"

Jacob looked toward him in feigned suspicion. "Who are you?"

"I am the god of this world."

The initial part of the endowment was a rough retelling of the creation story of Genesis. Elohim (the Father), Jehovah (the son), and Michael created the Earth. Michael became Adam. Elohim and Jehovah created Eve from Adam's rib. Lucifer arrived to tempt Adam and Eve, who Elohim and Jehovah then drove from the Garden and into the Lone and Dreary World.

The participants covenanted to obey the Law of Obedience, wherein men promised to obey the Lord and women promised to obey their husbands. In Eliza's case, this meant her future husband. The Law of Sacrifice followed:

"We covenant to sacrifice all that we possess," Stephen Paul said, "even our own lives if necessary, in sustaining and defending the Kingdom of God."

The endowment moved to the rituals of the lower, or Aaronic Priesthood, which would be followed by the rituals of the higher, Melchizedek Priesthood. They represented higher and lower states of spiritual awakening. Stephen Paul, now playing Peter, instructed Jacob, as Adam, in how to put on the robes of the Aaronic Priesthood, and in the first token of the Aaronic Priesthood, its name, and sign. Stephen Paul's brother, Aaron Young, filled in the other roles when three men were required on stage.

The name of the first token was the new name that Eliza had been given in the washings and anointings. The sign was a handshake with thumbs over knuckles. And then the penalty, for those who might be tempted to violate the covenants they had made in the temple.

"We, and each of us, covenant and promise that we will not reveal any of the secrets of this, the First Token of the Aaronic Priesthood," Stephen Paul continued, "with its accompanying name, sign, and penalty. Should we do so, we agree that our throats be cut from ear to ear and our tongues torn out by their roots."

Jacob watched Eliza. Her face illuminated in understanding, followed almost immediately by a grimace of horror.

The tokens, names, and signs were the meat of the endowment. Jacob took them as symbolic; he didn't think angels would ask for secret handshakes and whispered signs and countersigns when you died and if you had a crappy memory, then oops, you'd be con-signed to a lower kingdom. But why take blood oaths to protect a secret with only symbolic meaning? God knew that *someone* had taken them seriously.

Amanda Kimball. And whoever had killed her.

They had cut her throat and torn out her tongue. But why? Was it for discovering that they had murdered the gentiles? For then threatening to go to the police? And he couldn't wrap his mind around the original crime itself: the brutal murder of a woman and her unborn child. Why?

Jacob thought about what his father had said. The Quorum of the Twelve had wrestled for many years with the inherent flaw of any breeding program involving a small population. It didn't mat-ter that they doubled their population every twenty years and that they might someday number in the hundreds of thousands or even millions.

Take golden retrievers. Inbred with others descended from the same pedigree, it didn't matter that there were millions of them. They still suffered from hip dysplasia, vision problems, and epilepsy because they didn't have enough genetic diversity.

In humans, inbreeding also involved cognitive deficiencies, which was the antithesis of what the church elders sought to accomplish.

That they should breed themselves like animals filled him with disgust. *Golden retrievers. Is that all we are?*

Well, not exactly. Unlike a purebred animal, the stock could be improved by bringing in outside females. Some members of the Quorum of the Twelve had driven down that road before being turned aside by other, more practical voices.

The Jupiter Medallion.

The thought came unbidden to his mind, and he almost dismissed it. But he could see it in his mind now, the picture of the wall where someone had painted its symbols in the blood of a murdered baby and her mother.

And suddenly, everything came into focus. He knew what had happened, and why.

CHAPTER TWENTY-ONE

I am God.

Enoch stood on the far side of the veil in the Celestial Room of the temple. The Celestial Room was brightly lit, with white carpets and white marble walls. Even the door on the far side was white, as was the veil that separated them from the Telestial Room. The only color came from the reddish browns of a Victorian cameo-backed couch with a hand-carved floral apron. His third great-grandmother had carried it across the plains, and his Grandpa Griggs had refinished the upholstery and the claw feet.

The room was quiet as Enoch waited, with only the quiet murmur of voices from the other side of the veil carrying itself into the Celestial Room. Stephen Paul Young would present Jacob and Eliza at the veil. He wondered what Jacob had told the other participants, if Eliza and the Young brothers knew that Enoch would be the one to draw them through the veil, acting as proxy for the Lord, or if they'd be expecting someone else.

"God," Enoch whispered to himself. It was half prayer, half affirmation of his role in the endowment.

He would tell Jacob everything he knew. It started with Elder Kimball, elder of Israel, and ended with his son, Gideon. Elder Kimball laundered money in Las Vegas, stole tithing from the church. He had bribed doctors and nurses and hospital administrators. Spied on people. Blackmailed. And he had given Gideon free rein to kidnap, murder, and intimidate.

Enoch would greet his brother through the veil, and here, in the Celestial Room, he would tell Jacob everything. And then Jacob would do everything in his power to destroy Elder Kimball, no matter what damage he might inflict on the church.

But Enoch had to do it. He'd stood at the point of murdering an innocent woman. And he'd known that his actions were not of God.

Enoch wore temple white, pilfered from the changing room. Over this he wore his robes, his green sash, his cap. It was the clothing of the endowment and of a temple sealing. It was also the clothing they dressed you in at death. So that you would be prepared to give the real God the signs and tokens.

The others did as Enoch had told them. They passed first through the creation, then through the signs and tokens, one by one. The participants spoke in loud voices, and he could hear them clearly as they recited their lines even though he couldn't see them through the veil.

And they reached the Second Token of the Aaronic Priesthood, with its penalty:

"We, and each of us, covenant and promise that we will not reveal any of the secrets of this, the Second Token of the Aaronic Priesthood, with its accompanying name, sign, and penalty. Should we do so, we agree to have our breasts cut open and our hearts and vitals torn out from our body and given to the birds of the air and the beasts of the field."

"An appropriate phrase, don't you think?"

Even as Enoch turned with heart pounding, a fist crushed him in the solar plexus. He grunted and went down, and the three men who'd come in behind him were on top of him.

Gideon Kimball. Israel Young. Eric Froud.

They were too strong. He was stunned from the blow. Within seconds they had him pinned. Eric held his legs, while Israel had his hands around Enoch's throat. Gideon sat on his chest with a knife in hand. He pressed it against Enoch's gut.

"Very clever," Gideon said. "Coming to the temple. It's the right place to make peace with the Lord, don't you think?" The knife pressed harder, and Enoch felt it pierce the skin. Only a prick, but the slightest pressure would slide it right in.

How had they found him? Maybe they *were* on the side of God.

And then he remembered the look on Jennifer Gold's face. Enoch had stood over her, ready to cut her unborn child from the woman's womb. No angel had directed those actions. No angel of God.

Israel Young choked Enoch's air supply. Gideon leaned harder on the knife. It eased slowly in. An eighth of an inch, a quarter.

"One scream," Israel said. "One single scream and your life will come to an end." His grip relaxed on Enoch's throat. Air burned back into his lungs.

He could barely breathe with Israel's hands around his throat. "Why?" he whispered.

"You have sinned against the spirit," Gideon said in his ear. "You made covenants, accepted penalties. This is your chance to atone—it is the only way to be forgiven of your sins. Now do you understand? Accept it and the Lord may yet show you mercy in the world to come."

That wasn't what Enoch had meant. He knew why Gideon wanted to kill him, and the twisted logic of blood atonement was a front for Gideon's own wickedness, a way to convince himself that he stood among the righteous.

"Jennifer Gold?" Enoch said. "Why her?"

"A Jew," Gideon said. "Native intelligence. And carrying a daughter. What does it matter?"

"Not yours?"

"What, the baby? No. Samuel Gold's sperm and Jennifer Gold's egg. We bring the child back, breed her with our own. It's called hybridization vigor. It works with plants. It works with cattle. It will work with humans. But what does it matter?" he repeated. "You're confused, Enoch. Taking these babies. Spreading our own seed. Those are only tactics. Individual battles. It's the war, Enoch. That's what matters. You forgot that. And so you forgot where your allegiance lies."

Gideon claimed that it didn't matter, but spread throughout the West were hundreds of vials of sperm. Gideon's seed, much of it. Whatever breeding or random evolutionary mix had formed this monster, it would be spread to hundreds of children. Taking the information fed back by the clinics, the Lost Boys would kidnap some of the girls and return them to Zion. Other children would remain, like sleeper cells to be awakened by a future church fed and nourished on Gideon's sickness.

"It's all a lie," Enoch said. He groaned from the unbearable pain and pressure of the knife pushing into his flesh. "The angel, everything. It's you, Gideon. It wasn't even your father. It was all you."

Gideon leaned closer. "We are who we were born to be," he whispered. "That's all. You were ordained by God to fail. I was ordained to lead His kingdom."

"My brother will stop you."

Gideon smiled as he drew back. Was that uncertainty behind that smile? The man nodded to Israel, and the grip tightened once more about his throat.

"And now, Enoch Christianson," Gideon said in a low voice, "having violated thine covenants, thy breast shall be cut open and thine heart and vitals shall be torn from thy body and given to the birds of the air and the beasts of the field. Vengeance is mine, sayeth the Lord."

* * *

Jacob drew in his breath as the pieces fell into place.

He'd read about the murdered woman, but the gruesome details and the occult-like symbols of the Jupiter Medallion painted on the wall had distracted him. Made him believe, as had the police, that the killers had consumed the woman's baby in a black mass.

They had not killed the baby. That had been misdirection, and an effective one, aided by the gruesome murder of the baby's mother. Of course the police would take the note at face value. He had.

But the truth was, the baby had never died. Jacob would consult the article, but certainly the child had been a girl. As would have been the other two children. They had kidnapped the children and brought them to Zion to improve the breeding stock. Instead of adopting the children of drug addicts and prostitutes—as his father had put it—they had kidnapped the daughters of academics and scientists.

He remembered what Fernie had told him. Amanda had disappeared to Denver six months into her pregnancy, just when she'd have started to show through the loose-fitting, ankle-length dresses the women of the church wore. Premature labor, supposedly, requiring bed rest out of sight of her sister wives. And then she'd come back from Denver with a baby.

It was so obvious now. Sophie Marie didn't look like a Kimball. Dark, curly hair, a darker skin tone than the pale complexion common in the Kimball clan. They'd said she looked like Amanda's brother, killed as a child. The human mind searched for patterns and found them where they did not exist. In truth, she was not related to Amanda Kimball in any way.

But how had they convinced Amanda to take the baby? Maybe Elder Kimball had scorned her for being infertile, had threatened her if she didn't go along with the plan. Or maybe he had told her this was a gift from God. An abandoned child. Infant Moses, found among the bulrushes in a basket.

Whatever the reason, she hadn't known the horrific truth. Until one day, perhaps when she was in Cedar City with her sister wives, she had seen something on television or caught a glimpse of a magazine. Maybe she had seen the Jupiter Medallion, its symbols marked on the walls of Sophie Marie's murdered parents' house. She had thought of her unexpected gift and the pendant worn around her husband's neck. Amanda Kimball had done her research.

And there had been similar cases in New Mexico and Los Angeles. Prominent academics who had lost their lives and their infant or unborn daughters. Jacob thought about their names, Stein, Feldman, Rosenberg.

Jewish names. That would be no coincidence. The Church of the Anointing was a covenant people, chosen by God and set apart, as He had set apart the seed of Abraham, Isaac, and Jacob. And so each member of the church must be adopted into the House of Israel to receive his or her inheritance in the Celestial Kingdom. In the church, this usually meant the House of Ephraim or the House of Manassah. Outside the church, only the House of Judah had the same claim on the Lord.

That they were scientists, high IQ individuals, both mother and father, was similarly no mistake. What better way to improve the intellectual foundations of the church than to adopt—if butchery and kidnapping merited the word adoption—females from a proven genetic heritage?

Jacob knew what they had done. All he needed from Enoch was names.

The time came to present Eliza to the veil. They had to shift their robes from the left to the right side preparatory to receiving the signs and tokens of the Melchizedek Priesthood. They had to form a prayer circle, and then approach the veil to be admitted into the Celestial Room and the symbolic presence of the Lord.

The veil was a sheet that hung between the ceiling and the floor and divided the Terrestial Room from the Celestial. It had holes placed to perform handshakes and other tokens through the veil; these holes matched the signs of the compass and square on the temple garment itself.

Jacob wore a robe that draped over his right shoulder, a sash around his waist, and a hat on his head that looked something like a baker's cap. Everything was white except for the green apron embroidered to look like a cloak of leaves; it represented the apron worn to cover Adam and Eve's nakedness as the Lord drove them from the Garden of Eden.

He stopped Stephen Paul as they made their way to the veil. The man was about to slip through the veil to play the part of the Lord. "I know what I told you," Jacob said in a low voice. "But I need you to present me at the veil."

"I thought that was my brother's job," Stephen Paul said. "You want me to present at the veil and Aaron to go into the Celestial Room instead?"

"That won't be necessary. Someone is in there already. You will present, he'll play the part of the Lord and pull me through. Once I'm in, you'll present Eliza and I'll bring her through."

Stephen Paul frowned. "What are you talking about? Who's in there?"

"My brother. Enoch."

"The Lost Boy?" He kept his voice low, but it was angry. "You let an *apostate* into the temple?"

"He let *himself* in." Jacob decided to take a risk. "It's about Amanda Kimball."

Stephen Paul's frown deepened. He'd have heard the same rumors of her murder as everyone else. "Go on."

The others watched from a few paces back, Aaron Young and Charity with their own frowns.

Jacob whispered, "That's the real reason I'm in Blister Creek. Brother Joseph himself wanted me. Eliza's marriage is secondary. And Enoch knows something. He's going to play the part of the Lord, and when we're inside, he's going to tell me who killed her. It was the only way he'd cooperate."

Stephen Paul stared for a long moment. "You should have told me."

"I couldn't. I'm sorry."

"Well, let's get going then. And you'd better not be lying."

Jacob approached the veil. He saw nothing moving through the thin fabric. There was nobody on the other side. Had Enoch changed his mind? And then a shadow moved behind the sheet. Stephen Paul approached the veil and gave three raps with a mallet against a carved wooden post.

A muffled voice came from the other side: "What is wanted?"

Stephen Paul hesitated, then said, "Adam, having been true and faithful in all things, desires further light and knowledge by conversing with the Lord through the veil."

"Present him at the veil and his request shall be granted." His brother spoke so softly that Jacob had to lean forward to hear.

The Lord's hand—or Enoch's, in this case—reached through the veil to receive the First Token of the Aaronic Priesthood. Jacob took the offered hand and gave the appropriate sign and its name.

But his mind was racing. The hand presented to him was not Enoch's.

Had it been the left hand presented to him, or even just a normal handshake, he might not have noticed it. But the first Token of the Aaronic Priesthood involved placing the thumb just so on the recipient's knuckle. Enoch had broken the thumb on his right hand fly-fishing as a boy, and the thumb had never been entirely straight ever since. This man's thumb had no such deformity.

Who was it, then?

Stephen Paul stood at Jacob's shoulder, his face calm, a look of concentration. He didn't seem to notice anything wrong.

They reached the Second Token of the Melchizedek Priesthood, where Jacob reached through the veil to put his left hand on the man's right shoulder while the man on the other side did the same through an opposite hole. With their right hands, they gripped in a handshake with little fingers interlocked. "Health in the navel, marrow in the bones, strength in the loins and in the sinews," the man began. Jacob and the other man stood inches apart, locked in this intimate embrace but separated by the fabric of the veil.

He felt vulnerable. A strong grip on his hand and shoulder. No hands free for movement. For either of them. But supposing the other man wasn't alone. The man on the other side of the veil shifted on his feet but didn't break his grip.

Jacob glanced down and saw something dark move toward him at waist level. The grip on his hand and shoulder tightened. He couldn't break it. Instead, he lurched to one side. A knife thrust through the mark at the level of his navel.

"Jacob!" Stephen Paul cried. He put his hands on Jacob's shoulders and jerked him backward.

The blade withdrew. It glistened with blood. Jacob reached a hand to his gut, but it came away clean and he felt no pain. The blood on the blade was not his own.

Moving shadows and muffled shouts came from the other side of the veil. Running feet. Jacob pushed aside the veil, and Stephen Paul followed him into the Celestial Room. It was bright on the other side, and it took a second for Jacob's eyes to adjust.

The Celestial Room was a small room with a few white plush armchairs for quiet contemplation and a Victorian couch against one wall. A chandelier of cut crystal lit the room. A door slammed on the far side of the room.

Enoch lay on his back in the middle of the room. The carpet around his feet was a butcher's block of blood and guts. His temple robes lay in bloody shreds, centered around a gaping hole in his middle.

Stephen Paul stood at Jacob's side. "Oh sweet Jesus Christ." The man turned and was sick.

Jacob could not look away. A single, strangled word came from his mouth. "Enoch."

They hadn't had enough time to crack Enoch's chest and take his heart, but they had done a fair job of the vitals. Severed intestines and other innards lay half spilled onto the floor. A bloody trail led across the floor in the direction of the slammed door on the far side of the Celestial Room.

Jacob heard sounds at his back and remembered the women. "Quick," he told Stephen Paul. "Don't let the women through the veil. Especially not Eliza." The man recovered enough of his wits to obey.

Enoch, Jacob was horrified to discover, was still alive. He clutched at the seeping guts, as if trying to push what was left of them back inside. Intestines squirted through his fingers.

Jacob stared, mouth agape. *I agree to have my breast cut open and my heart and vitals torn out from my body and given to the birds of the air and the beasts of the field.* The penalty of the Second Token of the Aaronic Priesthood.

"Dear God," Jacob said as he snapped from his stupor and hurried to his brother's side. "No, Enoch. No." He knelt. He reached for the wound, as if hands could close it again. All around him were bits of tissue and chunks of innards. Much of it was missing, taken away.

He must not lose control. It was only meat. Just meat in a butcher's shop.

My brother.

"Oh Enoch. What happened? Oh God. Please, no."

Enoch looked up at Jacob, his eyes semi-glazed. Blood foamed at his lips. "The veil," he whispered. "I can see the other side."

Jacob knew he had only seconds. "What happened?"

"Grandpa, what? I'm forgiven?"

Jacob had no idea what he was talking about. "Who did this to you?"

Enoch's eyes turned toward him. "Gid…"

"Gideon?" When Enoch gave a faint nod, he pressed. "And Taylor Junior? Was he involved, too?"

Too late. The light faded in his brother's eyes. His soul left his body. And the body hung there, limp, lifeless. An empty glove. Dead.

Jacob lifted bloody hands to his face. He felt like he was going to pass out.

Stephen Paul came back then. He wouldn't look at the body. "I told my brother, but not the women. Eliza is okay. She doesn't know what to make of the delay. Fernie and Charity will be asking questions any moment, though. We'd better come up with something, and quickly."

Not yet. He needed more time. Jacob had to clear his mind and start thinking rationally. It was all he could do not to take his brother in his arms and weep. But he couldn't afford that luxury.

"This is your brother?" Stephen Paul asked in a half-strangled voice. "Oh Jacob. I'm sorry." A silent moment. "Someone ran through that door. We need to go after them."

"Yes," Jacob said, trying to pull out of his stupor. He stood up and wiped the blood from his hands onto his white temple clothes. It made an appalling mess. He ran his sleeve across his face. It came away red, too.

"Who would do such a thing? Who would desecrate the temple?"

"Lost Boys. Gideon Kimball. Others." *Taylor Junior. Bastard.* "There were at least two in here, one to hold me at the veil and the other with the knife." He looked down at Enoch's sprawling body, but he had to look away in a hurry. He took two deep breaths. "My brother was a strong man. And we heard nothing while they cut him open, alive. At least three, then. Did you see a face?"

"No, but the man I saw was wearing his robes and everything. I saw the green of his apron."

Jacob had seen white, but not the green. So the murderer had dressed in his complete temple clothing in preparation for ordinances. Whatever for? Had they performed their own endowment session? Why? Had they been surprised to find Enoch in the Celestial Room, or had it been their plan all along to murder Jacob's brother and then stab him through the veil?

Jacob's mind was racing. The door on the right side of the room led to the changing rooms. The one on the left led to the sealing rooms. The murderers had fled to the left. He had assumed at first that they had taken that route because it led further in, past the Holy of Holies to the offices of the temple president. From there, one could take the back stairs and flee through a side door.

Even as he turned this over in his mind, he heard a woman's scream from behind him. He turned, expecting to see that Fernie, Charity, or Eliza had come into the Celestial Room and seen Enoch's butchered body. But the veil was still drawn and the women on the other side.

He turned back to the door where the murderers had fled. Fled in their temple clothes. Enoch's attackers didn't mean to leave the building. Their destination was the sealing rooms. It was there that a man would take a woman in celestial marriage.

Eliza. They'd come for his sister.

CHAPTER TWENTY-TWO

Eliza had known something was wrong even before Stephen Paul returned from the other side of the veil with his face ashen and wiping at his mouth.

It was her first time in the temple, and so she was letting events push her. Take off the robe, put it on the other shoulder. Repeat these words. It was surreal and more than a little creepy. Especially the oaths. The only thing that kept her going was her brother and sister. They had done this before. Surely they knew what they were doing.

And so she hadn't been immediately concerned when Jacob and Stephen Paul rushed through the veil. But Fernie and Charity stood on either side of her, short of the altar that stood in front of the veil. They exchanged worried looks that crossed in front of Eliza. Stephen Paul's brother, Aaron Young, stood between them and the veil, waiting his turn to pass into the Celestial Room. He shifted from foot to foot as if not knowing whether to go forward or to stay where he was.

"What's wrong?" she asked. "What's going on?"

Charity put a hand on her wrist. "I don't know. I—"

But before she could finish, Stephen Paul parted the veil. He looked at Charity. "Keep her in here. Do *not* come through." He turned and went back through.

My brother. Something had happened to him. To Jacob, or maybe Enoch. Perhaps both. She started forward, but the two women took their charge seriously. They each grabbed her wrists and held her in place. Aaron Young, too, held out his arms to stop her.

"Let me go," she said. She opened her mouth to cry for Jacob, but just then she heard a commotion from the back of the Terrestial Room.

Coming up the aisle then, to her surprise, ran three more men. All three wore white temple robes with green aprons, the same as the women and Aaron Young.

She didn't recognize any of them, but she knew who the leader was. He had the same narrow eyes as Taylor Junior and the same forehead as Elder Kimball. It must be Gideon Kimball.

One of the men carried a plastic garbage sack that he'd tucked under and tied off at his belt. It hung round and damp, and she saw now, to her horror, that blood dribbled down its side. Good Lord, what was in that sack? More blood splattered like paint flicked from a brush across their robes. There was blood on their hands and even faces.

The three men moved swiftly down the aisle. No hesitation. Running straight at them. Charity and Fernie moved just as quickly to maneuver between Eliza and the approaching men. "Leave her alone!" Fernie cried.

The men shoved the two women aside. Eliza moved to help Charity and Fernie, but from behind her, Aaron Young grabbed her to drag her back through the veil. Keep her safe, at least.

Or so she thought. Instead, he wrenched her arm behind her back. It was a sharp pain, and as she turned, she could see the betrayal in his eyes. He was not here to protect her. He had come as an enemy.

And now she screamed. It was a short cry, aborted by the hand of Aaron Young clamped over her mouth. "I must obey the angel, Eliza."

Angel? What angel?

Aaron dragged her, kicking, struggling, scratching, toward the door. Like his brother, Stephen Paul, Aaron was a tall man and powerfully built, with muscles built by long hours of farming and ranching. She could not free herself or even get out another scream.

The other men grabbed her legs. Charity and Fernie followed them to the door, punching and pleading. They reached the far door.

"You," Gideon said to Charity when the struggle had reached the doorway at the far end of the Terrestial Room. "You will come with us." He yanked back on Charity's hair. The woman cried out and grabbed at her scalp. The man with the bloody bag at his belt grabbed her feet, while the other punched Fernie in the mouth. Eliza's sister fell with a muffled grunt.

Eliza stared down in horror at Fernie, lying stunned on the ground. She had never seen a man punch a woman like that. Charity flailed as Gideon yanked her this way and that by the roots of her hair.

"Sorry, Eliza," Aaron Young said in her ear. "It's the will of the Lord. We don't always understand his purposes."

"You don't speak for the Lord," she said.

With Fernie out of the way, the four men dragged Eliza and Charity into the hallway. The women fought back. Eliza felt such hatred and loathing that she thought she would burst. But she was also terrified, and already exhausted by the struggle.

"Leave us alone!" Charity cried. "Elder Kimball—"

Gideon slapped her across the mouth. "My father isn't in charge here. I am. You, you will be our witness." He turned to Eliza. "You, well, today is a special day." He gave her a toothy grin. "The happiest day of your life. Your wedding day."

* * *

Jacob and Stephen Paul left Enoch's body and rushed back through the veil and into the Terrestial Room. Jacob blinked twice in growing confusion. The room was empty. Whatever had happened had ended in seconds. Fernie, Eliza, Charity, and Aaron Young were all gone.

And then he heard a moan from the far side of the room. They found Fernie lying on the carpet near the door, dazed. Jacob felt a twist of fear to see her down, but she was okay. She climbed slowly to her feet.

Fernie wept. "I tried to stop them. They were too strong. What could I do?"

Jacob said, "How many?"

"Three. They came through the door. Gideon Kimball, Israel Young, and someone else. A boy."

Stephen Paul said, "My cousin, Israel. That's no surprise. But what about my brother? He could have taken Israel. Maybe Gideon, too." He shook his head and looked around the room as if expecting to find his brother unconscious and bleeding behind some chair.

Jacob had already guessed what had become of Aaron Young, but Fernie confirmed it. "Your brother went with them." She wiped a trickle of blood at the corner of her mouth. "Willingly."

Stephen Paul stared. "I don't believe it. Not Aaron."

"Yes, Aaron." Some of the fear left her voice, replaced by anger. "He grabbed Eliza from behind. Dragged her out of here himself."

"But my brother? He's not a Lost Boy."

Jacob said, "So what? He's with them. Doesn't matter why."

"They took Charity, too," Fernie said. "Dragged her out by her hair. Bastards."

Stephen Paul still hadn't made the connection. "Why Charity?"

Jacob thought he knew. "It's Taylor Junior's first marriage. His mother must vouch for his faith and righteousness before the officiator can proceed." After the first marriage, the senior wife would stand in to give approval.

Stephen Paul said, "But why force it? You said your father had already approved a marriage to Taylor Junior."

Yes, that was the problem. They had killed Enoch in revenge and escaped without being spotted. There was nothing overt to tie this murder to Taylor Junior, any more than there had been to link him to the death of Amanda Kimball. So why send Gideon for Eliza? Unless...

His thoughts crystallized in his words. "They didn't wait because it's not Taylor Junior who is going to marry Eliza. They're going to force her to marry Gideon."

Fernie said, "That doesn't make sense, Jacob. Charity is not Gideon's mother." She frowned. "Or Taylor Junior's, for that matter."

"No, their mother is dead. Which means—"

"—that his father's senior wife must stand in her place," Fernie completed.

He looked back toward the veil. Behind lay his brother, broken and lifeless. He had to leave Enoch to save his sister. He turned to the others. "There are only three sealing rooms. We can find them quickly. There are four of them, and the three of us plus Eliza and Charity. That makes five."

"What about Enoch?" Fernie asked. "He'd make six."

"Enoch won't be coming." Jacob tried to wipe emotion from his face.

Fernie studied his face and looked at the blood on his hands and robes. "What happened in there, Jacob? Where is your brother?"

"Not now, Fernie," Stephen Paul said.

"He didn't...he isn't... Your brother..." But then she shook her head and didn't press further. "Okay then. But think, Jacob. Three of your five are women. Charity isn't young. Our enemies will be armed. We won't stand a chance."

He thought of the attack in Enoch's apartment in Las Vegas. He had stood down two men—probably Gideon and Israel. This time he had Stephen Paul on his side, a large, enraged man who could certainly deal with his own brother even if that meant that Jacob had to face the others on his own.

"Simple, Fernie." He marshaled every ounce of confidence. "We will defeat them because they're cowards. And their purposes evil. Our cause is righteous."

"Yes," said Stephen Paul, his face red and glaring. "For the arms of the wicked shall be broken, but the Lord upholdeth the righteous."

Sure, thought Jacob, as they left the room. But wasn't every man the righteous hero of his own story? Did Gideon Kimball, even now, think that he was doing the will of the Lord?

Clumps of Charity's graying blond hair marked their path to the right. It was the direction of the sealing rooms, as he had guessed. They moved down the hallway, swiftly, but not running. There were branching hallways and doors to restrooms and the offices of the temple workers. Jacob didn't want to risk ambush should one of the Lost Boys be waiting behind one of those doors. They had time. The sealing would take several minutes, even if performed quickly.

They passed into the sealing wing. It was a short hallway with three doors that alternated on each side of the hall. Inside the sealing rooms, the couple would kneel across the altar in their temple robes, while the officiator sealed them for time and all eternity. The only higher ordinance was the second anointing, which the prophet performed in the Holy of Holies for the elders in the Quorum of the Twelve.

Jacob put his hand on the first doorknob and gave a slight twist. Unlocked. He looked back at Stephen Paul. Fernie looked afraid, but there was a determined set to her mouth. Stephen Paul gave him a grim nod. Jacob threw open the door and made to charge in.

The room was dark. The air inside was still, neutral smelling, and undisturbed.

They went to the second door and tried it. Same result.

By the third door, Jacob's heart was pounding. He'd had too long to consider this moment. What if there were more of them in the room than Enoch's three murderers, plus Aaron Young? What if they were armed with more than knives? He flung open the door.

Dark and empty.

"Damn it," Stephen Paul said.

"I don't understand," Fernie said. "Are we wrong?"

Jacob cursed himself for wasting valuable time. He had taken them down this unused passageway, bursting into dark, empty rooms, and all the while the attackers had been fleeing in some other direction. The whole hallway had a stale, unused flavor, although the lights were on. But the lights meant nothing. They'd been switched on for the whole building.

He rethought his assumptions. Jacob had seen clumps of Charity's hair heading in this direction, as if they'd dragged the woman by her hair. There was nothing here, though. He looked down at the carpet, walking up and down the hallway. The carpet was a plush cream.

"What are you looking for?" Stephen Paul asked.

"The murder was a grisly affair. And they took trophies."

Fernie stopped short. "Murder? You mean they killed Enoch? Oh, I'd hoped…"

He turned, remembering that he'd turned away her questions at first. "Yes, that's right."

"Oh Jacob, I'm sorry. And Eliza…" Her voice trailed off. "What do you mean, trophies?"

I agree to have my breast cut open and my heart and vitals torn out from my body and given to the birds of the air and the beasts of the field.

Jacob said, "It wasn't a clean killing, Fernie. They took part of Enoch with them."

She had nothing to say to that.

They backed their way out of the sealing wing to the main hallway. The three of them searched the carpet again.

"Here," Fernie said. "Is this blood?"

It was indeed. Spots, like flicks of paint from a brush, already turning black, together with larger splotches.

"Look," Stephen Paul said. He bent over something.

A piece of tissue, ground into a partial footprint. It must have caught up between the treads of one of the murderer's feet as he fled the Celestial Room. The prints led further down the hallway. There was a stairwell back there, as well as offices used by Brother Joseph and his counselors from the Quorum of the Twelve. Had they fled the temple, then?

And then he realized something. The sealing was only the *second* highest ordinance performed in the temple. There was a room dedicated to the second anointing, and any lower ordinances might also be performed in that room. It was down this hallway, beneath the spire of the temple.

He turned to the others. "The Holy of Holies."

CHAPTER TWENTY-THREE

Eliza did not follow meekly as the men dragged the two women down the hallway, but kicked and fought every step of the way. She cried out for Jacob, all the while fearing they had killed him in the Celestial Room.

They pulled her into a room and threw her to the floor. It was dim inside, and her eyes adjusted slowly, even as she struggled to catch her breath. She didn't know where she was.

There was an altar in the middle of the room, and her first thought was that it looked like pictures she had seen of the Ark of the Covenant in the Old Testament. The ark was carved wood, possibly cedar, with two gold-winged cherubim on top. The ceiling was higher than in the Terrestial Room, maybe forty, fifty feet high. She was beneath the temple spire. Men in temple robes crowded the room.

Two other figures sat among them. Brother Joseph and her father.

The prophet sat with his hands tightly bound in front of him and his cane at his feet. A red welt raised on the side of his head, and his face looked gray. They had gagged Abraham Christianson with duct tape. He looked at her with a dark expression. Was it defiance? Defeat?

"Father."

There was another member of the Quorum in the room. Elder Kimball. Taylor Junior and Gideon's father. Her would-be father-in-law. He stood next to the altar, prepared to officiate the wedding.

"I should have known," she said. "All of this, everything. It's all your doing." She fixed Elder Kimball with a look of scorn. "Where is your pathetic son, then?"

"Son?" There was confusion in his voice.

It was a tone of voice she had not expected. It matched the bewildered look on his face. No triumph, no confidence. "Yes, Taylor Junior. Where is he?"

He licked his lips. "Ah, Taylor Junior." He made a sideways glance to the prophet, then looked away quickly. "You see, he's not here."

Gideon chuckled. "You thought you were going to marry Taylor Junior? That's funny. No, you're not marrying Taylor Junior. You'll be marrying my father's *other* son."

"Gideon," said Elder Kimball. "Son. This is too hasty. It's not time yet."

Gideon cut him off. "Be quiet, old man." A hint of violence colored his voice.

Elder Kimball blinked hard, but did not speak again.

Eliza stared at Gideon in growing horror. "You're the one who killed Amanda. You cut her throat. You are the murderer."

"It's not murder to cut down the enemies of God. The blood of the wicked must justify the souls of the righteous."

"And what? You'll kill the prophet, too?"

He looked shocked at the idea. "Why would I do that? The prophet always obeys the Lord's will." He turned to Aaron Young. "Bring her to the altar. And my *mother*." This last bit he said with a sneer.

Aaron Young dragged Eliza to the altar and forced her to her knees. They brought Charity to the altar and stood her to one side. It was she who would stand as witness for Gideon's character.

During this conversation and while they'd forced the two women to the front, the Lost Boys passed around a goblet, from which they drank deeply. When they'd finished, they handed it to Gideon, who took a wine bottle and filled the goblet a second time, then passed it back among the men.

Gideon knelt across from Eliza on the opposite side of the altar. Elder Kimball took his place to one side, uncertain, looking now to his son for his cues.

"What happened to Enoch?" she asked. She almost suffocated on the words as they came out of her mouth. "Please, you didn't hurt my brother. You wouldn't kill him."

"Come, Eliza," Gideon said. "Your cooperation is the only thing keeping your father alive." He hesitated. "And Enoch. Nobody will get hurt. Can we continue?"

"You're lying. There's blood on your robes. It's Enoch's, isn't it?" She thought she was going to be sick.

A cough from behind her. Eliza looked back at her father. He gave her another shake of the head. *Keep quiet.*

Yes, quiet. And she would obey. Because Eliza had a secret of her own to play out. Manuel and Eduardo had given her a wire to tape to her breastbone. She'd had to take it off when putting on the sheet for the initiatory, afraid that Fernie or someone would see what she was carrying. But nobody had touched her clothes when she'd returned, and she'd taped it back in place. She'd thought only to prove to the agents that she was being forced into marriage. They had much more reason to come now. What had they heard? More than enough.

With any luck, the FBI agents had picked up on the struggles in the Terrestial Room and even now were on their way here. That had been what? Ten minutes ago? If only she knew where in the temple they had taken her. She could tell them.

"Underneath the temple spire," she whispered.

Gideon turned toward her. "What did you say?"

"This isn't a sealing room, is it?" she asked him. "Why did you bring me here? What room is this? It has an oak door with a sunstone." She glanced up. "It looks like we're under the spire."

"Be quiet." Gideon looked at Elder Kimball. "Father?"

Elder Kimball cleared his throat. He addressed his son in a voice that began shakily, but gained strength as he continued. "Brother Kimball, do you take Sister Christianson by the right hand and receive her unto yourself to be your lawfully wedded wife, for time and all eternity, with a covenant and promise that you will observe and keep all the laws, rites, and ordinances pertaining to this holy order of matrimony in the new and everlasting covenant; and this you do in the presence of God, angels, and these witnesses of your own free will and choice?"

Gideon bowed his head and said, "Yes."

"Sister Christianson, do you take Brother Kimball by the right hand and give yourself to him to be his lawfully wedded wife, and receive him to be your lawfully wedded husband, for time and all eternity, with a covenant and promise that you will observe and keep all the laws, rites, and ordinances pertaining to this holy order of matrimony in the new and everlasting covenant; and this you do in the presence of God, angels, and these witnesses of your own free will and choice?"

Eliza said nothing.

Gideon smiled. "You will be the prophet's senior wife. A Kimball and a Christianson. Through you, my seed shall be as the dust of the earth."

"No, it won't," Eliza said.

He turned to one of the Lost Boys. "Israel, if she doesn't say yes in three seconds, cut Abraham Christianson's throat."

She blurted the word at once. "Yes."

A sham. It had no authority.

Elder Kimball said, "By virtue of the holy priesthood and the authority vested in me, I pronounce you, Brother Kimball and Sister Christianson, legally and lawfully husband and wife for time and all eternity; and I seal upon you the blessings of the holy resurrection, with power to come forth in the morning of the first resurrection, clothed in glory, immortality, and eternal lives.

"I seal upon you the blessings of kingdoms, thrones, principalities, powers, dominions, and exaltations, with all the blessings of Abraham, Isaac, and Jacob; and say unto you: be fruitful and

multiply and replenish the earth, that you may have joy and rejoic-
ing in the day of our Lord Jesus Christ.

"All these blessings, together with all the blessings appertaining
unto the new and everlasting covenant, I seal upon you by virtue of
the holy priesthood, through your faithfulness, in the name of the
Father, and of the Son, and of the Holy Ghost. Amen."

Gideon sprang to his feet. A strange glow lit his face. "It is
done."

"What now?" Elder Kimball asked.

"Now?" Gideon looked down at his new bride, still trembling on
her knees. "Now I will consummate my marriage with my beautiful
wife."

Elder Kimball stared at his son with horror. "Here? Now?"

"Are you deaf, old man? Yes, here. That way everyone will
know. There will be no mistake that Eliza is my wife. And I am the
new prophet."

"You're insane," Elder Kimball said.

Eliza flailed as Gideon and two of the outcasts grabbed her
hands and legs and threw her on top of the altar.

* * *

Fernie, Stephen Paul, and Jacob ran down the hallway toward the
Holy of Holies. Jacob could see the door, and he was certain now
that he would find the murderers inside with his sister.

"Hold it right there." It was a hard voice that left no argument.

The three stopped short and turned. It was the younger of the
two FBI agents. Eduardo, gun drawn. He emerged from one of the
offices they'd overlooked while running toward the sealing wing,
apparently conducting his own search. He wore a headset, held in

place by a nylon band. There was a microphone, and he spoke into it now. "Come back upstairs. I've got three of them."

Relief flooded through Jacob to see Eduardo instead of one of the Lost Boys. "They've taken my sister. She's just down this hall. Hurry. Please, we have to stop them."

The man watched Jacob warily. "What's the blood?" He didn't lower the gun, but used it to gesture at Jacob's clothing.

Jacob looked at the stains on his temple clothes. "My brother's." His throat was tight. "We got there too late. Please, you have to help. My sister is in there."

Stephen Paul said, "He's telling the truth. We need your help."

Eduardo looked from Jacob, to Stephen Paul, and then Fernie. He nodded. "Eliza is wearing a wire. They're forcing her into marriage, threats of violence, but it's a mess. What do you mean they killed your brother? Where? What the hell is going on?" He lowered the gun.

"They murdered him in the Celestial Room," Jacob said. "We've got to get to Eliza. They're in the Holy of Holies." He pointed. "Right there. Hurry."

"I don't understand," Fernie said. "Who is this? What are the Mexicans doing in here?"

Jacob said, "He's FBI. They're here to help."

Manuel arrived in a rush a moment later, carrying his own gun. Eduardo held up a hand to stop his partner. It took a few seconds for Jacob to explain as best he could what was happening and who was involved.

"How many men are we talking?" Manuel asked Jacob, voice low.

"At least three," Jacob whispered back. "Possibly more. They have a knife. Maybe a gun."

"Did you call for backup?" Manuel asked Eduardo.

"No signal."

"Bad cell coverage on this side of town," Jacob said.

Manuel said, "Yeah, we thought we were coming in here to rescue an unwilling bride, not face down a bunch of armed men."

"And my sister is in there. Be careful."

A nod, and then they advanced toward the Holy of Holies. Nobody spoke. They stopped in front of the door. "Stand back, all of you," Manuel whispered.

They stood outside the door, the FBI agents with weapons drawn and the other three standing two steps back. Eduardo and Manuel nodded at each other and then burst through the door.

CHAPTER TWENTY-FOUR

The two FBI agents held their guns steady.

Jacob couldn't see clearly past them into the dim light of the room, but there were numerous shapes inside, more than they'd expected.

"FBI! Step away from the girl!" Manuel shouted. "All of you get back."

When they did not get the hoped-for response, Eduardo and Manuel stepped carefully into the room with their guns held at the ready. Jacob and Stephen Paul advanced into the room behind them. Jacob could see now that there were a good dozen men in the room. Too many for two agents, armed or no.

Jacob's eyes adjusted to the dim light. Eliza lay sprawled across the altar in the middle of the room. Israel Young stood to one side her. Elder Kimball stood on the other side, next to his wife, Charity, her eyes swollen from crying. Gideon Kimball was crouched on the alter over Eliza, pinning her wrists.

Most of the others in the room were also Lost Boys, but there were two others sitting on the benches, bound. The only two not in temple robes. Father and Brother Joseph.

"You," Manuel said in a calm voice. He gestured with his gun at Gideon. "Let go of the girl. I *will* shoot."

Gideon hesitated, then nodded. He released her hands and stepped back.

Eliza stumbled from the altar. She looked shaken. And in that moment, Jacob saw Gideon shift slightly to his right. His hands did not move. His right leg twitched, as if stepping on something that Jacob could not see.

Light blossomed overhead like the sun. It drowned out the dim bulbs of the chandelier and radiated heat. Jacob threw up his arm to shield his eyes.

"The angel!" someone cried. The Lost Boys rose to their feet.

Other voices joined. "The angel. The angel has come!" The room erupted. Cries, movement.

Jacob did not think for a moment that the light came from an angel. He had seen that shift in Gideon's posture. The man had done this, and the first cry of, "The angel!" had come from him as well. Jacob was certain of it.

A gun discharged. A second shot. By then Jacob's eyes had adjusted enough that he could see Gideon and Israel fighting with the two FBI agents. The guns pointed at the ceiling. Some Lost Boys moved to help, even as others stared slack-jawed at the light on the ceiling.

Jacob looked for Eliza. There she was, helping Charity untie the hands of Brother Joseph and Abraham Christianson. He grabbed Stephen Paul, and together they forced a path through the Lost Boys toward the fight over the guns.

And then the mob fell upon Jacob. A pair of hands seized his wrist. It was a weak grip, and he jerked back his free arm and smashed his assailant in the face with his elbow. He tripped over a leg. Someone else grabbed him.

He turned to lash out at this new attacker.

"Jacob, it's me."

Brother Joseph. The prophet had gained his feet. He had taken Jacob's arm with duct-taped hands. Jacob blinked, only slowly recognizing the prophet through the noise and the lights.

"The cane, Jacob. Take it."

Brother Joseph's cane. It was solid oak and topped with a brass handle in the shape of a beehive. Jacob saw it now for what it was. Not a historical artifact or a family heirloom. Nor a staff for an old man. A weapon. He took it.

Jacob brained the first man who tried to stand against him. Another came forward, but he smashed this man in the nose with the brass beehive. Stephen Paul regained his feet, and together they cleared a path toward the main knot of fighting that surrounded the FBI agents.

And then everything went dark. Someone had cut the lights. Shouts. Confusion. Cries of dismay that the angel had abandoned them. Only gradually did Jacob regain his vision from the light that trickled into the room from the hallway.

Far from turning the battle against them, the loss of the light ended it. It was over even before Charity Kimball found the dimmer switch on the ground and turned the chandelier back on.

Manuel and Eduardo forced men to their bellies. Stephen Paul pushed another down, and Jacob's father and the prophet bound a man's hands with his own temple sash.

Eduardo bled from one shoulder. Jacob looked down to see fresh blood sprayed across his own clothes. The recipient of one of his blows with the cane lay on the floor, clutching his nose. Blood streamed down his face.

There was no sign of Gideon and Israel among the men on the floor. Jacob looked frantically for his sister. She too was gone.

"They've taken Eliza," he said. He rushed into the hallway and looked each way. No sign of the two men or his sister. They'd fled during the confusion.

"My husband is gone, too," Charity Kimball said.

Jacob looked around for Elder Kimball and saw that she was right. How many others had slipped away?

While the FBI agents finished binding the Lost Boys with their temple sashes, Stephen Paul propped his brother Aaron against the altar. "Where did they take her?"

The man shook his head with a glazed expression. "Take who?"

Jacob looked from face to face among the Lost Boys. They all wore the same vacant expression. There was a wine goblet overturned by the altar, and Jacob blinked in surprise. They had been drinking. They looked drunk, or even drugged. No wonder the battle had ended so quickly once their "angel" abandoned them.

Stephen Paul tried again. "Gideon and Israel. Where did they go?"

"They left the temple," someone said. It was Eric Froud, bleeding from his lip.

Jacob pushed his way to Eric's side. "How?"

"The desert. We always come and go through the desert. Witch's Warts."

*   *   *

Eliza didn't stop struggling even as Israel and Gideon bound her hands behind her back with her temple veil and her feet with the sashes from the men's temple robes. She kept struggling as they carried her through the halls of the temple. But they were too strong.

They ran into Elder Kimball just before they reached the back door. He stared at Gideon but shrank against the wall.

"Elder Kimball," she begged as her two captors rushed past. "Help me."

But the coward did nothing.

Now outside, Israel carried her over his shoulder as they made their way into the maze of sandstone fins and hoodoos stretching beyond the temple. They hit Witch's Warts at an angle, doubled back on their own trail twice, and crossed through the narrow gap where Amanda's body had been discovered last week. Eliza could still see the stones that had held the tarp in place and the disturbed sand, only partially smoothed over by the rain.

At first she thought the two men were lost. She could feel the hesitation in Israel's body as she rode over his shoulder. He was following Gideon, and perhaps the other man was similarly confused.

"Just run," she urged them. "Put me down and run. I'll slow you down. Put me down and you can get away."

"Yes, go ahead and put her down," Gideon said. "Put her down and I'll bash her fucking head in. How does that sound, Eliza? No? Then shut up."

They weren't lost. Gideon had just taken time to walk through the area closest to the temple, already confused with multiple sets of footprints. Disguising the trail. He soon led them out of the sand and onto the bare rock. It was a low-lying hump of stone that gashed into the middle of Witch's Warts, and when it sank back into the ground some thirty yards further, it ended just before another lip of stone. Gideon jumped over the sandy gap. Israel passed her across to Gideon and then took her back a moment later. They continued over stone.

The two stopped briefly when they emerged onto sand again a couple of minutes later. Israel dropped her to the ground while the men stripped off their temple robes and stuffed them behind a boulder.

They'd only been in the open for ten minutes, but already sweat drenched their clothes. Israel bent to pick up Eliza, still dressed in white, except for the green apron.

She said, "Just let me go. You don't have to do this. It doesn't make sense."

Israel turned to Gideon. "She's right. What's the point of this?"

"Of what?" Gideon snapped.

"The girl. Let's leave her."

Gideon scowled. "You know what the point is. She's my wife."

"No, I'm not, you bastard," Eliza said.

Israel said, "Your so-called wife is slowing us down. I don't know if this is a pissing match with your father or if it has something to do with Jacob Christianson. Or maybe even Taylor Junior. Doesn't matter. There are two armed gentiles back there. Not to mention Jacob and my cousin. We can move twice as fast without her."

"She's not going back."

"She doesn't have to go back," Israel said. "We're close now to where we left the old man."

"What old man?" she asked. She felt a fresh surge of terror.

In response, Gideon yanked off her shoes, tossed them to one side, and then stripped off her socks. He tied the socks together and then used them to gag her.

Israel said, "We've got to go. And we can't take the girl."

Gideon blinked at Israel without answering, then turned and slammed his fist into the sandstone wall. He turned with his face shaking with anger and blood streaming from his knuckles. A moment later he was as calm as ever.

"You're right," he said at last. Voice measured. He wiped his knuckles on his shirt. "Pick her up. We'll dump her in the sinkhole."

* * *

The trail grew jumbled at the edge of Witch's Warts. Kids often played along its outskirts, and Jacob himself had added to the confusion as he'd wandered around, looking for clues to Amanda's murder. There were too many footprints to decipher.

Abraham Christianson and Brother Joseph had remained in the temple with Fernie and Charity. The prophet had called one of his sons to join them. The Lost Boys were drugged and now bound; Jacob didn't expect further trouble from them.

Jacob found the presence of the two FBI agents comforting, together with the determined figure of Stephen Paul Young by his side. Together they faced Gideon, Israel, and possibly Elder Kimball, burdened with Eliza. But their enemies knew Witch's Warts. Jacob did not.

Eduardo had his cell phone out, trying to get a signal. "Still no service," he told his partner.

Manuel turned to Jacob. "You know the country better than we do, and what these guys might be thinking. What's your call?"

Jacob considered. "Witch's Warts goes all the way to the Ghost Cliffs and is what? Two miles wide?"

Stephen Paul nodded. "More or less. We always say eighteen square miles. You can get lost inside, that's for damn sure."

Manuel said, "But unless they're planning to live in here, they've got to have an exit."

"There's a ranch road that hits the east side," Jacob said. He turned toward Stephen Paul for confirmation. "Could be there that they plan to come out. Anywhere else to stash a car?"

Stephen Paul shook his head. "Not that I can think of. But that road still leaves a good three miles to search. By the time we look up and down every ravine and dry wash where they might have hidden their car, we'll have lost an hour."

"Say we go find a cell signal," Jacob asked the agents, "and you call for backup. How long are we talking?"

Manuel shook his head. "An hour and a half, if we're lucky. Nearest agents are in Cedar City. But we could probably get the Garfield County sheriff here in thirty, forty minutes."

Jacob stared into the maze of stone and sand, trying to figure how long it would take Gideon and Israel to get through. They'd be burdened with Eliza. Still, to get law enforcement here and seal off the road from both directions would take a minimum of an hour. Maybe longer.

Manuel seemed to come to the same conclusion. "Too long." He turned to Eduardo. "And we don't have time to fool around looking for a signal anyway."

Jacob looked to Stephen Paul. "Take your truck. Find others to help, if you can do it quickly."

Stephen Paul said, "After what my brother did, I don't know who to trust."

"Members of the Quorum. And women. You'll have to take your chances. Get as many cars on that ranch road as possible. Block it off. The three of us will go after them on foot." He glanced at the two FBI agents. "What do you think?"

Manuel gave a curt nod. "Right. Let's do it."

Stephen Paul turned at once and rushed off. The one man among them who knew the area. Jacob eyed the sky and the rapidly dipping sun to the west. Gideon and Israel would be burdened, and trying not to leave tracks. Jacob could waste time looking for those tracks or cut in a straight line toward the ranch road, then look for tracks once he got far enough in. That meant remembering the position of the sun in the sky or he would get lost.

He turned to the FBI agents. "Ready?"

* * *

Eliza had only one more chance. She had to make it count. A scream, a blow, something at the right moment. In the meanwhile, all she could do was delay.

She shifted her weight to make herself as heavy to Israel as possible. Her hands, bound behind her back, had been working at the green apron at her waist. She could at least drop it to signal their passage. She at last untied the apron's knot, but didn't let it fall. Not yet.

Gideon and Israel stopped where a fissure separated two conjoined sandstone fins. Working together, the two men hauled her up the stone, panting and cursing. As they climbed, they pushed past a juniper tree high on the bald slope. She felt the apron snag on a branch, and let go of the strings. Neither of the men saw what she had done.

They reached the sinkhole. The rain had filled it with water. The surface sat smooth and quiet. The stone curved up around the sinkhole like clay on a potter's wheel, shaped by fingers of water and wind. It was here that they meant to murder her.

Israel dropped her to the ground. The men gathered loose rocks and broke off flakes of sandstone, which they stuffed into her robes and down her dress. Gideon shoved her into a seated position at the base of the sinkhole, with the water to her back. He pulled the gag from her mouth.

"This is your chance to plead for mercy," he said.

"Go to hell."

He looked disappointed in her response. "It could have turned out differently, Eliza. I didn't want to kill you." He shrugged. "Well, these things happen. It might take a few years to recover from this setback."

"There will be no recovering. My brother will kill you."

"Why do you always argue with them?" Israel asked Gideon. "Just do it."

Gideon's voice changed. "Eliza Christianson, we now seal thee unto death. May the Lord have mercy upon thy soul."

He reached for her, and Eliza leaned forward as if she would resist. Instead, she prepared to fall back when he pushed. Off-balance, he might stumble into the water after her. Maybe she could grab his clothes as the stones pulled her down.

Suddenly he stopped and looked down with a frown. "Where's your apron?" He looked behind him, then back at Eliza. "Where the hell is her apron?"

"Did she have it when we left the temple?" Israel asked.

"Of course she had it. The only thing green on a white dress. Don't you think I'd have noticed?"

Eliza smiled. "You'll never find it. And that's not the only thing I did," she lied. "I've left other clues along the way. They'll find you easily."

Gideon whirled to face Israel. "Quickly. Go look. But don't go far. We don't have time."

Israel made his way back down the fissure. Eliza had bought little time. He'd find that apron in about ten seconds.

Gideon jerked Eliza to her feet. She found it difficult to stand straight with the stones weighing down her clothes. He put his hands around her neck and choked. She gasped, but couldn't breathe. He released his grip. "Where did you put it?"

"And if I don't tell you? What are you going to do? Murder me?"

"Shame I have to kill you," Gideon said. "You'd be an interesting challenge." He started to squeeze again.

"Found it!" Israel shouted from just beyond view. "She left it on the juniper bush just down the slope."

Gideon released his grip and smiled at Eliza. "There, what did that accomplish?"

A gunshot. Shouts.

Gideon turned toward the sound. Almost as quickly, he turned back to Eliza. But she did not waste the moment. He stood too close, right on the edge of the sinkhole with her, where the stone was smooth from centuries of erosion by wind and water. She drove her shoulder into his. He stumbled, flailing for balance. Eliza gave him one more shove, and he fell into the water with a splash.

Eliza dropped to her knees at the lip of the sinkhole and watched.

Gideon thrashed at the water below her. He came up on the near side, but the lip was too high to pull himself out. So he paddled to the far side, where the edge was lower. He started to pull himself from the water, sputtering and cursing.

Still on her knees, Eliza pulled a chunk of stone from the front of her dress. She lifted it over her head, took aim, and hurled it at Gideon's head. The man was only about five feet below her, and not much further away laterally. Hard to miss. The stone struck him a glancing blow on the temple. He fell back to the water.

No chances.

She found a bigger stone on the ground, a sheared-off piece of sandstone so big she lifted it only with difficulty. Gideon bobbed up. She didn't wait to see if he was unconscious. This rock flew down and struck him squarely on the head.

Another gunshot sounded over her shoulder. A moment later, Jacob and the two FBI agents scrambled into the bowl.

"Are you okay?" Jacob asked as he hurried to her side. Eduardo bent to untie her hands while Manuel scanned around the sinkhole for others.

All eyes looked down at Gideon. He floated facedown in the water. Blood spread across the surface. The three men bent over the edge and fished out his body. The second stone had caved in his skull.

Eliza felt stricken. "I killed him."

"Good for you," Jacob said as he pushed Gideon's body to one side with a look of disgust. "Israel is dead, too. Elder Kimball?"

"Not here. We passed him in the temple, but he didn't come with us."

It was then that they saw through the clear water and saw a second body at the bottom of the sinkhole. The men went into the water to retrieve it. Weighted down with stones, it took all three to pull him out.

It was Elder Griggs. Jacob's grandfather.

CHAPTER TWENTY-FIVE

"Let's get one thing clear," Manuel said, his tone firm. "This is a courtesy meeting only. A chance for you to clear your heads and make the wise decision."

Eliza sat between her brother and her father, with Brother Joseph to Jacob's left. The FBI agents were all business now, sitting confidently on the other side of the table, but if they thought that the members of the church would fold before the authority of the badges they had taken pains to show, they would soon learn otherwise.

Jacob, Eduardo, and Manuel had laid the three bodies together at the sinkhole, then returned to the temple. Brother Joseph's sons had arrived in the meanwhile, together with more members of the Quorum of the Twelve to take temporary custody of the living conspirators.

It was here, less than an hour after the deaths of Gideon and Israel, that the situation had begun to break down. Manuel and Eduardo had prepared to call for backup. Brother Joseph and Abraham Christianson had insisted that they would not cooperate if the agents did so. Manuel shot back that cooperation was unnecessary. Jacob suggested a meeting in the office of the temple president.

As the meeting began, Jacob had told the others everything he knew. Eliza reeled when she learned how the Lost Boys had kidnapped infant girls to bring to Zion. And Sophie Marie was one of these children. Even the FBI agents had looked stunned by what Jacob told them.

"Of course we want to do the right thing," Abraham Christianson said after the FBI agents delivered their warning. "This has been a terrible business, and the sooner we put it behind us, the better. On that, I'm sure we're in agreement. But it appears we have different ideas of how to do so."

"Our position is nonnegotiable," Manuel said. "You can cooperate or you can face charges for obstruction of justice." He fixed each man with a stare in turn, then directed his gaze to Eliza. She refused to flinch. "There might even be accessory to murder charges."

Eduardo stepped in. "I'm sure it won't come to that." He spoke in Manuel's direction, though Eliza knew the words were meant for them. "Everyone in this room understands that we need to take care of the bodies, to look after the wounded, to investigate the crime scene while it's fresh. Get statements, check for fingerprints, et cetera."

Eliza's father said, "Look, I'm not trying to be difficult. I'm really not. First, you have no idea how grateful I am that you helped save my daughter's life." He leaned forward. "But from my point of view it looks like everything is wrapped up."

"You know better than that, Mr. Christianson."

"Do I? The murderers are dead. The others—accessories, as you might call them—are in custody. But does it matter the words we use to punish them? Couldn't they be tried for other charges?"

"And you're suggesting," Manuel said, "that we keep all of this quiet from the outside world?"

"That's exactly what I'm suggesting. My son told me you came to investigate fraud, and you found it. Isn't that enough to put away Elder Kimball and his Lost Boys?"

"You can't be serious," Manuel said. His astonishment didn't seem feigned this time. "We killed two men out there. My partner shot one of them. He took a knife to the shoulder. And there's the old man from the sinkhole and the man cut open in the temple. That makes four dead bodies, not even counting Eliza's cousin Amanda, murdered by these thugs. And that's just the start! Jacob says there are murders in New Mexico and California. And kidnapped children—what about that?"

"They killed my son," Abraham Christianson said in a tight voice. "You don't think I want to see justice served?"

"Fine. You can't hide this. Why would you want to?"

Abraham Christianson said, "You know what happens if the outside world hears of this, don't you? The media will descend like a plague of locusts. We've seen it before. They love a juicy polygamist story. They'll camp in front of every house, school, and church. Not just here but in Alberta and Montana. Every apostate, polygamist crusader, and anti-Mormon will come out of the woodwork. We're already vulnerable. The extra attention will tear us to pieces."

"Not our problem," Manuel said. "And most certainly not our fault."

"I never said it was. But it's *our* problem."

"And you're suggesting what as an alternative?" Manuel asked. "A massive cover-up?"

"The question is not whether or not we're going to cover this up. I prefer to think of it as keeping our own business private. The question is whether you will make this difficult for all parties."

"You can't cover this up," Manuel insisted.

"You'd be surprised," Abraham Christianson said. "You can't even confirm the identities of the dead men without our help. And for all you know, we've moved the bodies already. Are you going to throw us all in prison until you get what you want? Because I'm pretty sure that's a media storm that *you* don't want. Surely you've heard of the Short Creek raid."

Eliza had grown up hearing stories of the raids on the Short Creek polygamist settlement in the 1950s. The national media had published photos of screaming children pulled from their mothers' arms. Fifty years later and the authorities were still hesitant to go after polygamist communities.

The two agents looked furious. Manuel said, "What, are you an independent kingdom, above any laws? You just do whatever you want?"

"What *God* wants," Brother Joseph corrected, speaking for the first time. "And yes, we are a kingdom. The Kingdom of God on earth."

The two men looked at each other, and Eliza could see the confusion at being thwarted in their legitimate duties. Confusion and
anger. And Eliza thought it was a dangerous game her father played.
The government could come down on them hard. But something else had occurred to her. Something her father didn't know
about.

Jacob, who had remained quiet during this exchange, caught
Eliza's eye. He gave a significant glance toward the door. He wanted
to talk to her alone. She gave a slight nod in response.

Jacob rose to his feet. "Father, Brother Joseph, I have to talk to
Eliza alone. Will you excuse us please?"

"Right now, Jacob?" Father asked.

"Yes, now. Just a minute."

Alone, in the hallway, Jacob asked Eliza, "You have something.
What is it?"

She hesitated. It didn't feel right. Eduardo and Manuel had
saved her life.

"It was Eduardo that night."

"What night? When?"

"When Taylor Junior attacked me and I tried to tell you why I
thought God was punishing me. It was Eduardo that I saw. I kissed
him. I let him touch me."

"Ah, I see."

"I told him I was eighteen," Eliza said. "He doesn't know that
I'm seventeen. You know what I mean?"

She could see Jacob thinking, weighing the ramifications. "Yes,
I see. Seventeen-year-old girl. FBI agent seducing a naïve polygamist girl. For sex or to further the investigation, who cares? We'd

tell the media and it would explode. The threat of it, I think, might make these two back off."

It was along the lines of what she'd been thinking, but she didn't like hearing it voiced. It felt wrong. "Should we do it?"

Jacob said, "Liz, Father's right. This story will be huge. It has everything to attract the media sharks. Pregnant women murdered. Secret eugenics programs. A polygamist sect and its secrets. It might be better for the church if we covered it up."

Only he didn't sound like he thought it would be better. He sounded like he thought it would be worse. "Unless...?"

"Unless we're going to do the right thing. That's what it comes down to, Liz."

"It might be the end of the church if we tell the truth," Eliza said.

"Maybe. Hopefully, we'll be strong enough to weather the storm."

"Then we have to do it. We have to tell the truth. And go against Father."

"He'll get over it."

She hesitated. "Okay, I'm ready if you are."

They returned to their room and took their seats. Jacob looked right at Manuel. "Here's our proposal."

"Jacob?" Father said. "What are you doing?"

"We'll cooperate with the murder investigation. And the fraud investigation. All we ask are a few small conditions."

Father sat bolt upright. "You are *not* in a position to speak for us!"

Manuel held up his palm to their father. "We want to hear this."

"What are you talking about, Jacob?" Father asked. "What possible reason do we have for cooperating?"

"Most simply, because we should tell the truth."

Father said, "The truth? Yes, for those who are ready to hear it. But in cases like this, not everything that is true is useful."

"A morally bankrupt point of view, Dad."

Father asked, "Didn't you hear what I said? The media frenzy will eat us alive. There will be gentiles living on our doorstep. Media, law enforcement. All manner of unsavory individuals. They'll come to White Valley and Harmony, too. Not just Blister Creek."

"And then what?" Jacob asked.

"Apostates will appear on TV to air their grievances. Church members will doubt. Finger pointing. Gentiles will mock our sacred rituals and claim we're abusing our people."

"And then what?"

"Many saints will fall away."

"Some, but not all," Jacob conceded. "Is that all?"

"Is that all? Are you insane, Jacob?" In spite of his words, a subtle change had taken place between the two men. It was Father pleading with his son, not the other way around. "That is everything."

Eliza said, "Father, even the worst trials come to an end."

"And we don't have a choice," Jacob said. "You want to pick a fight with the federal government? There's no way to win that fight. And I guarantee you, even if we *could* get away with it, we can't just pretend this never happened. Then it will never go away. But above all, Dad, it's the right thing to do, and every person in this room knows it."

Abraham Christianson looked angry enough to burst, but Brother Joseph put a hand on his arm and murmured a few soothing words to him.

The prophet then turned to Jacob. "If we do this, Jacob, will you be our representative? Will you speak to the media and direct our efforts with law enforcement?"

"Of course, Brother Joseph."

Brother Joseph turned back to Abraham Christianson. "My dear friend, your son is right." He shook his head. "It's the honest thing to do. And the best way to put these terrible events behind us."

Father still didn't agree. Eliza could see that on his face and knew this was a fight they would have to win later. He had not surrendered, but he had retreated from the battlefield.

"What are your conditions?" Manuel asked. He still sounded suspicious.

Eduardo was looking at Eliza again, and she could see new respect in the man's eyes. That look gave her a twinge of guilt. He didn't know how close she had come to turning her back on him. If Jacob had pushed, she would have poisoned everything by claiming that Eduardo had taken advantage of her.

Jacob said, "First, the kidnapped girls. Will you allow us to return the girls to their families before the media gets involved?"

Manuel nodded, but it looked like a nod of understanding, not agreement. "Anything else?"

"Yes," he said. "I'd like to convince Elder Kimball to cooperate with the investigation. He's one of the ringleaders, but I don't believe he sanctioned the murders. Let him surrender and we can almost certainly find every single one of the conspirators."

And Taylor Junior? Eliza wondered. *Could he not be involved as well?*

But it didn't matter, did it? Elder Kimball was disgraced. His family, tragic as that may be for people like Fernie and Charity, was disgraced as well, from top to bottom. There would be no marriage (second marriage, if you could consider the horror with Gideon to be a first) with the Kimball family.

"If you can do that," Jacob added, "I can almost guarantee that the Lost Boys will cooperate."

"How will you do that?"

"Securing Elder Kimball's cooperation is the key. He'll command the others to obey. You'll get prison terms for every man involved."

"What, are you a lawyer now?" Manuel asked.

"You're right, I'm not."

"Can you give us a minute?" Manuel and Eduardo stood and retreated to a corner of the room where they conversed in low voices for several minutes in Spanish. At last they returned to the table.

"Here's the thing," Manuel said. "We can't make a deal like this, not on our own. Something this big might need to go all the way up to the deputy director. But if you come through, we can propose an arrangement."

"What kind of arrangement?" Jacob said.

"We'll contact the families. You can deliver the children under FBI supervision. Meanwhile, we keep the investigation low-key, but not for long. It's our butts on the line if we wait too long to call in help."

"Sounds fair," Jacob said. "How long do we have?"

"Twelve hours. Provided you find Mr. Kimball and secure his cooperation. Otherwise, all bets are off."

* * *

Elder Kimball's head had cleared as he fled through the halls of the temple. He had come late to the Holy of Holies and found that the Lost Boys had already taken most of the wine. He'd only consumed a few sips and had been less muddled than usual during the ceremony. And so he hadn't seen the angel, just a bright light.

He'd escaped in the commotion. And when Gideon and Israel Young ran past holding Eliza, he shrank against the wall.

My son is dead. If they haven't killed him yet, they soon will.

The truth was, Gideon had been dying for some time. Suicide in slow motion.

And everything that Kimball had thought about Gideon was wrong. What he had taken for contrition had been a scheming obsequiousness. What he had taken for obedience, subterfuge. Gideon had intended nothing less than a complete takeover. Only a blind man would not have seen it.

Or a father.

All his work, carefully building the seeds for genetic domination within the church—and ultimately, the world at large—had come to a grinding halt with Gideon's overreach. Personal greed had destroyed everything.

And you brought Gideon in. You gave him power.

Elder Kimball made his way to the Celestial Room. And found Enoch.

The young man lay dead on the ground. Butchered in the most savage way. They had taken his entrails to feed to the birds and the beasts. His son had done this.

Elder Kimball buried his face in his hands.

"Taylor Kimball."

He turned, and there, standing over Enoch's body, was the angel. He floated several inches off the floor. He held his sword in his left hand, a black, shadowy thing. He raised his right arm to the square and said, "The Lord is greatly displeased, Taylor Kimball. Because of thy cowardice, the enemy has thwarted the will of God. Thou art hereby rebuked for thy disobedience."

You're not real, he thought as he shrank back. *You never existed.*

But he was doubting the words even as they came to his mind. A finger of terror twisted around his heart.

"And what would you have me do?" he asked.

"To regain the favor of the Lord, you must obey my commands or face eternal damnation. You must fly from this place at once. Go to Las Vegas, to Gideon's apartment. There, you will receive further instructions."

And Elder Kimball realized that whether or not the angel was just his own madness or something real, he was certain of one thing: It was not an angel of the Lord. And if he let it rule him now, he'd never escape.

Slowly, with a quiver in his voice, he held out a trembling hand to the angel. "Will you shake my hand to seal our agreement on this matter?"

If it be the devil as an angel of light, when you ask him to shake hands he will offer you his hand, and you will not feel anything; you may therefore detect him.

The angel grew angry. "Do not tempt the Lord thy God."

"Shake my hand," he insisted. He held out his hand. "Shake it. Shake it if you are real."

The angel held out his hand. Elder Kimball reached forward before he could lose his nerve. There was a cold sensation, like icy water flowing around his hand. And then nothing, just the air. He withdrew his hand and lifted his own right hand to the square. "And now I rebuke thee. Get thee hence, Satan."

The light faded. The shadow departed with it. Elder Kimball bent to the ground, weeping over Enoch's body.

"Taylor?" It was Charity. She had come up behind him and put a hand on his shoulder. He tried to shield her from Enoch's body, but she had already seen. She looked away with her face pale. But Charity was a strong woman. She looked back at him a moment later.

He looked her in the eyes. "Why are you here?"

"I came to find you. To stop you from whatever it was you came to do. You're not well." She gave him a hard look. "In any sense of the word. The only thing for it now is to go back and face your responsibilities. You must think of the church and of your family."

"The church? My family? What does that mean to me? Brother Joseph will excommunicate me. Yes, he will. And I deserve it."

They both knew what that would mean. Excommunication would dissolve his sealings. His wives would be given to other, more faithful men. His children, sealed to new fathers. Elder Kimball knew he should kill himself instead.

"It's not over," Charity said. She took his face in her hands, and he saw real kindness there. It was something he didn't deserve. "Will your children remember you as a coward? A man who refused to admit his errors, even as his people drove him from Zion?"

"Does it matter?"

"Of course it does. There's still time to earn a small measure of redemption. Help them. Tell them everything you know. Settle Amanda's death. Punish the guilty. Even if you number among them. Admit your sins and beg forgiveness."

Kimball bowed his head in shame. "They'll never forgive me."

"You don't know that. And it doesn't matter. Because your family will see your example. I know that you don't think much of your sons, but some of them are on the cusp of manhood. They could go either way, follow their sisters' examples, or turn out like Gideon and Taylor Junior. You can still influence them."

He looked down at Enoch's body. He'd long wished for sons like Abraham Christianson's, but in the end, Abraham's son had fallen, too. Enoch had been corrupted by the same madness that had taken hold of the others.

At last he lifted his head and nodded. "Okay. I'll go."

CHAPTER TWENTY-SIX

It was a terrible business, wrenching babies from the arms of their mothers. The women had taken the girls without knowing their origins. They had been gifts from God, presented by Elder Kimball as rescued orphans from Romania, and he'd told the mothers to keep them secret. That they belonged to some other family, that they had been brutally acquired, did not ease the pain of losing those children.

Eliza's heart broke for the women.

Tess, who everyone had assumed had either been one of Elder Kimball's favorites, or had simply become pregnant very easily, lost two of her three children. One of the girls was almost five, and the other only eight months. Tess had begged and pleaded, had threatened to kill herself if they took her children, and had even tried to flee in the middle of the night for parts unknown.

She had been brought to Brother Joseph, who had spoken to her, given her a blessing, and told her that it was the Lord's will that the girls be returned to their biological families. In the end, Tess had gone with Jacob and Eliza to New Mexico and California, and when the time came, had handed over the children herself.

Finally, there was Sophie Marie. She was four. Old enough to understand a little of what had happened. Gideon had killed her mother, but the girl still loved her aunties and her many siblings. It was the only life she had known.

Jacob, Eliza, and Fernie drove Sophie Marie to the Bay Area. It was a long, uneasy trip. They would spend the night in San Jose before rising the next day for the meeting with Sophie Marie's biological aunt and her husband.

Something passed between Fernie and Jacob during the drive from Utah. Eliza had picked up on it less than five minutes from Blister Creek. They were awkward when they spoke to each other and always conscious of Eliza in the car with them.

"He said he could see through the veil," Jacob said without warning somewhere in the middle of the sagebrush expanse that was Nevada.

"Who saw what through the veil?" Eliza asked from the back seat, where she took her turn sitting next to Sophie Marie.

Jacob turned off the radio. "Enoch. He said that to me when I found him dying in the Celestial Room."

"He could see the other side," Fernie said. "He was dying, and so he probably saw people waiting on the other side.

"He said he saw his grandpa," Jacob said.

"It must have been his Grandpa Griggs," Fernie said. "Gideon killed him, too, and so he came back to welcome Enoch through to the other side."

"But he also said he was forgiven. The blood atonement stuff is nonsense. The only covenants he violated were the evil ones. He'd repented of that the moment he decided to turn against Gideon and the other Lost Boys."

Eliza thought about this. "Did he specifically say anything about blood atonement or breaking his promises to the Lost Boys?"

"No," Jacob said.

"Then maybe he was talking about something else," Fernie said.

"Maybe," Jacob said. Like always, he didn't sound convinced. "I keep wondering if he really saw something or if he was hallucinating."

Eliza thought this was more about Jacob wrestling with the death of his brother than from any lingering mystery. He couldn't let it go. She said, "He was dying, Jacob. Either the next world was right there or he was thinking about it."

"I can't help thinking he was trying to tell me something, is all." He reached over and turned the radio back on. "Maybe it doesn't matter."

That night, they took two rooms at a Motel Six. Eliza and Fernie turned on the television in their room. They watched a show that starred a dozen women and a man living in a house together. The women degraded themselves on camera for the affections of the lone man. At the end of the series, the man would marry one of the women. While the women bickered, gossiped, and backstabbed each other, the man stood aloof, feigning interest in each of the women, and sorrow when he had to send one of them home. The more vacuous the woman, the more artificial her appearance and manner, the more interested in her the man seemed.

"Here's the solution," Eliza said. "He can marry them all. Problem solved."

Fernie sat on her bed with her head propped against the pillows. She turned with her mouth quirked into a half smile. "Sister wives. I like it. That'll put an end to the bickering, eh?"

Eliza laughed. She found that she liked her sister's dry sense of humor. It reminded her of Mother.

"So you've narrowly avoided marriage," Fernie said, turning off the television. "Elder Johnson dead, Stephen Paul Young uninterested, and Taylor Junior is nowhere to be found. What now?"

Taylor Kimball Jr., that pasty-white, raspy-voiced weasel, and the architect of his father's fraudulent activities, had disappeared. He'd stolen money from the church, had filed fraudulent tax returns for his father's wives, claiming them as single mothers with lots of dependents, and had organized a string of dummy bank accounts, most of which the FBI had punctured, but not before Taylor Junior had cleared out several of them to the tune of hundreds of thousands of dollars.

The FBI was looking for him, but since he'd apparently been uninvolved in the murders, he was not a high priority. More important was tracking down a handful of Lost Boys who'd fled for Las Vegas. With Elder Kimball's assistance, authorities were arresting the remaining conspirators one by one.

"I don't know," Eliza said. "Jacob is a member of the Quorum now. Father is still simmering over what happened when we met the FBI agents, but I don't think he can pressure Jacob anymore about marrying me off. I've got a few more years, anyway. Maybe I'll go to college." It was an exciting thought, albeit only half formed.

"Sounds great. I wish I'd had that opportunity." Fernie shrugged. "Maybe someday. Life, I've discovered, is a lot longer than you think it is when you're a teenager."

Eliza watched. She got the impression that her sister had something else she wanted to talk about.

"I need your advice, Liz." Fernie had picked up on Jacob's nickname for Eliza somewhere in Nevada. "You know my husband is going to prison. Could be ten years before he gets out on parole, according to Manuel Cardoza. Maybe longer."

"Yes, I'm sorry."

"He's lucky it's not for life. They could have charged him with murder. Probably made it stick." Fernie shrugged. "Question is, what do I do in the meanwhile?"

"You're wondering if you should wait for your husband?"

"Well, you know that with his temple ordinances dissolved, he's no longer technically my husband. I am currently the unmarried mother of three. But Brother Joseph said that if my husband returns humble from prison, he'll be allowed back into the community."

"Really? I'd think he'd go the way of the Lost Boys."

"Oh, he'll never be a leader again," Fernie said. "But he's got children. And wives who are still faithful members. Charity is waiting for him. So are Clara Sue and Dolores. I don't think the others will." Fernie stroked the hair of Sophie Marie, who slept on her bed.

"And you?" Eliza asked.

She looked up and her eyes were shining. "Brother Joseph said I could choose a new husband. Can you believe that, *choose?*

Would it be disloyal not to wait? I mean, that seems wrong. But then I thought that maybe the Lord is offering me the chance to be happy."

Eliza studied Fernie. There was a flush on the woman's face, and Eliza saw a new facet to her sister. She was not just an older sister, or a mother, or some man's eighth wife. Fernie was a woman. Fernie was in love. And not with her husband. "Who is he?"

Fernie looked at her carefully. "You mean you don't know?"

Eliza didn't have to think very hard to piece it together. It explained so much about Jacob's behavior, for one, as well as the strange vibes she'd picked up between Jacob and Fernie on the drive from Utah.

"Jacob."

Fernie hesitated, and when she spoke again, she sounded anxious. "Would you be able to accept that? I mean, it's weird from your perspective, having your brother and sister marry each other, even if they're not related to each other by blood."

It would bring Eliza's relationship with her brother and her sister full circle in a way incomprehensible to the outside world. And Jacob was in the Quorum now. How long before they pressed him to take a second wife, then a third? Fernie and Jacob's moment of happiness might be just that, a moment.

Eliza came over to Fernie's bed and gave her sister a hug. "So you'll be both my sister and my sister-in-law. Yeah, that's weird." She hesitated. "But I'm okay with weird if you are."

"Thanks, Liz."

* * *

They rose early. Jacob drove through the streets of Berkeley while Fernie navigated with a map. They stopped the car at a park. Eliza and Fernie took Sophie Marie by the hand.

They dressed like gentiles, Jacob in slacks and a button-down shirt, Fernie and Eliza in jeans and long-sleeved blouses. The women had braided their hair, so that it wasn't simply free-flowing to their waists and at least semi-modern in appearance. Eliza had never worn pants before; they felt uncomfortable and immodest. Eliza would have attracted more attention in her ankle-length, wrist-length dress. Still, she fought the sensation that she was walking through the park in her underwear.

Eliza spotted Eduardo and Manuel standing by a black Ford Expedition. They'd come separately and quietly to the park to verify that the hand-off happened as promised. They were too far away for her to see their faces. She found herself wondering what Eduardo thought of her now, if he had pleasant memories about that kiss in the trailer or if he thought about it with guilt and embarrassment. She was surprised to discover that she felt no shame when she turned over the incident in her own mind.

A young couple waited for them on a bench next to the playground. The sister of Sophie Marie's biological mother and the woman's husband. The couple had a six-year-old son who had just started kindergarten, according to Jacob.

They stood up when the three of them approached with Sophie Marie. They looked wary, even though Eliza knew that the FBI had called and briefed them on the exchange.

"Mr. and Mrs. Dennings?" Jacob asked. "I'm Jacob Christianson. The one Mr. Cardoza told you about."

The woman looked down at Sophie Marie. "Oh my God, she looks just like Sarah," she said to her husband. "It must be her."

Eliza and Fernie let go of Sophie Marie's hands.

The woman hesitated, then picked up Sophie Marie. The girl looked back at Fernie, trusting, not yet afraid. That would change, Eliza knew, when they got in the car and drove away. Poor child.

"You remember what I said, sweetheart?" Fernie said to Sophie Marie. "This woman is like one of your aunties." She stroked the girl's hair. "You'll be with her for a little while."

"Okay."

"The girl's name is Sophie Marie," Fernie said. "At least that's what her mother—I mean, the woman who was taking care of her—named her."

Jacob looked back to the woman and her husband. He held out a parcel wrapped in brown paper that he'd carried from the car. "There are people who love Sophie Marie. We wanted to send her with something from her other family."

The woman opened the package to uncover a stained glass window made by Brother Joseph. It was a wild rosebush climbing a wall, an intricate and beautiful design composed of several dozen pieces of cut glass.

CHAPTER TWENTY-SEVEN

Ron Chen waited uneasily in the parking lot. His contact had called himself Ezekiel. Always some weird-ass Biblical name with these guys. It had been several months since Chen had heard from them. So long, in fact, that he'd grown worried; he needed the money.

Chen had spent his money quietly, but spent it he had. A new stereo, a remodeled kitchen. More meals out. A trip to Italy with his brother. He'd sold his six-year-old Accord and picked up a Nissan Z. Three hundred horses under the hood gave it a nice gallop. Great for picking up chicks, he'd thought, though so far it hadn't worked any magic. Oh, and he wanted to put in a home theater system, but he was still a few thousand short.

In fact, he was a few thousand short just about everywhere. Weird how he'd taken eighty thousand tax free and now he had a higher balance on his cards and a new home equity loan to worry about. It was like they said, it doesn't matter how much you make, at the end of the month you always eat beans.

But then the e-mail had come. No explanation for the delay, just another shipment, this one smaller. Less money, too, but Chen had stretched his credit cards to the limit and couldn't afford to argue.

The man kept Chen waiting for almost thirty minutes in the parking lot before he showed up. It was Wednesday afternoon, the half day at the clinic. Dr. Stephens had gone home, and Grace and Anna as well. But these rendezvous felt risky anyway. Someone might see.

And then the man who'd called himself Ezekiel arrived. Another van. White, unmarked, with Nevada plates. Chen thought he should memorize the plates. Write them down somewhere, with a note in case something happened to him.

A man stepped out of the van. He held a cooler in one hand and a manila envelope in the other. Ezekiel was pasty white, and there was something unpleasant about his eyes and the set of his mouth. He set the cooler at Chen's feet and held out the envelope, but just beyond reach, as if he would snatch it back should Chen grab for it. Chen reached instead for the cooler.

Don't be greedy. Don't make a mistake.

Santa Cruz County Medical Institute, or Scummy, as it was known by its overworked and underpaid employees, was not the biggest fertility clinic in Northern California. And most IVF procedures used sperm from the husband or partner, not donor sperm. But the clinic had produced over four hundred sperm-donor babies—including multiple births—in almost two hundred and fifty different women in the previous dozen years.

These days, most of the sperm came from the coolers given to him by men like Ezekiel. What's more, the clinic resold Scummy sperm to a host of smaller facilities throughout the Bay Area and Northern California. Chen pictured billions of tiny swimmers, like salmon swimming upriver to spawn, migrating from the clinic and into the wombs of women.

Rivers of sperm.

Chen shook his head in disgust at his own role in this business. Billions and billions of sperm. Only one purpose. Find egg, fertilize. God only knew whose sperm came from those vials.

-end-

ABOUT THE AUTHOR

Photograph by David Garten

Michael Wallace was born in California and raised in a small religious community in Utah, eventually heading east to live in New England. An experienced world traveler, he has trekked through the Andes, ventured into the Sahara on a camel, and traveled through Thailand by elephant. In addition to working as a literary agent and innkeeper, he previously worked as a software engineer for a Department of Defense contractor, programming simulators for nuclear submarines.